Into the Promised Land

*A family's true story
of faith, courage, and
finding their way home.*

SARAH HEATWOLE

Into the Promised Land
by Sarah Heatwole

Library of Congress Control Number: 2025941437

International Standard Book Number: 979-8-89674-038-4

Masthof Press
219 Mill Road | Morgantown, PA 19543-9516
www.Masthof.com

TABLE OF CONTENTS

Dedication | v

For my children—
Asher, Jubilee, and Zion—
third-generation torchbearers of the faith.

ONE

Andy

Spring 1933, Troyer Farm, Middlefield, Ohio

Andy stopped at Mamm and Dat's bedroom door; he wasn't supposed to be here. His bare feet stuck to the wood floor.

"Ohhh," came another low guttural moan, slipping out of the bedroom like the painful bellow of a sick cow.

He hadn't meant to disobey; he'd only come in to grab a glass of water and an apple from the cellar for a snack. Chores made him tired, and the thin porridge they'd had for breakfast was already wearing off.

His stomach clenched. *Was that Mamm?* He should have obeyed Dat, stuck to his chores, and never come into the house. His body turned to flee, but his legs stuck to the ground. It felt wrong to go in and worse to walk away. Fighting his fear, he gulped and gathered his courage as he pressed his hand against the door, the creaky hinges giving way.

His eyes adjusted to the darkness and fell on Mamm in the middle of the bed, her plump figure swallowed by the pile of quilts. Sweat beaded on her brow, and wisps of dark hair stuck to her forehead. Her head covering sat off to the side on the dresser. He'd never seen Mamm without her *kap*. Something must be very wrong. With closed eyes, she pulled in deep breaths.

"Mamm, are you ill?" His voice wobbled as he stepped inside.

At his words, her eyes fluttered open, and she grimaced. "Oh Andy, I'm glad you're here," she whispered. "I need you to get Dat. It's important."

Andy froze at her request. *How could he explain to Dat why he'd abandoned his chores?*

"Go on," Mamm commanded, her voice hardening to an edge. "Hurry. It's time."

Time for what? He'd never seen Mamm in such a condition. He pivoted his almost eight-year-old frame and fled out of the room onto the front porch, racing past his cousin Maryanna, minding his three younger siblings.

"What's the hurry?" Maryanna hollered after him.

He didn't respond as he ran to the barn to find Dat. When he didn't spot him, he checked the chicken coop, but the cackling hens, annoyed with the interruption, fluttered away with no sign of Dat. He wished he could stop for a minute and dig for eggs; he liked all the different colors he found, but he didn't have time to waste.

Next, he went to the outbuilding where they kept the buggy. Hunched over, Dat sat replacing a spoke in a wheel, his back to the door as he whittled away at a piece of wood. Andy slowed his run and bent over, trying to catch his breath. His heart beat fast from all the running, but also in anticipation of Dat's reaction.

"What is it?" Dat asked, turning around.

Andy moved the dirt around with his toe, careful to keep his eyes downcast. "Mamm needs you at the house."

"What does she need?"

"She's sick in bed and said it's time."

Dat stood; his brow creased with worry instead of anger. He rubbed the sawdust off his dark pants, closed the door to the firebox, and strode back to the house. Andy followed in his long steps, but had a hard time keeping up.

On the porch, Dat turned, his face pinched. He removed his hat and scraped his hand through his hair. "Go back to your chores. Can't have you in the house right now."

Andy nodded, careful to keep silent and obey, but before he reached the bottom step, Dat stopped him. "Wait. I may need your help while I fetch Aunt Rachel and the midwife."

The midwife? Again? He'd noticed Mamm's belly expanding over the past few months but hadn't paid it much attention. *I should have known*, he thought as he stood waiting on a cold patch of dirt.

Maryanna and his little brothers played two games of hide and seek before Dat exited the house. "I'm going to collect the midwife and alert Aunt Rachel. Keep your Mamm company till I get back."

Certainly Maryanna could sit with Mamm? Seems more like women's work. Andy trudged up the steps, careful to keep his complaints to himself. Then again, laundry was women's work as well, and he did that all the time. *What if something went wrong while Dat was gone?* His palms began to sweat. If that happened, there would be trouble to pay. Dat would for sure farm him out to work for wages. He knew nothing about birthing babies. *Just do as you're asked*, his inner voice pushed him.

Mamm panted and clenched at her belly. All the moaning made tears rise to Andy's eyes. He'd seen a cow give birth but felt ill-prepared for birthing babies.

Mamm pointed to the chair pulled beside the bed. "Come sit. Don't worry, this is normal. Help is coming soon."

Andy didn't want to sit; he wanted to flee. He went to the window and looked down the lane. After a few minutes, he returned to Mamm's side and sat on his hands. "Do you want some water?"

"*Jah.* That would be nice."

He went to the kitchen and poured a glass, grateful to put some distance between him and Mamm's whimpers of pain. After pacing back and forth between Mamm and the window to look for Dat's buggy, he finally spotted the black speck coming down the lane. Relief flooded him. He'd made it, and Mamm hadn't gotten any worse.

Aunt Rachel rushed through the door, clucking her tongue as she shooed Andy out. "Go back to your chores. There's no place for a boy in here."

Aunt Rachel meant business, and Andy knew it. The knot in his stomach released now that she had arrived, and he wanted to stay. He would rather see what happened than go back to the stinky laundry chores, but he obeyed, knowing the house would be off limits until later.

Dat added, "Once you're done with the laundry, go on to school and walk your brother home."

The thought of going to school brightened him. If he did the laundry quickly, he could make it in time for the lunch period. Even though Wednesday wasn't a day he normally attended school, and he hated reading and writing, he loved lunch period where he got to eat his slice of bread with bologna and play with his friends. Arriving early would give him an extra recess this week.

In the washhouse, Andy took the wood bucket to the pump and filled the large wash basin. Then he lit the fire underneath the basin. When the water started steaming, he gathered an armful of chore clothes caked with mud and dung and dumped them in the pot. He picked up the wooden paddle that reached the top of his head and stirred the clothes around until the water became tepid and brown. Next, he used the homemade soap Mamm made to scrub some of the more stubborn stains, then dunked the clothes in the rinse water, and wrung them out. Now the laundry was ready to hang out to dry. He drained the dirty water back into the buckets, which he dumped on the spring garden.

He worked the better part of the morning carrying buckets of clean and soiled water in and out of the washhouse until his arms ached. No matter how quickly he worked, it seemed the pile of dirty laundry hardly diminished.

His stomach rumbled again, reminding him of the snack he'd never gotten. When he saw two baskets left, filled to the brim with soiled clothes, disappointment engulfed him. He wouldn't make it to school in time for lunch. Worried about Mamm's well-being, he glanced at the house. Maryanna and the siblings kicked a rubber ball around the yard, shrieking with laughter. He wanted to go inside and grab a slice of bread, but didn't dare cross Aunt Rachel's demand to stay out. He'd already disobeyed enough today.

Finally, in mid-afternoon, he finished the last load and set off towards the school. During the mile-long hike, he thought long and hard about his life. *Why did everything fall on his shoulders?* Do the laundry, mind your brothers, complete your chores. There was never any time and space for anything he wanted.

By the time he arrived in the schoolyard, children were spilling out the front doors and tumbling down onto damp earth, eager to play while Mrs. Yoder swung the big brass bell.

"We missed ya today," Mrs. Yoder commented. "Everything okay at the house?"

Andy nodded. "Needed my help with chores." He mumbled, not wanting to answer anymore of her prying questions.

"You need to be in school more often. Learning is important, gives a person better opportunities in life."

Andy kept his head low. He wished he could go to school every day like his brother David, but how could he when there was so much work to be done, and he was the oldest? What opportunities did Mrs. Yoder mean?

"I just may need to pay a visit to your folks and talk with them about it."

At her words, his head snapped up. "I don't think a visit would be good right now. My folks are so busy." He hoped his words staved off her ambition.

David appeared in the doorway, and Andy sighed with relief at his timing.

"Come on, David, we need to be heading home."

David, a year younger than him, liked to talk nonstop. Dat had joked one evening that together they made a whole person—Andy thought and David talked. Dat howled with laughter at his own joke, but Andy didn't think it was funny. He wished Dat would see him differently, not as half a person, but as a man.

They started down the road towards home. The recent spring rains and melting snow softened the dirt. Buggy wheels carved deep ruts into the muddy lanes, and Andy avoided the slimy muck.

Oblivious, David stomped in the nearest puddle.

"Stop it, David. You're getting your pants all muddy, and it takes forever to get those stains out."

David ignored him, talking on and on about a game his best friend Alvin had taught him. "Two lines face each other. You hold the hand of the person next to you, and chant, 'Red Rover, Red Rover,' calling over a friend to join your line. The friend must run as hard as they can to break the chain of hands. When Alvin called me over to his team, I—"

Andy didn't want to hear anymore about the fun he had missed out on. "Did Mamm seem different to you this morning?"

David shrugged, "Not really. Why?"

"She was sick in bed, and Dat fetched the midwife."

"A baby?" David exclaimed, wide-eyed.

They turned off the road and started down the lane to the farm. Over the crest, their two-story farmhouse appeared. Its worn and sagged front porch dipped like a welcoming smile. For an entire year, they had called the place "home," the longest Andy could remember. No one had escaped the hard times, as Dat called them. Not even the Amish.

Aunt Rachel's horse and buggy sat hitched to the post in front of the house. "Why is Aunt Rachel here?" David shouted as he took off at a jog.

"I told you; I think Mamm had a baby."

They pounded up the front steps.

"No, no," Aunt Rachel scolded, meeting them at the door. "You boys scrape the mud off of those boots before you go flying in here."

They scraped and stomped their boots against the chipped and peeling door frame, eager to enter.

"Did Mamm really have a baby?" David asked with excitement.

"Come on in and see for yourself." Aunt Rachel held the door open with a twinkle in her eye.

They entered the kitchen. Dat sat at the table with a mug in front of him. His eyes were glassy, but his thin lips carved into a tense smile. "*Buva*, we've had an eventful day. Your Mamm gave birth while you were gone."

Dat's mood seemed jovial. All must have gone well.

David grinned. "I knew it!"

Andy wanted to roll his eyes at his brother, but thought better of it.

"Come and see." Aunt Rachel motioned to them from the bedroom door.

They tiptoed into the room off the kitchen. Andy glanced over at Mamm. She seemed pale and exhausted, but smiled at him. Her *kap* back on her head in its rightful place.

She directed their eyes to the long dresser with the three drawers across the top pulled out. "Go on and look."

Andy and David peeked their heads over the top of the drawers. Tucked inside on soft blankets lay three squirming little babies, so small they could almost fit in the palm of Andy's hand. Their new rosebud mouths opened and shut making tiny squeaks. Andy held out a finger, and a baby grabbed hold of it, its tiny sliver of skin warm against his rough hands. *Three? How could there be three?* He'd never heard of such a thing.

"Now you see for yourself," Dat boomed from the doorway. "We've got triplets! Three babies, a boy and two girls rounding out our family to ten."

Andy looked at Dat, unable to discern the emotion on his face. Three more mouths to feed. Dat grumbled now about the cost of everything, and it seemed no matter how hard they worked, they never had enough food.

"What are their names, Dat?" David asked, grinning while jumping up and down.

"Alvin, Alma, and Alta."

"Yippee!" he squealed with delight. "Wait till I tell my friend Alvin I have a brother with his name."

Aunt Rachel interrupted David's joyful moment. "Boys, dinner will be ready soon. I'll be staying on for a few days to help get you all situated. Now go on and get to your chores. Those cows can't milk themselves."

David groaned but scurried out the door towards the barn. Andy's stomach growled at the mention of food. He hadn't eaten since breakfast. He gave Mamm a nod as he headed towards the door, annoyed David always got away with grumbling.

"Andy," Mamm called out softly.

He turned.

"Thank you for helping fetch Dat earlier. I don't know what I would have done had you not come in to check on me."

Warmth filled Andy's core at Mamm's words. He had made the right decision.

On his way out, he overheard Mamm and Aunt Rachel discussing dinner plans.

"There are a few potatoes I dug yesterday, and a cabbage from the garden. I planned on making vegetable soup."

"Do you have any meat to add?"

"There is only one jar left of last year's beef. I was going to make do without."

Dat's powerful voice piped in. "Use the meat, Mary. You need it."

Andy's tongue watered at the mention of beef. He could almost taste the rich chunks on his tongue. It had been a long time since Mamm had used a jar of beef.

The next morning, Andy woke up to the rooster crowing. The familiar sound lulled him out of his comfortable cocoon. He rubbed the sleep from his eyes and pulled the quilt up to his chin to keep out the cold. The blocks of worn trousers and shirts cut up and hand stitched together covered his bed and made for a heavy weight on his slight frame. His three brothers, David, Roman, and Eli, snuggled up to him in a tangle of limbs and morning breath.

It took a few moments for yesterday's events to register. Mrs. Yoder's words echoed in his head. *You need to be at school more often.* Why couldn't he be like all the other children and only do chores before and after school?

He wanted to gather his courage and ask Dat if he could go to school like David, but he knew his words would be a waste of breath. Dat needed his help more than ever. Hopefully, Mrs. Yoder wouldn't cause more trouble by visiting. He didn't want Dat thinking he'd put those thoughts in her head.

He sat on the edge of the bed, imagining his life as a regular boy, going to school, playing games with friends, a life without the heavy burden of work and hunger. *What would that be like?*

Daisy the milk cow's moo interrupted his thoughts. He needed to get moving. His limbs felt like heavy logs as he pulled on his chore clothes. There was lots of work to be done before breakfast and even more after. Today would bring pots and pots of boiling water, the paddling of clothes, diapers, and soiled sheets.

"I wish my life was different," he whispered aloud.

Sylvia

Fall 1933, Slabaugh Farm, Burton, Ohio

Sylvia sat on the kitchen floor fiddling with the bonnet strings of the doll she'd received for her fifth birthday. She listened as Mamm fed her baby sister, wishing Mamm would pay her the same attention she always gave Betty. Ever since Betty joined their family, Mamm didn't play with her like she used to.

"Look at her," Mamm cooed as she spooned oatmeal into Betty's mouth. Betty accepted the rich porridge while her grubby fingers smashed a string of beads sitting on a wooden tray in front of her.

Dat looked up and smiled at Betty overtop *The Budget* Amish newspaper spread out on the table. She returned his smile and shoved a bead into her mouth.

"Betty, don't you try to eat those beads. You'll choke," Mamm scolded as she fished the plastic bead out of her mouth. Mamm turned her attention to Dat. "I know it's been a while since I had a *bobblin*, but I don't remember Sylvia being this active. Did I tell you she tried crawling yesterday? Six months old and already on the move."

Betty smacked her hand on the highchair, causing Dat to raise his head out of the newspaper again. "Ahh, little one, you're vying for my attention, eh?" He reached over and lifted her out of the chair, tossing her high into the air. Her blonde curls danced in the shafts of morning sunlight across the kitchen floor. Betty squealed at Dat's attention, her smile wide and her giggles bubbling. The playful commotion caused Sylvia's older siblings, Clara and John, to come skidding into the kitchen.

A well of jealousy sprang up in Sylvia's heart. Betty had taken her place. Now even Dat had lost interest in her. She curled up in her corner of the kitchen, quiet and still, as if she weren't even there.

"Eat your breakfast before you head off to school." Mamm set bowls of steaming porridge with slabs of creamed butter and scoops of brown sugar on the table. Clara and John slid into their seats.

"You too, Sylvia," Mamm called. "Time to eat."

Cross with Mamm, Sylvia ignored the request until she felt a gentle tug on the two dark braids that hung down her back. She scrambled up, went to the table, and plopped down next to Dat, forgetting her envy for a moment.

She peeked over his shoulder at the newspaper. "What does it say, Dat?"

"There's a livestock auction over in Middlefield this weekend. I've got in mind to add some cattle to my herd." He sighed. "It seems like there are more and more auctions these days. Folks need the money just to buy basic supplies. I feel guilty profiting off their misfortune."

Mamm browsed his newspaper as she put Sylvia's bowl in front of her. She placed her hands on Dat's strong shoulders. "The Lord has blessed us. If you don't buy them, someone else will. Your bidding will help ensure a fair price."

Dat chewed on the end of a toothpick. "You've convinced me. I think I'll go to the sale this Saturday."

Mamm replied, "I'll pack a picnic."

Sylvia couldn't hide her smile at the suggestion, and Betty followed suit by clapping her hands. Mamm looked over at Dat, and they chuckled like they shared a special secret.

Sylvia's glee faded. She loved going on family outings, but now with Betty along, Mamm and Dat would show her all the attention.

Clara and John rose from the table to leave for school. Mamm reached for their lunch pails and held the door open as they grabbed their book straps and headed out.

"Looks like there was a house fire down in Middlefield." Dat clucked his tongue. "The family lost everything. Such a pity."

"Are they taking up a collection? I know it's not our district, but we could spare a few dollars to help fellow church members," Mamm replied.

"I'll ask about it when I'm in town and see who's collecting."

Mamm caught Sylvia's eye. "It's just us today. What would you like to do?" She wiped off the mess smeared all over Betty's face.

A warmth spread through Sylvia at the idea of Mamm's attention for an entire day. "Can we play with dolls? Then bake some cookies and take them over to Mummie and Daughty's?" She tried to squeeze in all the things she missed doing with Mamm.

Mamm smiled. "Of course. That's a great idea. Let's start with the baking."

Dat folded up the newspaper. "I wouldn't be at all disappointed if you girls baked up some whoopie pies."

Sylvia jumped up and down. "Yes, yes, can we Mamm? I love whoopie pies."

"Come on, then, and help me pick out the ingredients." Mamm turned and opened the corner cupboard and reached for the cocoa powder on the upper shelf.

Dat folded the newspaper and put it under his arm. "I'm headed out to the barn, then I'm going into town to pick up some supplies. Do you need anything from the general store?"

"No, I think we're good." She grinned. "Us girls will whip up some special treats for you while you're gone."

Cars and buggies lined the street leading up to the auction. Sylvia jumped down from their buggy and looked up at the sea of people inspecting the property and livestock. There were Amish in their dark bonnets and hats, and *English* ladies with their belted dresses and gloves, accompanied by men in fine suits. Other spectators wore flour-sack dresses with baggy stockings and worn trousers with threadbare shirts.

"You think you're going to win those cows bidding against all these people?" Mamm asked Dat.

"*Jah*, most of these folks are here just checking it out. Free entertainment." Dat smirked.

John and Clara waved goodbye and disbanded into the crowd, eager to meet their friends.

Dat handed Betty off to Mamm. "I need to hurry and get my number before they sell off the animals," he commented as he headed to the registration tent.

Mamm took Sylvia to the back of the auction tent, where they waited for Dat to return. A hum rose over the crowd, and the air filled with the scent of coffee and frying oil from the donut booth. Sylvia hoped Dat would snag her some donuts. She climbed up onto a chair so she could see the stage and held tight to Mamm's hand.

The auctioneer began his rhetoric. "Okay folks, it's time to auction off the livestock. We are going to start with the pigs. This here is a nice young sow, good for breeding and butchering. Who'll start me off with five cents a pound? Who will give me five cents?"

The crowd buzzed, but no one lifted their bidding cards.

"How about three? Anyone give me three?"

A hush fell over the crowd.

"Two and a half? Someone give me two and a half."

A man in the back lifted his card. The auctioneer's shoulders relaxed a bit. "We got two and a half. Who will give me three? Give me three?"

When there was no response, he hit the gavel on the podium. "Sold for two and a half cents to the man in the back row." A murmur rose through the crowd.

"Ay, yi, yi," whispered Mamm. "Lowest price I've ever seen."

Dat slid in beside them with his bidding card in hand, but no donuts.

"Are you sure you want to spend the money?" asked Mamm.

"*Jah*, we have reserves. Milk still goes for a good price."

The auctioneer started again. "Next up are the cows. First the steers, then we'll move on to the milking heifers."

More people bid for the cattle than the pigs, but the steers still sold for a low price.

"Who will give me fifteen for this here milker? She's a beaut, a Guernsey. Fifteen? Do we have fifteen?" Dat raised his card. The auctioneer pointed at him. "We have fifteen. How about sixteen? Do I have sixteen?" A man across the aisle lifted his hand, raising his eyebrows at Dat in a challenge.

Dat and the man bid against each other until the auctioneer declared the winner. "Going once, going twice, sold to card number six eleven in the back for nineteen dollars." The wooden gavel made a hollow thud as it landed, sealing the deal.

Dat's smile stretched from ear to ear. "Hopefully, I can get several more at that price. That's a good bargain."

Mamm elbowed him playfully. "Don't let your eyes get bigger than your stomach. Think of all the work they'll add."

Dat tickled Mamm in return, and she shooed him off.

Betty reached for him. "Dada," she clucked.

He took her in his arms and held her tight. "Do you want a calf, little one? Dada will buy you a calf, and we'll name it Betty."

"Jake, you'll spoil her," Mamm chided.

Betty beamed up at him with her toothless grin. Her love radiated like the sun melted snow on a cold winter day.

Sylvia hung onto Dat's pant leg feeling left out. She wished he'd buy her one, too.

When the calves came up for sale, Dat raised his card, and the auctioneer pounded the gavel. "Sold."

Dat squeezed Sylvia's shoulder affectionately before fishing a wad of cash out of his pocket and handing Betty back to Mamm. He headed to the register to pay.

With an empty heart Sylvia watched Dat walk away. He did love Betty more.

Later, Dat returned with a sack of donuts; he handed them to Sylvia. She dug her fingers into their sticky goo and thrust them in her mouth as fast as she could. Betty looked at her eagerly and reached for a donut. Sylvia stuck her tongue out at her and made a nasty face.

"Stop it, Sylvia," Mamm chided. "What's gotten into you?" She grabbed her arm and dragged her along back to the buggy.

Pain blurred the edges of Sylvia's eyes as she swallowed her anger.

Mamm scolded her, "Since you can't share willingly, I am going to take those donuts from you." She reached for the half-empty bag and tucked it beside her skirts.

Sylvia turned toward the window and lay her head against the hard interior. Dat clucked the reins and the horses took off. The rhythmic jostling of the buggy focused her thoughts. She licked the sugary glaze of the donuts off her fingers with contempt while Betty fell asleep in Mamm's arms.

Out of the corner of her eye, Sylvia saw Mamm run a finger down Betty's soft cheek and heard her whisper, "Why has the Lord blessed us with so much while others struggle?"

Sylvia pressed deeper into her corner, shrinking.

Dat reached over and squeezed Mamm's hand. "Don't worry Lizzie, John and I will do the extra milking," he teased.

Mamm squeezed his hand in return and adjusted Betty in her lap. Sylvia wondered what it meant to struggle. Her only unhappiness came from Betty. Betty had ruined everything when she came along. *How could she get Mamm and Dat to love her again?* An idea formed; she'd show them she was better than Betty. She'd be the best daughter—always obedient, cheerful, and kind. They would see.

Andy

Fall 1933, Troyer Farm, Middlefield, Ohio

The cool autumn breeze ruffled Andy's hair as he stood at the top of the knoll. To the west, farmland stretched to the neck of the dark woods, where Andy prepared to join Dat for his first hunt of the season. He straightened his shoulders in anticipation. If he could get his first big kill, perhaps Dat would see him as a man and not a child.

He closed his eyes and listened to the wind whipping through the dry leaves. He imagined Dat leading the way in the dark woods, holding the Winchester, pushing back the brush as they tiptoed forward. In his vision, Dat tapped him on the shoulder and knelt beside him, helping him position the gun. Together, they aimed at the twelve-point buck. Time froze, and just before he pulled the trigger, Andy shifted. The chomp of a crispy leaf broke the silence, startling him back into the present from his daydream.

He frowned, disappointed at the failure of his imagination. Hopefully, the real hunt wouldn't meet the same demise.

The dinner bell tolled. He glanced one last time over the harvested fields. A whiff of acrid smoke floated in the air. In the distance, a neighbor burned a gigantic pile of leaves. The smoke billowed towards the sky, evaporating into the expanse of the horizon.

Mummie Troyer always said fire meant change whenever she scooped the pile of ash out from the bottom of the wood stove.

Hopefully, this fire signaled pleasant change. They sure could use some good fortune.

He snapped his pocketknife closed and shoved it in his pocket. In May, Mamm and Dat had given him the knife for his birthday. He could hardly believe they had found the money to give him such a gift, now his greatest treasure. Whenever he could steal away for a few moments, he sat in his favorite spot at the top of the knoll and whittled away, dreaming. He imagined skinning the coons and other small game he'd trap with his new knife. *How proud Dat will be.* Shivers of excitement raced through him as he hurried back to the house for dinner.

The screen door slammed shut behind him. Mamm spun around. "Shush, child, the babies are down for the night. Please take care not to wake them!"

Andy slid into his spot on the bench, and Dat settled into his chair at the head of the table. They all bowed their heads, sitting in silence for a moment reminding Andy of birds before a storm. Finally, after what seemed like too long, Dat raised his head and cleared his voice, signaling the start of the meal.

Dat served himself first, tearing a thick slab of bread into pieces and placed a scoop of canned blackberries on top. Andy licked his lips in anticipation, eager for the hunger in his belly to subside. Scattered on the table sat pitchers of warm milk and little jars of honey to add sweetness to their bowls.

David groaned, "Blackberry soup again?"

Mamm hushed him. "You'd better be grateful for what we have."

Andy grew tired of the same foods all the time, too, but his hunger pangs always overcame any objections.

Dat gave David a steely stare. "You complain again, and I'll take you over my knee."

Andy sat still and quiet, picking at his bowl. Blackberry soup had been on the menu more frequently since Mamm found the bountiful blackberry patch in June. He remembered the prick of the briars in his hands as they spent hours plucking the tiny berries from their snares at the edge of the woods, but the plentiful harvest had allowed Mamm to put away over two hundred quarts of blackberries—a tremendous help she said.

After dinner, Dat clapped his hands together. "Time for stories."

Andy rose from the table, and his siblings followed suit, taking their bowls and plates to the dry sink and trailing after him into the living room for their favorite time of day.

Dat sat down in the rocker. David, Eli, and Roman circled at his feet. Andy sat off to the side in a corner too old to sit at Dat's feet. He wouldn't admit to anyone how much he looked forward to story time, particularly when Dat told stories about his childhood. He liked imagining Dat young and free.

Dat began. "At age sixteen, my parents sent me to work for the Schrocks to help pay some bills. I gave my Dat all the money I earned every month except for three dollars he let me keep for myself."

Andy's eyes widened. Three dollars seemed like a fortune. Maybe someday he would earn his own money, too.

"Every day I rode my old horse Bessie to work. One day, I noticed she walked gingerly because the nails in her shoes were coming loose, so after I received my pay, we rode into town to the ferrier. The price of her new shoes was exactly three dollars. I remember counting out those bills, knowing I'd have to wait a whole month to get change in my pocket again, but Bessie was my horse, so I needed to take care of her.

"After my visit in town, I headed back home eager for a slice of my mamm's cherry pie.

"When I got to the old crossroads on Pine Street, I met a neighbor girl named Annabelle riding along on her pony. Annabelle was a feisty little girl with hair as red as a rooster's comb. She challenged me to a race to see who could get to our lane the fastest. I knew old Bessie could beat her silly little pony any day. So, we set out. Bessie flew over the road a full body length ahead of Annabelle and her pony. When we reached our lane, I slowed down and dismounted, and Annabelle went on her way.

"As I walked Bessie up the hill into the upper part of the barn, she suddenly seized, fell over, and plumb died. I reckon' from exhaustion. I'm ashamed to say my first thought was the three dollars I put into those horseshoes rather than the dead horse." Dat slapped his knee as he chuckled.

Andy's eyes followed his siblings as they sat in rapt attention on the braided rug, wide-eyed, imagining the horse belly up.

"What did you do next, Dat?" asked David.

"We buried poor Bessie out in the pasture, new shoes and all. From then on, I had to walk to work or get Dat to take me. We made do, like we do now. I should never have raced that old horse. Her poor heart couldn't take it."

He glanced at the clock. "Well, it's getting late. Andy, help your brothers up to bed."

Dat handed Andy a lantern and his little brothers trudged behind him up the stairs. He led them to their room, careful not to wake up Linda Ruth, who slept in the room beside them.

Andy readied for bed by taking off his chore trousers. He grimaced at the thump they made when they dropped to the floor. *The pocketknife!* Gently removing it, he placed it on the bedside table and crawled under the comforter, soon falling fast asleep.

After only a few hours of sleep, Andy woke up to yelling. At first, the haze in the room confused him, and he thought he was in a dream, but as his heavy eyelids lifted from their slumber, a powerful scent stung his nostrils. He sat on the edge of the bed, orienting himself. Tiny tendrils of smoke seeped under the door and into the bedroom curling up to the ceiling. The moon shone brightly outside, accentuating the smoky wisps.

Dat's heavy footsteps pounded up the steps. "Everyone out! The house is on fire!" The bedroom door flung open. "Andy, get your brothers downstairs!" Dat yelled as he raced down the hall to the second bedroom.

Time seemed to move in slow motion as Andy pulled on his trousers and roused his brothers. He got everyone out into the hallway, now full of smoke. Holding his brothers' hands, he dragged them to the bottom of the stairs. Dat followed behind, with Linda Ruth in his arms.

The living room filled with billows of smoke that rolled in from the kitchen, accompanied by a roaring radiating heat. Mamm's jars of blackberries fell off the shelves and hit the floor with high-pitched pops. His hands tingled where the briars had dug in at the sound of shattering glass. All that work gone to waste.

Mesmerized, he watched as the flames licked higher and higher, working their way toward Dat's rocker. He stopped and ran his hand over the smooth wood. Here on this rug, they sat only a few hours ago.

Scared, his little brothers released their hands and ran towards Dat, who called for them from the door. Andy stood paralyzed like the heirloom clock on the mantel, unable to move. Seconds ticked by, and the fire seemed to consume time.

"Andy!" Dat screamed. "Move!" Fear laced his voice, and it shook Andy from his stupor. He bolted for the door.

Mamm had set the triplets on the cold, dewy grass under the oak tree. They shrieked frantically. Their little arms and legs pumped up and down as they rolled around. David took two of them in his arms and Eli the other, trying to shush their desperate cries.

Mamm furiously began pumping water into buckets. "Andy, you're in charge. All of you stay together here under this tree. No one is to move an inch."

She handed the buckets off to Dat, who hauled them back into the house, the process painstakingly slow. Mamm pumping and filling up the buckets, Dat running them and pouring them on the fire. Eventually, Mamm had filled enough buckets that she helped run them to the house as well. Water sloshed over the sides, dripping down her nightdress, as her plump frame leaned to the right, pulled down by the heavy weight of the bucket.

They kept at it for a long time. Finally, Dat exited the front door, panting. "It's no use, Mary. It's too far gone." He bent over, trying to catch his breath, both hands on his knees, then he wiped the sweat from his brow. Shoulders forward, they headed back to the children pressed together under the tree.

Huddled together, Andy watched as their home burned, blazing like a bright fireball against the midnight sky.

Eventually, Dat buried his head in his arms. "*Favas Gott?* Why God? *Es glevenich us du uns geva hosht is alles veg gawa?* The little You gave us is gone. *Even es dach iva unsa kop.* Even the very roof over our heads."

Andy knew better than to cry. He should be strong at a time like this, but he couldn't stop the trickle of silent tears running down his cheeks as his father prayed. He had never seen Dat so weak.

His pocketknife. In all the commotion, he had forgotten to grab it. Panic gripped his heart. He stood prepared to run into the flames. Before he even took a step, Dat tugged on his shirt.

"Where are you going?"

"My pocketknife. I left it upstairs!" Andy cried.

"You can't go in there. Sit down." Dat gripped Andy's arm.

A lump formed in Andy's throat as he folded himself back into the dirt, burying his head between his knees. *Why did life keep knocking him down? Now I won't be able to go hunting.* With the loss of the knife, his hopes of impressing Dat died. They would be too busy rebuilding for frivolous hunts. He clenched his fists tighter. Another dream vanished into nothingness, just like the house disintegrated into a pile of smoldering ash.

The sound of horses' hooves competed with the pops and crackles of the fire. Andy lifted his head. A buggy cut its way down the lane through the inky blackness, the only light coming from a lantern that bobbed up and down with the familiar clip-clop of the horse. Dat rose to his feet and went to meet the guest.

Their neighbor David Gingrich hopped down from the driver's seat. "Everyone get out?"

Dat nodded. "*Jah.*"

"I went over to the Smiths and used the telephone to call for help when I saw the glow in your direction. The Middlefield Volunteer Fire Department will be here soon." He pulled blankets from the buggy and handed them out. Mamm pulled one tight around her shoulders, covering her nightdress.

Eventually, the shiny red Seagrave came streaking down the lane, but it was too late. As the firefighters jumped out of the truck, the structure caved in with a mighty crash of splintering timber.

While the firefighters worked, and with his parents distracted, Andy seized the opportunity to inspect the fire engine. His fingers grazed the shiny red paint, feeling the smoothness beneath his touch. He could see his reflection in the chrome piping—a soot-covered nose and a shock of blonde hair sticking up in all directions. As he looked at his image, he wondered, *Why am I so different? Why can't we drive a car or have a phone?* He imagined himself as a firefighter behind the wheel, twisting and turning down the roads at breakneck speed, racing toward the fire. How fun it would be to have the wind whipping his hair in every direction.

He didn't feel Dat come up behind him and jumped at the sound of his voice. "What are you doing?" Dat hissed in his ear.

Embarrassed, Andy dropped his fingers from the shiny paint. "Nothing."

"Well, get your nothing back to your brothers. Stay away from the *Englishers*, we don't belong with them."

A firefighter noticed them standing there. He placed a hand on top of Andy's tousled hair. "I'm sorry we couldn't save your house, son. Do you want to sit up in the driver's seat of the fire engine?"

Dat's grip on his arm tightened, and he answered, "No, thank you. He shouldn't be interrupting your work."

"It's no trouble." The man smiled.

Dat dipped his head in acknowledgment and pulled Andy away, back to the tree where everyone gathered. A nagging question settled in Andy's stomach, *Where did he belong in this world?*

Later, after the excitement settled, Mr. Gingrich invited them to stay at his place, but Dat declined and pointed to the barn. "We can bed down there for the night and regroup in the morning."

"*Jah*, I'll let the Bishop know what happened. You'll have the church's support; we'll get through this." Mr. Gingrich put a hand on Dat's shoulder before heading back to his buggy.

Dat directed everyone to the hayloft. They climbed the ladder wearily and settled into their nests in the hay. Mamm tucked the babies and Linda Ruth in beside her, and Eli, David, and Roman lay bundled under the horse blankets beside Andy.

Eventually, everyone's breaths slowed and soon they were fast asleep, but Andy lay there in the stillness. He looked up at the barn roof. Moonlight crept in between the slats. He tried to count the stars exposed through the tiny slivers, but the wood obstructed his view. *Who controlled the stars? God? Why would He let this happen to them?* Unable to sleep, he got up and climbed down the ladder, hoping to get a peek at the house once more.

There in the moonlight stood Dat, leaning against the frame of the barn door. His slender body silhouetted by the half-moon. Dat's nose with its creases and bulb on the end outlined against the night sky. Dat hooked his thumbs in the pockets of his trousers and stared straight ahead at the burnt shell of a house, silent.

Andy hid in the shadows. He observed the frown on Dat's face, the way half of his body glowed in the moon and the other half hid in the shadows. The moon slipped behind a cloud, and Dat faded into blackness.

Andy shivered. A resolve settled in his gut. *I'm going to find answers as to why the light is disappearing from our lives.*

When the moon reappeared, he climbed back up the ladder into the hayloft and crawled beside his brothers. Pulling the blankets close to keep the autumn chill at bay, he drifted off into an exhausted sleep.

The next morning, word spread. The owner of the farm came from Chardon to survey the damage and start an insurance claim. Neighbors and church members rolled in at midday bringing food.

All their furniture, dishes, clothing, rugs, beds, and bedding were gone. The biggest loss of all, though, was the food they had prepared for winter. Andy hated the thought of eating cornmeal mush every day. Aunt Rachel would be sure to donate jars of her "famous" pickles to the cause. His stomach clenched at the thought of the turpentine-tasting pucks, but without the support of the family and church, how would they survive?

Later that day, they loaded the donations into the buggy, hitched up the horse, and headed to Mummie and Daughty's house to stay until they found more permanent housing. Andy wondered what their lives would look like if Mamm and Dat moved into town and chose a home with electricity and a phone. Dare he dream? Dat would never allow it.

Throughout the winter, the community regularly dropped off bags of flour, potatoes, vegetables and canned goods. The church even took up a special collection to buy new fabric to sew clothing and bedding for the family.

Gratitude filled Andy's heart when Aunt Rachel dropped off fabric for Mamm to sew him pants, as he could see straight down the leg of Johnny Yoder's donated britches only held up by stretched-out suspenders. However, Dat hung his head in shame every time a donation rolled in. Andy knew he hated accepting charity.

By the time spring rolled around, Mamm and Dat had found a new place to live, and they moved onto another leased farm to start all over again.

Sylvia

Spring 1934, Slabaugh Farm, Burton, Ohio

Sylvia pushed her feet against the cold packed dirt to make the swing go higher. Tiny leaves squirreled their way out from the bare branches of the tall oak. Soon there would be a full canopy of green above her. She loved the breeze against her face and legs and pushed harder, determined to go higher than ever.

Mamm yelled from the back door. "Time to come in, Sylvia! I need your help minding Betty."

Sylvia stopped pushing her feet against the ground and let the swing come slowly to a stop before climbing off and plodding up to the house. Why did she have to watch Betty all the time?

All winter, Sylvia had worked hard to help Mamm with any-thing she needed. She transformed into Mamm's best helper. Dat had even taken to nicknaming her *"Leiffe helfa."* She had made head-way in her quest to earn back Mamm and Dat's affection, but to-day the spring sunshine and warm air beckoned her, and she wished Mamm had called Clara to do the minding.

Mamm met her at the door. "Clara went down to the chicken house, and John is out with Dat doing chores. Betty is too much for me to handle while I'm making lunch. Can you keep an eye on her?"

Sylvia nodded in obedience and followed a toddling Betty into the living room. Most days Betty wore her out because she was so active. Today she gravitated toward the stairs, trying to climb them. Sylvia followed behind her scolding, "No no, Betty, you mustn't do that. You will get hurt." She picked Betty up under her chubby arms and carried her back to her toy chest countless times, only to repeat the cycle all over again every few minutes.

Finally, Sylvia, tired of the routine, put a few of the dining chairs in front of the steps to block her. "Come now, let's go find Mamm in the kitchen and look for something different you can play with." She picked Betty up, plopped her on her hip, and carried her away to the kitchen, depositing her on the floor close to Mamm. She gave her a big wooden spoon, which Betty used to hit everything in sight.

Sylvia plopped into a chair at the kitchen table and buried her head in her arms, attempting to drown out the clanging of Betty's spoon. She wished she could go back out and swing. Maybe she could if Betty would behave for once. After a few minutes, the noise stopped, and Betty became distracted with her string of beads. Sylvia watched her for a few minutes, then took her opportunity, got up, and slipped outside. Mamm might be cross with her, but she didn't care. She would rather swing.

"Sylvia! Get back in here!" Mamm opened the back door and hollered across the yard again.

Sylvia heard the disappointment in Mamm's voice, and she felt a flush rise to her cheeks at her disobedience. As she hurried back to the house, she heard Mamm scolding Betty through the open door.

"Betty, get down from there."

"Mama ama yay!" Betty cried in response.

Here she goes again, Sylvia groaned. *She's always getting into everything.*

Sylvia made it to the door in time to see Betty standing on the chair where Sylvia had sat minutes ago. Betty had pulled it to her play area and climbed shakily aboard. Now she took her antics to a new level and reached up on her tippy toes, shifting her weight against the back of the chair.

"No!" Mamm reached for her as quickly as she could, but Betty's weight caused the chair to become unbalanced, tip, and crash. Sylvia heard the sickening thud as her sister's forehead hit the ground, and she lay still as a discarded doll.

Sylvia raised a hand to her mouth, stifling a scream. She wanted to run away and pretend this never happened but couldn't move. The pot on the stove boiled over splattering brown gravy down onto the floor and filling the kitchen with its burnt odor.

Mamm reached Betty first and turned her over, but no sound came from her parted lips. Her rosy cheeks faded to white. Picking her up, Mamm's hands gave tiny pats to her cheeks, trying to coax the life from her. "Betty, Betty. Wake up. Come on."

Betty didn't respond. She lay limp in her arms. Mamm put a hand on Betty's neck. Her small chest lay still and flat. "No, no, no. Lord, please." Mamm yelled, "Help! Help!"

Sylvia still stood in the open doorway with wide eyes, feet frozen with the consequences of her actions.

Mamm spun and saw her. "Run and get Dat, quick."

The panic in Mamm's voice unglued Sylvia's feet, and she raced across the yard to fetch Dat.

When she reached the barn, she struggled to speak. Her words were swallowed by the gasps of air heaving from her lungs.

"What is it?" Dat asked.

"It's—" She couldn't get the words out before Mamm's howl. Dat raced towards the house.

"What happened?" Dat asked as he met Mamm in the lane between the barn and house. He reached for Betty. His forehead pinched into a deep valley.

"You know how active she is. I was just chopping vegetables when I turned around and found her standing on the chair. She tipped it over before I could get to her. She's hurt, bad."

Dat cradled Betty in his arms and spoke as if he could command the life back into her. "Come now, *Liefje*, come on. Now isn't your time. You belong with us." He strode with purpose towards the house. "Let's get her inside."

Dat's words twisted inside Sylvia's gut. *You belong with us.* Sylvia had always wished for the opposite, for Betty to disappear.

In the kitchen, Mamm hurriedly cleared the salt and pepper shakers off the table and Dat gently laid Betty down in the center. He examined the knot forming on her forehead and checked her breathing. Finally, his eyes rose to meet Mamm's. "She's gone."

Sylvia heard the words escape his lips, as if he didn't want to speak them into existence.

John rushed through the back door, breaking the intensity of the moment. "What can I do to help Dat?"

"Go fetch the doctor."

The door slammed behind John as he ran out to the shed to hitch up the buggy and take off towards Burton.

Sylvia peeped up over the edge of the table and stared at Betty's blue fingernails. Mamm slumped down into a chair next to her. Sylvia's stomach twisted tight. Bile rose up her throat, and she gulped, swallowing the disgusting liquid. *This was her fault.*

Dat tenderly scooped Betty up while they waited for the doctor and guided Mamm to the rocker in the living room. He placed Betty in Mamm's arms, and Mamm buried her face in Betty's curls. Only the creak of the rocker sliding back and forth on the wood floor broke the silence. Unable to bear her guilt any longer, Sylvia fled to her room.

—⟨◇◇◇◇◇⟩—

Within an hour, the doctor's automobile arrived in the lane. Sylvia crept down the stairs and watched while the doctor gently examined Betty while Mamm held her. Maybe he could bring her back. He put a tiny disk with tubes that connected to his ears to her chest, then placed two fingers on her wrist and neck, listening. He looked at the pupils of her violet eyes and pushed the blonde curls back from her forehead to examine the knot. After the examination, he placed his instruments in his bag and sat down. Sylvia searched his face for any sign of hope but found none.

He shook his head. "I'm sorry. It's no use. She's gone." His brow deepened, and he pinched the bridge of his nose. "The trauma from the fall caused her death. You best prepare for the service and burial."

Dead. His words didn't seem real. All her envy and selfishness had caused this sorrow. She should of never gone out to swing.

Mamm tucked Betty closer to her bosom at his words. Sobs overtook her body. Sylvia hated seeing Mamm so sad. She wished she could undo her actions.

Dr. Brunson closed the clasp of his black doctoring bag. He placed his long coat over his arm. "I am so sorry for your loss." Putting his hat on his head, he exited out the front door to his automobile that roared out of the lane to spread the terrible news.

Mamm continued to sit in the rocking chair, holding Betty. Dat stood behind her in silence, placing his hand on her shoulder. Sylvia remained in her perch on the steps, watching, waiting for their anger to chop her up into little pieces.

Bishop Mast arrived within the hour to help plan the funeral service the next day. Before long, other friends land neighbors also arrived to offer support. Clara stood at the door, greeting the visitors and accepting condolences. Sylvia wished she could help. Most of all, she wished she hadn't caused this. Soon she heard a familiar voice, Mamm's best friend Fannie.

"I heard the news and would like to see your Mamm. May I come in?"

Clara opened the door wider, giving space for Mrs. Yoder to enter the living room. Fannie went over and sat beside Mamm. In her arms lay a length of white fabric.

"I thought you'd be needing this for the burial dress. The ladies and I will be here in the early morning to help with the cleaning and preparation for the laying out."

Mamm stared straight ahead, lost in her sadness.

"I know this is a shock." Fannie set the fabric aside and knelt in front of her. She placed both of her hands on top of Mamm's and locked eyes with her. Tears leaked out of Fannie and Sylvia yearned for her kindness to be directed her way.

"Thank you, Fannie," Mamm finally spoke. "I should go prepare the burial dress." Her bottom lip quivered as she moved her body out of the rocking chair. She walked Fannie to the door, with Betty still in her arms.

After Fannie left, she motioned to Dat. "Can you bring the cradle down into the kitchen?"

Sylvia scrambled up the stairs at her words before Dat caught her snooping. She lay down on the bed and pretended to be asleep. She breathed a sigh of relief when he grabbed the cradle from her room and left. After a bit, she crept to her spot on the steps again, wanting to see what Mamm would do next.

Peeking through the spindles, she saw Dat place the cradle by the kitchen stove and Mamm bent over, tucking Betty in. She took care to even out the crocheted blankets and quilts, pushing them tight against Betty's little body to create a warm cocoon.

Then, Mamm got to work, carefully smoothing out the white fabric on the kitchen table. The kerosene lantern burned long into the night as her slight frame bent over, making every precise cut and stitch.

Occasionally, Sylvia glanced over at the cradle. She hoped Betty would stir, but she just lay there unmoving. Seeing Betty so lifeless tore at her soul. She felt like a piece of paper being ripped in half, and the darkness left in the middle seemed to swallow her whole.

Sylvia didn't remember climbing up the stairs and falling into her bed. She awakened when someone took off her shoes. Opening her sleepy eyes, she quickly removed her thumb from her mouth, feeling embarrassed.

"Dat?"

"Yes, *Liefje*, it's time for bed. Let's get you tucked in."

"Did Betty die?" she croaked. It was a dumb question; she knew the answer, but maybe this was all a bad dream. She squeezed her eyes shut, waiting for his response.

"I'm afraid so."

Sylvia sat up and launched herself into his arms. Dat held her close, and she felt her body quiver against his fingers. "It's my fault," she whispered. "I should have been watching her."

He smoothed the top of her dark hair, his hands running down the length of her braids. "It's nobody's fault. It's just an accident." He held her for a minute longer, then finally peeled her arms away from his neck, turned down the covers, and tucked her in. He sat with her until she pretended to drift off.

After Dat left the room, Sylvia heard his footsteps descending the stairs slowly. She waited till she heard her parents' muffled voices in the kitchen before crawling out from under the covers. *What were they doing with Betty down there?* She tiptoed down the stairs, careful to avoid the boards she knew would creak, and hid in the corner of a shadow on a step as she watched.

Dat fingered the white gown Mamm had sewn, then put his arms around Mamm's shoulders and gave a strong squeeze. "It looks perfect."

Together, they walked over to the cradle. Lamplight flickered over Betty's pale face. Sylvia put a fist to her mouth at the way Mamm's face crumbled.

"She looks so peaceful. I want to memorize every feature." As if on impulse, Mamm grabbed her sewing scissors, bent down and clipped one of Betty's golden curls. She gently folded it into her handkerchief and tucked it in her pocket.

Tears leaked down Dat's cheeks as he lifted the baby quilt and covered Betty's face. "Rest in peace, *Liefje*." He raised the cradle into his arms. "Go on to bed, Lizzie."

"What are you going to do with her?"

"I'm going to put her on the summer porch in the cooler air. It will help preserve the body until tomorrow. In the morning, the men and I will work on building her a box."

Mamm turned and walked towards the stairs. Sylvia froze, wishing she could melt into the wall and camouflage herself like she'd seen hares do against the snow in the middle of winter. Instead, she ran around the corner into the living room, tucking herself into a deep shadow, praying Mamm hadn't seen her.

Mamm didn't even look in her direction, her body shaking with effort as she climbed the steps. Sylvia wondered if Mamm would always love Betty the most. *How had their world fallen apart so suddenly?*

Dat returned to the kitchen from the summer porch with empty arms. Tears streaked his cheeks as he blew out the lantern.

Sylvia hugged herself to the wall and waited until she heard the creak of their bed before climbing the stairs. Poor Betty, all alone out on the cold porch. She'd never again feel the warmth of Mamm's arms, and it was all her fault.

—⟨◇◇◇◇◇⟩—

A few weeks later, after they heaped the last shovelful of dirt on Betty's little grave, Sylvia sat on her bed, playing with her doll.

"Sylvia," Mamm called up the stairs. "It's time for your breakfast."

Sylvia ignored Mamm's call. She missed Betty. A great sadness had descended upon their family like a wet blanket. No one laughed anymore.

A few moments later, Mamm poked her head in the door. "Did you not hear me?"

Sylvia looked up. "No, I'm sorry," she fibbed as she hung her head.

Mamm came over and sat on the bed, tucking her hands neatly in her lap. "This has not been an easy time for our family, no?"

Sylvia didn't reply.

"Do you remember the prayer we say every night? The Lord's Prayer?"

Sylvia nodded.

"There is a part in the prayer that has been helping me. The part that says, thy kingdom come, thy will be done on earth as it is in heaven. Sylvia, do you know what that means?"

"No."

"It means it was Betty's time to go. Nothing can stop the Lord's will. He took her to live with Him in heaven. I am so sad she is no longer here, but I imagine her up there giggling and getting into everything. It is one of the few comforts I have these days. It's a terrible thing to lose her, but it's *Gott's* will, so we need to trust Him."

Sylvia didn't understand. How could it be *Gott's* will that Betty leave their family? She had been the one to will it.

"Mamm, what does trespass mean? Whenever we pray that prayer, you ask *Gott* to forgive our trespasses."

"Trespass is another word for wrongdoing. We are to ask *Gott* to forgive us for when we mess up and we are also to forgive those that hurt us."

Sylvia paused for a long time, wrestling with the words. Finally, she could no longer hold in all the anguish from the past few weeks that erupted from her soul. "Mamm, please forgive me," she begged. "If I had watched her like you asked and not gone out to swing, maybe she wouldn't have died." Tears fell heavily from her eyes, and her body shook with the effort of her words.

Mamm's warm hands cradled Sylvia's cheeks as she lifted her head and looked deep into her eyes. "Listen to me, child, you bear no blame. It's my fault. I should have stopped her. I was the one right there."

Sylvia wiped tears away from her cheeks and stared at Mamm intently. She wanted to believe her words, but how could she? She had been the one to disobey. Maybe Mamm was right, and *Gott* had taken Betty to heaven because of His will. She still didn't understand what that meant.

The moment passed, and Mamm patted her hand. "Come now, your breakfast is getting cold and there is plenty to do today."

Sylvia tiptoed around the pieces of their broken family down the stairs to her cold breakfast. Even Mamm's forgiveness couldn't soothe the ache in her heart. *Would she ever find happiness again?*

FIVE

Andy

Summer 1935, Troyer Farm, Middlefield, Ohio

Andy lifted the gate of the pigpen. The three hogs snorted, snuffled, and grunted as they rooted and moved their scraps around the trough with their enormous noses. Flies buzzed everywhere and the heat of summer amplified the smell of rotten food and manure, making Andy pull up the bandana he wore around his neck to cover his nose.

Despite the stench, feeding the baby piglets always made him smile. This morning, he couldn't help but touch their soft pink skin. At his touch, the baby piglet squealed and ran away, its tiny curly tail bouncing as it made its way to its mama. He giggled at the antics.

His glee faded, however, when he noticed some of the soft pink color disappearing off the bigger piglets, their baby tenderness being replaced by a loud snorting jumble of flesh and muscle. They would need more food. All the scraps from the kitchen, peels, rinds and even yard waste went into the slop trough, but there was never enough. *How in the world would they feed three more full-size pigs?*

David came around the corner carrying two buckets of water. "Can you help me out here?" he whined.

Andy took the bucket from him and doused the sow with water. David walked away muttering about the stink. Andy kept quiet, keeping his complaints to himself. Pigs sure did add a lot of extra work, and mucking out the pigpen was the worst chore of all.

Since they'd moved to the new farm, Dat had taken care to

pick out a boar and two gilts; hoping they would reproduce and provide an ongoing supply of hams and bacon for the coming years, but their demands of food had exceeded his expectations.

One evening at dinner, Dat surprised the family. "You'll never guess what happened today." A twinkle caught his eye.

"I went into town. The crops have been growing well, and the orchard is full of ripening fruit, so when Mamm told me at breakfast her garden rake had rusted apart, I decided to pick up a new one rather than fix it.

"You know how Patchin's is. All the men were sitting out front smoking pipes and swapping tales. I stood out like a sore thumb, being the only Amish there. I overheard Mr. Dewey, the baker, talking about his problems. 'Business has been slow of late, with folks doing their own baking at home. With the price of flour these days, I hate to see my excess thrown into the garbage. Seems like I should be able to get a little coin for my day-old bread.'

"The men grunted in agreement. A few threw out some suggestions, but none seemed to strike a chord with Mr. Dewey. I pretended to look over a rake when the idea came to mind. I eyed Dewey, waiting for my opportunity. After a few minutes, he rubbed his hands on his apron and headed down the street, hollerin' that the oven was callin' his name. I didn't waste any time and called after him. "Dewey!"

"He turned around and said, 'What can I do for you?' He looked surprised that an Amish man had chased him down."

"I can help you with some of that day-old bread."

"How's that?" he said.

"See, I have a large family and several livestock to feed. I'll take it off your hands for a discounted price. We both win."

"Dewey twirled a toothpick around in his mouth. I didn't know if he would accept my offer, but then he broke into a wide grin and extended his hand. 'Less bother for me to sell it all to one person. One cent a pound and it's yours.'

"I'll take twenty pounds every week." I said, returning the handshake."

The twinkle in Dat's eye brightened. Then he gave the best news of all. "I also told him I'd send my boys, Andy and David, into town tomorrow afternoon to pick up the bread."

"You mean it, Dat?" David exclaimed wide-eyed. "A trip into town by ourselves?"

"Yup, I think you and Andy are ready for this responsibility. Dewey told me he should have a load ready tomorrow and every week thereafter. He said to have you boys come around back and he'll help load it."

Dat rubbed his hands together in glee. "I did a little jig on my way back to the buggy. I hit the jackpot. The *gut* Lord has provided for us."

Andy couldn't imagine Dat doing a jig. Later, when no one was watching, he tried to do one himself but failed miserably. He didn't care. Tomorrow was his birthday and his first solo trip into town. Nothing could squash his joy. The hogs in the pen watched him through slitted eyes. Andy thought they should be more grateful for the food Dat had just secured them.

The next day at breakfast, Dat gave Andy and David their instructions.

"Where should we go when we get into town?" David asked in anticipation.

"You'll go to Dewey's Bakery, next to Patchin's meat market."

Andy knew the exact location of Dewey's. The yeasty smell of baking bread baking from the small shop always made his mouth water.

"Go around the back and rap on the door. Let Mr. Dewey know you are Eli Troyer's sons." Dat pressed two shiny dimes into the center of Andy's palm. "Keep these coins in your pocket and do not lose them."

Dat paused for a moment, then placed a hand on each of their shoulders. "One more thing, when you go into town—you represent our family and traditions. I'm counting on you. One simple mistake can ruin a reputation, and then we must answer to the Bishop. Make me proud."

Andy stood in silence, contemplating Dat's words. He considered the recent shunning of Daniel Fisher for drinking at the town tavern and remembered the shameful whispers of the church members. He wanted no part of disappointing Dat. So, he bowed his head and nodded his understanding.

"Andy, repeat back to me how to get to Patchin's? I want to make sure you don't get lost."

Andy rattled off the directions, taking care to include local landmarks. He ended his recollection with, "We can do it. David and I will bring back the load for you and the pigs. We will make you proud."

"*Gut*," Dat replied. "Now go get the red wagon you normally use for weeding the garden and head out after lunch."

Andy's heart swelled. Finally, Dat had given him an important job, the perfect birthday gift.

After lunch, Andy and David started off on their mission. They began at a steady clip but quickly grew tired. It seemed much further than Andy remembered. The sun blazed down on his back, and his palms grew sweaty, having to squeeze the wagon handle. Eventually, the filling station appeared ahead, renewing Andy with vigor, and he increased his pace.

Andy and David entered town just as a train whizzed down the line towards the station. They had only seen a railcar once before.

"*Ufanstandi*! Look at it go!" David proclaimed. "The *English* sure know how to have more fun than we do."

"Don't talk like that. Someone might hear you. Remember what Dat said." Andy wanted to whoop just as much as David but heeded Dat's instructions.

"Let's get closer to the station!" David hollered. Andy took off after him. The little red wagon clattered behind him.

A single railcar resembling a caboose screeched to a stop. A handful of people exited its doors. Others stood waiting to board the train, dressed in their Sunday best and ready for a day in the city. Andy had a hard time averting his eyes from the ladies' exposed ankles and fancy hats. When a blush crept onto his cheeks, he looked away.

The train boarded, reversed directions, and headed back towards Cleveland, its large ocular headlamp shining bright. Andy and David stood and watched it disappear into the horizon until they could see it no more. Then they headed down High Street, looking for Patchins'.

Andy recognized its portico with the four slender wooden columns lined with ornamental corbels. The shaded porch held several benches where men rested and chatted. They quietly rolled their red wagon past the store, careful not to draw unwanted attention. Their mission lay next door at Dewey's.

The smells coming from Dewey's were tantalizing. Bread, sugar, and cinnamon drifted up in the air, drawing its patrons in the front door like a siren's call. Mamm always did her own baking, so there was never a need to go into Dewey's, but Andy always desired to see what went on behind those doors. Now he had his chance.

Following Dat's instructions, they passed the front of the store and turned down the little alleyway. The little wagon wheels crunched over the gravel. A screen door appeared at the back, just like Dat had said. The crackle of a radio drifted out the door with the excitement of an afternoon Cleveland Indians ballgame.

"The windup and the pitch, Linke throws a heater down the center of the plate, a strike for the Washington Senators starting pitcher!" the announcer cried. "That takes us to the top of the 4th folks, score is 1-1 with the Senators and the Indians in a tie. We'll be right back to the game after this commercial break."

Andy took the commercial break as his cue to knock timidly on the screen door. A man wearing an apron covered in flour came to the door. He was very tall, with a bulging waistline and dark hair that had lost its middle, leaving a large shiny bald spot. He sported round eyeglasses he kept pushing up with his index finger. "What can I do for ye fellows?"

David spoke up first. "We are Eli Troyer's young 'uns here to pick up the bread."

"Very well," chuckled the man. "Eli sure got a good deal on all this bread. He caught me at the right time. I've been saving them for a few weeks. Come on in while I grab them. I'll help you load the wagon."

Andy and David stepped inside. A big fan whirred in the corner, stirring the hot air cranking out from the ovens. A rack held pans of rolls, the snake-like ropes of dough rolled out and knotted up in small bundles to rise. Several loaves of sandwich bread were baking in the industrial oven. A workstation lined the other wall, full of bowls and giant spoons that littered the counter. Flour sprinkled over every crevice, even on the ceiling.

The radio sat on a small shelf above the workstation, ensconced in shiny cherry wood with two round circles on the front. One circle seemed to function as a dial, while the other had a mesh covering from which the sound came out. A small brass plate fixed to the front displayed the word "Admiral." The radio blared the newest advertisement for the 1935 Pontiac that promised 'sheer unadulterated thrills.' Andy had never heard such words and didn't know what they meant, but they sent a tiny shiver of pleasure up his spine.

Mr. Dewey came around the corner, dragging two large flour sacks bursting with goods. He headed out the door and heaved them onto the little red wagon. "There you go boys, come back again in a week and I'll have some more for ya."

Andy took the twenty cents Dat had given him out of his pocket and placed it in Mr. Dewey's beefy palm. Mr. Dewey pocketed the money and then got a spark in his eye. "I saw ye boys eyeing those sweet breads." He reached deep into his apron pockets and handed each boy a roll. "How'd ye like a cola to go with that?"

David's eyes got big. "We'd like that very much, sir!"

Andy elbowed David. He thought it'd be better not to take such an extravagant treat from the man. "Dat wouldn't like us taking handouts," he whispered to David.

Mr. Dewey grinned. "Don't you boys worry. This is my treat." He turned back inside to retrieve the colas from the icebox. "Now you come on back next week. I may not always have Coca-Cola, but I never run out of sweet treats."

Andy tentatively took the sweaty Coke from his hand, afraid of what it might cost him, but it was his birthday, after all. Mr. Dewey bid the boys goodbye and shut the door, humming a tune as he went back to work.

David and Andy stood for a beat, hardly believing their luck. "Let's sit and enjoy this Coke while it's cold," Andy whispered.

They moved to the back corner of the bakery building and sat on the dusty ground. Secretly, Andy wanted to listen to the rest of the game to see who would win. As the strains of baseball drifted out the screen door and down to the corner, Andy picked little pieces off his sweet roll and took tiny little sips of his Coke, willing the moment to last as long as possible.

Finally, the game ended, with Indians' pitcher Lee striking out the last player, and giving the Indians the 2-1 win. David and Andy had sat on that dusty spot for a little over an hour, lost in the game. Now the hard work really began, hauling all the heavy bread back to the farm.

Andy soon realized he'd lingered too long in town and tried to hurry to make up for lost time. The wagon was much heavier and took more effort to pull, but he didn't care. The excitement of the afternoon propelled him forward.

A little over an hour later they made it to the farm lane and as they rolled into the yard, Mamm came out on the front porch, hands on her hips and worry in her eyes.

"What took so long? We were about to hitch the buggy and come looking for you all," she fretted.

Andy kept his eyes downcast. He contemplated lying, but had never fibbed before. "I'm sorry, Mamm," he whispered. "Mr. Dewey gave us a treat, and we stayed a bit too long to enjoy it."

"Tsk. You shouldn't have taken the treat. He's already giving us this bread at a discount. Just politely decline next time."

Andy wanted to tell her about the radio and the baseball game, but the words wouldn't leave his lips. It wasn't necessarily a lie, he reasoned, just an omission. If he disclosed the truth, Dat would never allow him to go into town again. Listening to the radio would certainly earn him a trip to the Bishop and probably to the woodshed, besides why was it all that bad?

Andy could hear Dat's lecture now. "The *veech mon* has got your soul."

Dat often said the *gut mon* and the *veech mon* struggled for control of a person. One should always listen to the *gut mon* and do good. The more the *gut mon* won, the greater the chance of going to heaven. The only way to correct the wrongs of the *veech mon* was by confession to the Bishop and church. If the church forgave the wrongdoing, then you would be in correct standing before God.

The thought of confessing made his palms sweaty. It would bring such shame to Dat. So, he tucked his sin into his heart, the weight of it only a little pebble. Listening to the radio wasn't all that bad. He didn't mind carrying the pebble around for some time. Hopefully, David wouldn't spill the truth and would keep his mouth shut for once.

Mamm came off the porch and lifted the heavy sacks up out of the wagon. "Lindy Ru, come out and help the boys with this bread," she called through the front screen door to his little sister.

Four-year-old Linda Ruth came out on the porch, barefoot, and sat down on a step. They opened the first sack and found a mountain of rolls, bread, and a few cookies, each wrapped individually in brown paper. Andy undid the papers and discovered mold encrusted on several of the items. He picked the mold off and sorted it into buckets. Most of the buckets were for the pigs, but they put some of the good bread in a basket to eat later.

After completing the sorting, Mamm directed, "David, take these buckets down to the shed. Be sure to show your Dat what you collected." She stood up, dusted her apron, turned her back, and entered the house to attend to supper and their newest sibling, Mary.

Andy sat on the porch for a few minutes, reliving his wondrous day. Giving in to the *veech mon* should feel worse, he concluded. Yet, he was already looking forward to the following Wednesday when they would trek back to town.

"Andy!" Dat hollered from the barn. "Come and do your chores."

He got up and jogged down to the barn.

Dat stood waiting for him at the door, pitchfork in hand. "What is this I hear about accepting treats from Mr. Dewey?"

Andy's heart plummeted.

"I thought I made it clear you were to pick up the load and come right home."

"Yes, Dat."

"Your punishment is waiting. Head to the woodshed."

Had David only told him about the treats, or was Dat holding out, waiting for a confession? He was already getting a switching regardless of if he confessed or not. He knew he should come clean, but the words wouldn't leave his tongue, about the radio.

Dat's heavy leather switch hung from a nail in the rough lean-to. Andy hadn't been spanked before, but he deserved a spanking, especially for his hidden sin. Thankfully that sin would stay between him and God.

Dat didn't seem to remember today was his birthday as he delivered five perfect swats. Mamm looked at him with pity that night around the dinner table. Andy didn't care. Listening to the game had been his birthday gift, one he'd cherish, maybe even more than his burnt-up pocketknife.

Andy

1936, Troyer Farm, Middlefield, Ohio

Mr. Sanders' Model T came bouncing down the frozen lane on an early Sunday morning. The landlord's nineteen twenty-seven coupe with its box interior, round headlights and spoked wheels crunched to a stop in the driveway. Andy watched from the living room window as Mr. Sanders stepped out. The faded and peeling paint, smudged windows, and mud-splattered wheels matched his countenance.

Dat had worked for Mr. Sanders since the house fire, helping him farm his land a few miles to the south. In exchange for the work, Mr. Sanders had let them move into the small farmhouse and provided a modest salary. A new beginning for their family.

"*Gut* morning, Sanders," Dat bellowed from the front porch as Mr. Sanders slammed the car door. "What brings you over this morning?"

Why was he visiting on a Sunday morning? They reserved Sundays for church, rest, and visitation—not work. Today, Mamm had busied herself in the kitchen preparing a large breakfast for a time of fellowship. Andy's stomach growled, and he hoped Dat wouldn't invite Mr. Sanders to eat all their good food.

"Come on in for a spell and have a cup of coffee," Dat invited.

Andy slipped behind the open door that led from the porch into the kitchen. He peeped through the crack above the hinges, eager to eavesdrop.

Dat pulled out a chair at the table, and they sat. Frying sausages popped their grease on the stove.

Mr. Sanders rested his hand on his cheek while rubbing an eye with his index finger. The permanent creases above his brow deepened as his eyes darted about. "There's something we need to talk about," he said.

Mamm turned and gave Dat a look. The air in the kitchen tightened. This news did not seem like good news.

Mr. Sanders stammered, "You know my son Herman, who just turned eighteen? Well, he has taken a liking to a pretty girl out of Middlefield. They have become betrothed and plan to wed after the first of the year."

Dat's eyes narrowed. "Many congratulations to them."

The water finished boiling, and Mamm set the cups of steaming coffee in front of them.

Sanders took a deep, long dreg before continuing. "I need this house for 'em. Nellie comes from good stock. The only way her folks agreed to the marriage is if we can provide a place for them to start their lives. I'm sorry, Eli, I came to issue a thirty-day notice of vacancy."

The room went slack. The only sounds Andy heard were the occasional slurps of coffee and the spittle of grease coming from the stove.

Dat finally spoke. "I hate to leave this place. It has become home to us, Sanders, but what choice do we have? It's your property. How about the work I do for you at the other farm? Are you relieving me of that as well?"

At Dat's question, Mr. Sanders hung his head and issued a quiet, "Yes. I hate to do it, but I need to be taking care of my family. If there is anything I can do to help you find other work, let me know."

Dat's shoulders slumped, and the corners of his mouth turned down. Mamm kept to herself, frying the sausages. Dat extended his hand and issued a simple thank you.

Thank you? For what? Taking our home and work? Andy didn't understand why Dat didn't fight harder to save their home.

"I best be going. I'm afraid I've ruined your Sunday." Mr. Sanders placed his hat on his head and tipped it towards Mamm as he headed out onto the porch.

"Sanders," Dat called after him, following him down the steps. "Let me have the day off tomorrow. I need to go into town to look for work."

Mr. Sanders tightened his lips and nodded in agreement. Andy heard his car rumble to life and squeal out of the front yard and up the lane.

Dat entered the house muttering, "Those Model T's look just like electrified buggies." Andy had to cover his mouth to conceal the laughter that threatened to give away his hiding place. He shouldn't laugh, not at a time like this.

Shaking his head in disgust, and slamming a fist on the table, Dat picked up the folded piece of paper left on the kitchen table. Andy could see words scrawled across the top in bold print. Dat scanned the document and then read aloud near the bottom, "Eighteen ninety-seven Swanee Road must be vacated by January first, nineteen thirty-six." Andy glanced at the calendar; today's date read November thirtieth.

The next morning, Dat invited Andy to ride along with him into town. "Folks might have pity if I have a young 'un in tow while looking for work."

Andy hated pretending he hadn't eavesdropped. He had a

hundred questions about the situation. Mostly, he wanted to figure out how he could avoid getting into such situations in his own life when he grew up. He played along. The *veech mon* already had a little of his soul after last summer's radio listening. "Why do you need to look for work, Dat? Don't you have a job here?"

"I won't in a month. Sanders is giving the lease and work to his son."

Andy didn't respond. He wanted to shake Dat and tell him to fight for them, but the will to fight had long left Dat. What was the use? They had moved so many times that transitioning to the next house had become part of their normal rhythm.

After chores and breakfast, Dat hitched up the buggy and they headed into town. He stopped first at Patchin's store. As usual, the men sat out front, smoking and chatting. Dat hesitantly approached the group, muttering under his breath, "I probably should have gone to the Bishop first." Once he stood in front of the men, his demeanor switched and he exclaimed brightly, "*Gut* morning. How ya doing?"

The group grunted positively. "How'd your crop fare?" asked Mose Miller.

"Had a decent crop this year. Felt good until my landlord decided not to renew my lease." Dat wiped sweat from his brow despite the chilly autumn air.

Nerves crawled under Andy's skin, being so close to *Englishers*. He avoided Mr. Dewey's eyes. With a word, the man could expose his deepest secret.

"You know anyone looking for work? Wanting to lease a farm?"

"Actually, I heard word of a fellow up north who has gotten into the leasing business. Might be worth paying him a visit. The name is McNish. He lives up in Burton Station, about a mile past the train station on the right."

Dat placed his hat back on his head. "Appreciate the tip."

"Hate losing a good family around here, but understand you have to do what you need to do in these hard times." Mose also tipped his hat to Dat and offered him a genuine smile.

Dat gave a wry smile in return and walked back to the buggy. He patted Andy on the head. "Time to pay a visit to Burton Station."

Andy released the breath he'd been holding. Mr. Dewey still held his secret, for now.

Andy had never been to Burton Station before. Dat drove the ten miles through the countryside, gripping the reins tightly, his knuckles white. The chilly wind whipped around the buggy, spurring them forward up Old State Road and onto Burton Windsor. After riding past the whistle-stop, a large farmhouse, barns, and silos appeared on their right, just like Mose had said. A milk truck rolled out of the lane as they turned in. The horse clipped clopped forward and came to a stop in front of the house. Dat hopped out, tying the reins to a fence post. Andy dismounted and joined him.

Several porch swings swayed gently in the icy breeze on the wide porch. The glass-paned front door looked expensive. Through the wavy glass, a set of carpeted stairs rose to the second floor; a sitting room sat to the left and a dining area to his right. The house looked fancy; people with money lived here.

Dat smoothed back his sandy hair, adjusted the brim of his hat, and ran his fingers through his beard before he rapped on the door.

A slight woman with bright blue eyes and a tight white bun appeared in the hallway. She dressed in a wool grey skirt with a blouse tucked into the waistband; stockings and sensible shoes completed her outfit. Walking to the door, she cracked it open and peered out. "What may I do for you?" she asked in a clipped tone.

"*Gut* morning, ma'am, my name is Eli Troyer. Could I please speak with Mr. McNish?"

"Is he expecting you?"

"No, ma'am, Mose Miller in Middlefield told me I could find him here. I'm hoping to speak with him about leasing a farm. We need to be moving on from the house we live in. The owner's son is getting married and needs it for his kin, so I'm looking for a new place."

Andy could hear the desperation in Dat's voice. Despite his efforts to control it, the distress leached through; like the cold and went straight to his bones sending a chill up his spine.

The woman glared at Andy, making him shrink.

"Could I have a word with him, Ma'am?" Dat took off his hat and bowed his head forward. He all but knelt in front of this woman, begging.

A man came around the corner. "Delores? I need you to get lunch together for several of my—" he stopped speaking, seeing Dat in the doorway. "Well, who do we have here?" he asked, glancing over the top of his wire-rimmed glasses.

Dat lifted his head from its prostrate position and seized the opportunity. "Name's Eli Troyer." He extended a hand. "Mose Miller sent me up this way. I am looking for work for me and my family." Dat placed his other hand on Andy's head. "I'm a strong farm worker and will do whatever is needed in exchange for housing."

"Delores, doesn't that beat all? You won't believe this? Howard just gave me his notice." McNish slapped his knee. "He's moving to Indiana."

The man locked eyes with Dat. "He helped me with the overflow stock and sick animals. Kept them for me on a small property close by. It's not a large house, and the pay is mostly room and board, but if I can verify your story, the job is yours. I've always heard you Amish are hard workers."

"I currently work for Mr. Truman Sanders out of Middlefield. I've helped keep his stock and farmed his fields. He'll give me a good word."

"Where can I find this, Mr. Sanders?"

Dat gave him an address.

"Come back in two days' time and I'll have a final answer for you."

"Thank you, sir. Much obliged." Dat tipped his hat as they exited the porch and climbed into the buggy. The man gave a friendly wave as they circled around and took off back towards Middlefield.

Weariness instead of glee swirled in Andy's heart. This couldn't be the way to get ahead in life. Dat had found a home and work for them, but at what cost? *Why should a man have to grovel and plead for a roof over his head?* Dat's plea had been done with such earnestness that Andy almost believed he was genuine. The thought of another move made him tired. The appeal of starting over had lost its luster years ago.

Snow fell softly in mid-December when Mamm orchestrated the packing. "Lindy Ru, tie the clothing into bundles, using these sheets. Andy, pack the pots and pans in those wooden crates." She pointed to the corner of the kitchen, where a stack of milk crates sat. Make sure you get some hay from the barn to use as padding."

Dat had borrowed a wagon from a fellow Amish family and placed it in the shed. The boys loaded any unnecessary furniture ahead of the pending move.

"How are we going to get the pigs and cows over to Burton Station?" Andy asked, scratching his head.

"Mr. Sanders agreed to move them by truck."

"Life would be much more convenient if we could just drive ourselves." Andy hadn't meant to say the words out loud, and he clapped a hand over his mouth as soon as he realized they'd left his tongue.

Dat glanced over at him, surprised. "You know that's not our way. Driving is worldly. You best examine your heart, son, and confess. We can't have the *veech mon* taking a foothold."

Andy hung his head. "*Jah*. I'm sorry, Dat," he responded before scurrying off to the house, afraid Dat would reach for the switch next.

The next morning, the light dawned brightly. Andy bundled his belongings inside a sheet and knotted it tightly, just like Mamm had taught him. Then he helped his brothers and sisters do the same. Buggies streamed down the lane at nine o'clock after breakfast and chores. The women chatted while the men loaded three other borrowed wagons.

"Let's build a snow fort!" David cried, leading the charge as the children hustled outdoors, rolling in the fresh coating of snow and taking turns crafting snowballs to throw at each other. Once they were tired of the cold, they came into the house and stood around the kitchen stove warming their hands and noses, only to repeat the cycle all over again.

Andy threw a few snowballs but couldn't get in a festive mood. Tomorrow, none of these cousins, friends and church members would be in their everyday lives anymore. They would join a different district far away from everything they knew. He should be grateful that Dat found work, and that they didn't have to go live with Mummie and Daughty again, but he didn't want to leave. A better answer had to be out there somewhere. If Dat wasn't smart enough to figure it out, he would. Even if he only went to school a few days a week.

By noon, the trail of wagons clomped down the road to Burton Station, pulled by the draft horses. Andy looked anxiously at the horizon, yearning to see their new home. As they crested a hill, a squat white house nestled in a holler appeared. It was a far cry from the stately farmhouse the McNishes lived in. The front door had peeling red paint, far too worldly for an Amish family. He imagined a paintbrush in his hand by the end of the week.

Mamm clucked her tongue. "Did you ask to disconnect the electricity?"

"*Jah,* but he didn't take out all the plugs and switches, just flipped the breaker."

Mamm grunted. "I wish he'd at least cut the wires. Everyone will think we've gone worldly."

Andy liked the idea that the flip of a switch could electrify the house. He'd look for that breaker whenever he had a chance.

Dat responded to her. "The church knows we are doing the best we can in these hard times. At least *Gott* provided a roof over our heads. The basement contains an old coal furnace that can heat the house. The kitchen also has a wood stove alongside the modern electrical one. I'll have the men help me take the electric oven out to the barn while you unpack."

Andy didn't understand how Dat could think *Gott* had been gracious to them. All He seemed to cause was calamity.

They pulled into the yard, and Dat tethered the horse to the tree. The children helped unload the wagon carrying in crates of dishes and bedding. Mamm placed her canning on the shelves. The house didn't have indoor plumbing, but it had an upgrade, an indoor pump sink.

The most fascinating thing of all was the large window centering the living room with a bench built underneath for sitting and gazing out into the yard. All the children took turns looking out the big window while the rest marched in front, waving and laughing. Andy could hardly stomach their glee. The window seemed ominous, like a big eye opening into their lives, and he wished they'd never come to this place.

Moving day ended. People exchanged handshakes, and cousins shouted their goodbyes as the wagons exited down the lane. Mamm got busy preparing an inaugural dinner of fried potatoes and tomato gravy while the rest of the family settled their belongings and explored.

Dat needed to report to the McNish farm the next morning at eight o'clock to start work. Andy and David also needed to get up early to oversee the chores for Mr. McNish's small herd of livestock kept at the house, along with their own pigs and horses, so they went to bed after licking their plates clean.

Andy's eyes were heavy with sleep as he shifted on the straw-stuffed mattress, but he couldn't get the vision of the McNishes' plush residence out of his mind. He imagined stepping on the padded carpet and tucking in cozily next to the fire with an electric lamp next to him.

Life was easier for the *English*. If he was honest with himself, life was easier for most Amish, too. An uneasiness settled over him as a truth revealed itself. *Dat was the problem.*

SEVEN

Sylvia

Summer 1938, Slabaugh Farm, Burton, Ohio

The sun peeked its head over the eastern horizon. Sylvia cupped a hand to her forehead and scanned the morning sky. Painted strokes of red, pink, and yellow swathed across the pale blue sky. Dew on the grass absorbed the heat from the sun's rays and created a shimmering haze that sat close to the ground. *Weather's a coming,* she thought as she swung her tin bucket to the other side of a row in the garden.

She bent over the bushy plants, moving aside the leaves and checking underneath for the long, straight green beans. She moved swiftly, willing the chore to pass to go play with her best friend Alma, who lived across the street. They planned to run through the corn-fields until they saw nothing but the tassels overhead. Then Sylvia hoped they'd play house, carving out their own little burrows and pretending to raise little ones.

Sylvia finished up picking the last row when Mamm appeared at the doorway and called her in for breakfast.

"I've made your favorite, flapjacks with maple syrup."

Sylvia licked her lips. She loved flapjacks and maple syrup.

Dat had his own maple trees and every spring, when the snow melted, she tagged along with him to tap the trees. Dat punctured the trees with his hand-cranked drill, taking care never to put a hole in the same spot, always looking for the scar he created the year before.

This past spring, before he drilled the hole, he'd called for Sylvia. "Stand next to this root. Hmm… just a few inches higher than last year," he chuckled. "Before long, we'll need to borrow another child to be our height meter with the way you're growing."

Dat's words cut Sylvia deep. Betty should have been his measuring stick. No matter how much time had passed, moments like these were a constant reminder of her sister.

This morning, the warm tendrils of syrup swirling on Sylvia's plate stirred her memory of Betty's soft curls. She could almost feel her chubby body resting on the curve of her hip. She would do anything to have her back, to change her decisions on that fateful day.

Not wanting a speck of syrup to go to waste, Sylvia lifted the plate to her lips and licked it clean.

When she came up for air, Mamm looked at her sternly. "Where are your manners?"

Sylvia grinned. "Too good to go to waste. Thank you, Mamm, for the breakfast."

Mamm turned back to the pot she was stirring on the stove. "What are you and Alma up to today?"

"We are going to play in the cornfields until lunch, and then we might go to her house."

"Stay close by and be sure to come home for lunch." Mamm glanced at the gray clouds forming. "Looks like rain's coming; if those clouds thunder, come on home," she commanded with a creased brow.

"Yes, Mamm." Sylvia's mood darkened. Mamm had changed. Now it seemed she fretted over every move, always wanting to know where she played and what time she would be home—a relentless shadow that never left her side.

Sylvia wished Mamm would let her loose and give her permission to roam from dawn to dusk, like Alma's parents did, but knew she would never receive it. Her actions had resulted in her being forever tethered to Mamm's side as punishment.

Sylvia rose from the table, threw her dishes in the kitchen trough and let the screen door slam behind her as she raced across the lawn to Alma's, glad to be out from Mamm's scrutiny and away from her own thoughts. Her bare feet kicked up tiny puffs of dirt as her bonnet strings trailed behind her in a flurry.

Around noon, Sylvia heard the telltale "*Cheeeckkkk*" in Mamm's soprano vibrato.

Mamm loved hollering for Dat by his nickname. "Time for lunch!" she wailed.

Sylvia looked at the sky. Dark thunderclouds pooled together, their bellies full and swollen with the threat of rain. She took her time meandering back to the house, wishing the rain would go away and with it Mamm's strict schedule.

Entering the kitchen, Sylvia noticed rows of canned green beans lining the counter, fresh out of the boiling canning water. A pot bubbled on the stove. The salty brine of ham punctuated the air. "What's for lunch?" she asked, her stomach growling.

Mamm pulled a fresh loaf of bread from the oven. "Ham, green beans, and some potatoes I dug from the garden."

Sylvia took her place at the table.

Dat, John, and Clara were already seated, waiting for her.

"Those clouds sure look like trouble," Dat commented. "I better eat and get back out to make sure that the animals are secure."

Mamm didn't speak, but her face paled as she set the serving bowls on the table.

Sylvia shoveled the food into her hungry mouth. Dat finished first, followed by her brother, who grabbed a slice of bread to enjoy on the go as they headed back to the barn.

Dat and John jogged across the lawn as the sky grew darker and more ominous, and the wind picked up. The leaves on the trees flipped and showed their pale underbellies as the tops swayed their thirsty branches back and forth in a wave, welcoming the impending storm.

Mamm snapped into action. "Clara, go get the laundry in off the line, and Sylvia make sure that all the windows are closed."

Sylvia reached for the kitchen window, and Mamm got busy clearing the table, her jaw clenched tight.

The first drops of rain came in splatters. Fat, wet drops hit the ground, leaving circles of dust. Clara ran to the house with the clothes basket on her hip, and when she ducked onto the porch, the skies let loose, dumping their floodgates on the dry earth. It rained so hard that you couldn't even see the barn from the porch. Mamm latched the door tight behind Clara.

"What about Dat?" asked Sylvia. "Won't he need to get into the house?"

"John and Dat will stay in the barn with the animals. Come girls, let's sit down and wait for it to let up."

They all sat at the kitchen table looking out the back porch window. Rivers of water overflowed the gutters and splashed to the ground. Soon the steady drum shifted to a heavier pattern.

"Look, Mamm, there are marbles bouncing off the roof!" Sylvia exclaimed.

"Those aren't marbles, Sylvia, that is hail. It often happens when there is a severe storm," Mamm explained.

At first, the pellets were the size of pennies, but within a few minutes, they transformed into lethal round balls. Then came the lightning, slicing its path across the sky every few seconds, followed by deep bellows of thunder.

"I'm scared, Mamm."

"I know child, me, too. Let's pray." They huddled together at the table, their heads bent. Mamm began, "Our Father, who art in heaven—"

A loud clatter came from the upstairs landing, interrupting Mamm's whispered words.

Sylvia screamed.

Something else heavy hit the wood floor with a thump and then rolled to a stop.

"Stay here and get under the table," Mamm commanded. "I'm going to go see what it is."

Sylvia's heart raced as she crawled under the table. Clara reached for her hand and gripped it tight. They sat shoulder to shoulder, their eyes squeezed shut, waiting for Mamm to return. Sylvia counted her breaths. She got to twenty when Mamm returned.

"It's alright, girls," said Mamm in a relieved voice. "Sylvia, you left the hallway window open, and some of the hail came into the house. Do you want to see what hail looks like?"

Sylvia opened her eyes and scrambled out from under the table. Mamm opened her palm. An icy sphere pressed against her skin. The heat of her hand melted the outer layer.

"Wow." Sylvia picked up the translucent ball. "The sky is raining ice in the middle of summer. Who would have thought?"

"Go on and look upstairs. There are plenty more. We need to get them swept up and in a bucket before they melt."

The girls flew up the stairs. Hundreds of balls littered the floor like spilled marbles. Several had bounced down the stairs and pooled together on the first landing.

"Have you ever seen anything like this?" Sylvia exclaimed.

Clara shook her head in wonder. "Let's get a broom and bucket and get this mess cleaned up."

When the clouds broke, Mamm cracked open the door, and they looked outside. The air hung quiet and fresh. Dat and John approached the house, skirting the pieces of siding and tree limbs littering the yard.

"You all okay?" Dat shouted.

Mamm opened the door wider. "Everything is fine. How about you and the livestock?"

"The barn is good. Don't know about the cows yet. I came to check on you all first, then I'm going out to the pasture."

"We'll come, too." Mamm and the girls pounded down the back steps following Dat to the back pasture.

Sylvia couldn't think of another storm this ferocious. Daughty always talked about the one in '09 that leveled the crops. She picked up a piece of a shingle that had flown off the roof and tossed it aside. Limbs and branches were down all over the path leading out to the pasture.

As they rounded the corner, Sylvia's eyes widened. Five cows lay in a perfect semicircle underneath the shelter of the large sycamore tree. Their legs pointed upwards from their smooth, bloated bellies.

Dat walked over to the tree and looked up into its leafy branches, then his fingers trailed down the dark streak that had scorched its way down the thick trunk.

"Why is the tree burnt like that, Dat?" Sylvia asked as she reached his side.

"That's where the electricity transmitted and leapt into the cows that were sheltering underneath the tree. The lightning got 'em," he whispered.

She'd never heard of such a thing. She lurched forward to touch the tree, wanting to feel its power.

"Stay back," Dat commanded, as he grabbed a handful of her dress.

The telltale star on the forehead of the cow closest to her made Sylvia gasp. "Is that...." The words couldn't leave her mouth.

"*Yough*," Dat exclaimed.

Betty's calf. The reality gutted her as a picture flashed through Sylvia's mind of the day when Dat bought Betty her little calf. Betty's smile had lit up her entire face as her hand nuzzled its warm nose. Sylvia's dark jealousy had prevented her from enjoying the moment, and now one more piece of Betty was gone. All because of her.

"What do we do with the bodies, Dat?" John asked.

"I'll go get the draft horses, and we will drag them out of the field and bury them."

"Was it..." Mamm's words trailed off. She squeezed Sylvia tight to her side and reached a hand up to wipe a tear that fell down her cheek.

"I'm afraid so, Lizze. I'm sorry, *Leifje*," Dat patted the top of Sylvia's head.

It had been a long time since Dat had called her *Leifje*. Sylvia relished the way it rolled off his tongue. She wished Betty was here with them. Mamm held her close for a few more seconds before releasing her, but Sylvia still felt the imprint of her hand on her arm. She'd needed to be near Mamm, to bring her whatever comfort she could, to make amends for the worst mistake of her life. She had wanted to be the favorite daughter, but not in this way.

They turned back from the cows and headed towards the barn and house again.

Mamm fell in step with Dat. "Why us, Jake?" she asked. "God sure knows how to show His might, but where is His mercy?"

Sylvia wondered what she meant by mercy. *What was mercy?* God's might she understood. It lay all around her in the broken limbs and shattered pieces of their hearts. *Would they ever be whole again?*

EIGHT

Andy

Spring 1936, Lester Farm, Burton, Ohio

"One, two, three, four, five," Andy counted each bill as he laid them into Dat's outstretched hand. His wages for the week.

In late winter, Dat and Mr. Lester—Mrs. McNish's brother—had agreed that Andy would help the Lesters out with their spring work in exchange for wages. March rolled around, he moved into their home, did chores in the morning, caught the bus to the Burton School, then chored again in the evening. The Lesters covered his room and board and paid him twenty dollars a month. Twenty dollars seemed a fortune. When Mamm told Andy his wages were enough to cover all their staples from the general store, her words stuffed him with pride.

When Andy discovered he was being farmed out, he had a hard time sleeping. He'd never wanted to leave home; however, the opportunity to live with *Englishers* made him a little excited. He'd even get to go to school every day, an opportunity he'd always dreamed of. The mixture of excitement and trepidation played tug of war with his emotions. He knew eventually the day would come when he would be called upon to do more. That time had arrived, and Dat needed his help.

So, after dinner one night in early March, Mamm instructed Andy to pack a set of chore clothes and a set of school clothes because Dat was going to take him down to the Lesters'. Andy tied his clothing in a bundle, created a knapsack, and bound his schoolbooks together with a leather strap. He climbed into the buggy next to Dat. Mamm patted his shoulder, told him to be good, and that she'd make him some tomato gravy when he came home for a visit. Then they were off.

Dat held the reins loosely and didn't hurry the horses along. Their hooves hit the hard dirt, punctuating the silence on the way over to Andy's new home.

Andy sat small and quiet beside Dat. He didn't know if he should talk. Glancing over, he wondered if Dat was proud of him. Despite Dat's faults, Andy wanted his approval and hoped Dat could feel his desire in the silence. His stomach lurched. He felt as scared as he did several years ago when Mamm and Dad had brought up the idea of farming him out after the triplets were born.

Mamm had argued, "He's too young."

Dat reasoned with her. "We need the money, Mary. This is how it has always been done. What was good enough for generations past is good enough now."

Mamm won the argument, and Andy stayed at home for two more years. Two long years where he waited every day for the inevitable to happen. He pushed down the panic that climbed into his throat. This was happening.

As the buggy pulled into his new home, daylight faded, and electric lights flooded out the windows.

Electric. A new spark of excitement lit up his core. Maybe he could listen to baseball again.

Dat shifted in the seat before launching into a discourse. "Now remember to always work your best and abide by our ways. They have always served us well. You are part of something bigger than yourself, and your wages will help our family. Your efforts reflect me and our Amish traditions. Do you understand?" Dat's eyes bored into him seeking acknowledgement.

He didn't comprehend what Dat meant, but he gulped, and nodded his understanding anyway.

"I'll come for ya on Sunday and take you to church with the family."

Andy grabbed his knapsack and climbed down from the buggy. He followed behind Dat to the front door. Mr. Lester opened the door and greeted them before Dat even knocked.

"Evening, folks," Mr. Lester said in his booming voice. He shook Dat's hand, then moved to Andy. Mr. Lester's hand enveloped his hand like a heavy clamp. Andy tried to return the handshake, but his hand was unable to move under the pressure.

"Come on in, the Mrs. has got your room ready," Mr. Lester said warmly.

This might work out. They seem nice.

Dat rested his hand briefly on Andy's shoulder, then trudged back to the buggy, shoulders slumped, without looking back. Andy gave him a small wave, but Dat didn't see him as his wheels crunched down the lane.

He stepped into the house, the first *English* home he'd ever seen the inside of. In the living room sat two easy chairs. Between them on a stand sat a small radio. Melodic notes came from the speakers, meandering up and down in a strange rhythm. He'd never heard music like this before.

A woman he guessed to be Mrs. Lester hunched over a cross-stitch pattern, her nose almost touching the round frame that lay in her lap. A frown highlighted the severe angles of her face. Her white hair held back in a thin bun, and round spectacles rested on the bridge of her nose.

"Lottie, the boy's here!" Mr. Lester hollered.

"Ya don't have to yell," Mrs. Lester replied as she placed her project on the empty chair beside her and smoothed the wrinkles in her apron.

"Come on, boy, I'll show you to your room." When she spoke, her words echoed in tandem with the staccato notes coming from the radio. She gave instructions as she walked. Andy followed.

"There are a few rules you should know about. First, no hats in the house."

Andy swiped the hat from his head.

"We serve dinner at six p.m. sharp and breakfast at seven thirty. If you need any darning or mending, leave it in the basket in the hall. I don't have time for dramatics. Eli assured us you have a level head and wouldn't be prone to hysterics. The last hired hand bawled his eyes out after only two nights and had to go back home." She rolled her eyes and continued. "This farm takes all my energy. There isn't time for tears. I'll feed you three square meals a day and give you any clothing you need. You'll go on the bus to school after breakfast. We don't want to be accused of not providing a proper education. We expect your morning chores to be done prior to school, and your afternoon chores when you get home before dinner. Mr. Lester will show you the ropes in the morning." She paused at the bottom of a staircase and sighed, catching her breath. "Come, then." She motioned as she gathered her skirts and marched up the stairs.

Andy followed, his knapsack slung over his shoulder. This woman sucked the warmth right out of the room. The only words he could think to say were, "yes ma'am," as he scrambled after her.

His bedroom had a four-poster iron bed, a washstand, and a chair. A small cupboard stood in the corner with hooks inside for hanging clothing. Cotton curtains covered the single-paned window and tried to hide the moon that shone so brightly it carved a path of light onto the bed and out the door into the hallway.

"If you want to turn on the electric lights, you'll need to push this button." She punched the round switch on the wall, demonstrating how to turn off and on the electric lamp on the bedside table.

"I'll leave you to it, then. Mr. Lester will meet you outside at the barn at 5 a.m. I'll rap on your door at 4:30 a.m. to wake you up." With a twist and a flourish, she was gone. Her steps bounced down the hallway and then the stairs.

Andy stood in his new room for a moment, acclimating himself to the glare of the electric light. His mouth was dry, and he clenched his teeth, realizing the only two words he said since leaving home an hour ago were "yes, ma'am." His head spun from the sheer speed at which his life had changed.

He took off his boots, undid his clothing down to his cotton underclothes, and climbed into the bed. He reached to blow out the lantern, but his fingers brushed the porcelain lamp. Shoot. He'd forgotten to turn off the electric switch.

He rose, padded over to the small round knob, and pushed the button just as Mrs. Lester had shown him. Only the moon glowed. He punched it again, and the light glared. He did this several times until the novelty wore off. Andy wondered if David and Eli could see the blinking lights across the field coming from his bedroom window. After turning the light off for the last time, he made his way back to the bed, stumbling over his boots. He climbed in and pulled the covers up to his chin. He lay there for a long time thinking, before sleep finally overtook him.

A sharp rap on the door startled Andy from his slumber. His eyes darted around the room, disoriented until they fell upon the cotton curtains, and the events from yesterday came rushing back. *How should he respond to the knock? Should he acknowledge Mrs. Lester or just remain silent?* He decided that a simple "coming" would be adequate.

Dawn crept in the window, providing enough light to get dressed, and after he put on his chore clothes, he went downstairs. He nodded an acknowledgement to Mrs. Lester, who stood at the bottom of the stairs waiting for him, and headed out the back door, eager to use the privy before chores. He looked around for the outhouse but couldn't find it anywhere. Guess he'd have to hold it for now.

Mr. Lester had on an enormous pair of overalls and was using a pitchfork to shovel hay into stalls. "Good morning!" he sang. Andy's eyes were still sleepy and crusty. He did his best to give a half-hearted greeting in return.

"Ya know how to milk a cow, son?"

Andy nodded.

"Good, come with me then. We have ten of them to milk. That will be most of your chores, morning and evening." Mr. Lester led Andy into the cow barn. Each of the cows stood in a pen, chewing away on their feed. Mr. Lester provided a stool, and several buckets. Andy pulled on the cow's soft udders as a steady stream of milk hissed into the tin bucket.

"The milk truck comes every morning at seven-thirty. It's important to have the milk ready to go in these five-gallon cans here. When you fill one up, place it in the cooling vat right outside the door." After giving instructions, Mr. Lester exited the milking parlor and returned to his chores.

Filling the five-gallon milk cans wasn't much different from what his own family did with their supply, only Dat loaded up the wagon and drove their milk to the cheese plant a few miles up the road instead of the milk truck coming to cart it off. After he completed the morning milking, Andy headed back to the house for breakfast. He desperately needed to use the bathroom, and it took every drop of courage he had to ask Mrs. Lester where to find the privy.

"We don't have a privy. We have indoor plumbing. I suspect you'll like it a lot better than the outhouses you Amish use. It's right next to your bedroom upstairs."

Andy thanked her, excused himself, and walked up the stairs. He could hardly hold the urine that screamed for its release. The indoor outhouse held a toilet, something he supposed was for bathing, and a sink. He'd never used an indoor toilet before. He fingered the chain that hung above the gleaming porcelain bowl. *Should he pull it?* He gave it a light tug and watched his urine swirl down the hole. Feeling so much better, he headed back downstairs towards the smell of simmering sausages.

Mrs. Lester was an excellent cook and had laid out a spread of eggs, sausages, and toast with butter—more food than Mamm prepared at home. Andy took his fill, grabbed his schoolbooks, and then headed down the lane to catch the bus. *How would the English kids treat him? Would the speed of the bus make him sick?* He stood anxious with his thoughts as he waited for the bus to arrive. At least there were only two more months left in the term if it became unbearable.

Burton School was a large brick building on the town square. It had two entrances, one for boys and one for girls. Andy tried his best to blend into the crowd, but he was always aware of his differences. The boys had their modern trousers with zippers and buttons as opposed to Andy's hook and eye closures, their colorful jackets and sweaters in stark contrast to the plain white collared shirt and suspenders Andy sported. He could feel their eyes boring holes through his clothing, teasing him for his differences. A flush of embarrassment appeared on his cheeks.

Andy wished for once that he had David's personality; then he'd be able to laugh off the differences. Consumed by shyness, he instead stuffed his feelings deep down inside to think about later.

After school, the bus dropped him off at the crossroads that led to the Lesters' farm. As the bus pulled away, its exhaust puffed out blue fumes. Eli and David came from the other direction on their way home from the newly formed Amish school. Andy waved at them, and they ran to greet each other.

"Andy! When are you coming home?" Eli exclaimed.

"Yeah," David chimed in. "Ever since you left, I've had to do my chores and yours. It's time you came on home."

Andy smiled, thrilled to be in familiar company. "I bet I do more chores than both of you combined."

They continued ribbing each other and exchanging tidbits of information about their friends and neighbors until a lull in the conversation appeared. Andy hooked his thumbs in his pockets. "Well, I better get back. The Lesters are strict about me finishing the evening chores before dinner. Dat said he would come get me for Sunday church. Guess I'll see you then."

"Bye, Andy," David waved as he started in the opposite direction. Eli trailed behind him.

Andy headed down the road to the Lesters, but he only made it a few feet before he turned around. His brothers poked at each other and laughed as they made their way home. A longing to be with his family filled him.

A month later, in April, Andy started having nightmares. The first night it happened, he woke up in a panic, his heart racing and nightshirt drenched. In his dream, he stood on a distant knoll looking down onto their little whitewashed house. He could see Mamm in the kitchen cooking, his siblings playing in the yard, and Dat coming in from the barn. Then the earth rumbled and split open, and his entire family tumbled down into a great abyss, swallowed whole. Andy screamed and stretched out his arms, hoping to save them, but his efforts failed. He was alone, standing on that grassy knoll with no sign of his family to be found. The dream faded, its sharp edges cutting less into his soul, but it took him a long time to get back to sleep, and it seemed he'd only closed his eyes when Mrs. Lester's early morning rap came at the door.

The dream happened night after night. In it, his family disappeared in different ways. Once, he stood at the crossroads when the earth split open and swallowed his brothers. This version deeply troubled him.

Mrs. Lester took notice of the dark bags under his eyes and pale skin one morning at breakfast.

"Are you feeling unwell?" she asked sweetly.

"I didn't sleep well last night, but I'll be fine."

"I won't let anyone accuse me of working you to death. It's up to bed for you. Stay home from school today and get some rest. I'll bring up your lunch."

Andy didn't want to make a big deal. He remembered her opening words to him about hysterics, so he nodded, took a last swig of milk and climbed the stairs, glad for the opportunity to crawl back into bed.

He slept on and off all day, and when he awoke, big tears trickled down his cheeks. He didn't understand the tears, but knew somehow his soul had cracked open like the earth in his dreams. A deep yearning for his family bubbled to the surface. *Who could he turn to?* If he told Dat about his sorrow, he would surely disappoint him. If he talked to the Lesters, they would dismiss him. *Why had Dat put him in this position?* He needed to figure out a way to deal with the feelings that consumed him.

Later that afternoon, Andy, unable to postpone chores any longer, willed himself out of bed and got ready. He went out to the barn but couldn't find Mr. Lester. He soon spotted him near the house, helping a man unload a trailer.

The most beautiful horse he'd ever seen glided down the ramp. Its sleek black coat gleamed in the sunshine, accentuating the dainty white star on its forehead. What a fine specimen. Andy could tell she was gentle, barely nickering or pawing at the ground. As he approached, she turned her head and locked eyes with him. Her doe-brown eyes held the same sorrow as his and, without words, they understood each other. Andy approached her right side and gently placed his hand where her mane fell against the velvety skin. She trembled, but his touch calmed her.

"That boy has a way with horses, Lester," the man observed.

"You like her, Andy? Think I should buy her?" Mr. Lester asked.

Andy gulped, "Yes, sir." He knew he would do anything to stay close to this girl. "She is a fine horse. I think she will do well for you."

"Alright then, I'll take her." Mr. Lester reached into his pocket and pulled out a wad of cash. He paid the man and took the lead rope. "Andy, take her down to the barn." He handed her off. "Start brushing her and I'll meet you down there."

Andy grabbed the rope and guided his new friend towards the barn. He found an empty stall and led her in. As he brushed her, he forgot his heartache, putting his effort into rubbing her body till she shone.

Mr. Lester appeared around the corner; a smile plastered on his face. "Have little use for a horse, but figured I could make a good penny off her if I cleaned her up and sold her to an Amish family. What do you think? What should we name the ole gal?"

Andy had already been thinking about names and, without hesitation, he blurted out, "I think we should name her Marie Burton. She looks like a Marie, and she's from Burton."

Mr. Lester howled with laughter, his whole body jiggling. "Marie Burton it is. That beats all!" he exclaimed, slapping his knee. "Don't know where you came up with that name, but it's a good one." He ruffled Andy's head with affection and left hollering, "Don't forget to milk those cows!"

For the first time in a long while, Andy's spirits lifted. He had a friend to go to. He gave Marie Burton's neck a squeeze and hummed a little tune as he set about his chores.

NINE

Andy

Spring 1936, Burton, Ohio

The weeks wore on in the same pattern: morning chores, breakfast, school, afternoon chores, dinner, and bedtime. The monotony of it wore Andy down. At least he had Marie Burton to keep him company, but he looked forward to his Sunday visit home and counted down the days until Dat came to pick him up.

Finally, Sunday morning came and brought a bright, cloudless day. Andy woke with fresh energy. Today he'd go home. During breakfast, his ears and eyes peeled to the driveway, listening for any sign of Dat. At a quarter past eight, Dat's buggy came bouncing down the lane.

Andy could hardly contain his excitement. "Mr. Lester, do you think I could show Dat Marie Burton? He's a horseman, and I think he'd enjoy seeing her."

"Sure, son, take him out to the barn and show her off. Ya never know, maybe he will buy her from me."

Andy's ears perked. Wouldn't that be something if Dat bought Marie Burton? His glee quickly left with the reality of his situation. He worked for the Lesters to earn money, not to spend it. No way Dat could afford to buy an extra horse. Andy excused himself from the table and headed out to greet Dat.

Dat sat in the buggy waiting for him. "Ready to go?"

"There is something I want to show you first," Andy said, worried he may have miscalculated Dat's love for horses. "Mr. Lester said it was alright for you to come see."

Dat glanced at the sky. "Oh all right, I guess I have a few extra minutes." He folded his lanky body out of the buggy and followed Andy down into the barn. They stopped at the third stall. Andy's face pinked with pride.

"This here is my new friend, Marie Burton. Marie, meet my Dat."

Dat examined Marie. He ran his fingers down her shiny coat, muscular flanks, slender legs, and let out a low whistle. "She's a beauty son. What is Mr. Lester doing with such a fine horse?"

Andy's insides blossomed with his approval. "He is trying to turn a profit by selling her. He put me in charge of her care."

Dat rubbed his fingers through his beard, thinking. "We need a fresh horse. I wonder if Lester would exchange her for your services."

"What about the wages, Dat? Don't you and Mamm need them?"

"It would be a stretch for us not to have the money, but ole Cookie is getting up in years." He scratched the side of his face. "It's something to think about, but not today. Let's get you home. Mamm is eager to see you, and we have church at the Yoder farm in a few hours. They plan on choosing the new minister today."

Andy's face turned down. He wished Dat would go up to the house and talk with Mr. Lester about the exchange right now. Disappointed, he reached over and grabbed a handful of oats and placed them under Marie Burton's mouth. Her warm nose nuzzled his hand, and she ate willingly. He whispered to her out of Dat's earshot, "See ya later Marie, I'll miss you while I'm gone."

Dat drove the buggy down their lane until their squat white house became visible over the crest of the hill. Andy could see little faces pressed against the glass panes, wide eyes and smashed noses. He knew all his siblings awaited his arrival and news of the *English* world. Mamm stood in the doorway, hands on her round hips, a smile on her face.

Andy dismounted from the buggy before it even stopped.

Mamm gave him a pat on the head. "Come on in, son. We missed you this week. I hope you've got an appetite. I've made your favorite biscuits and tomato gravy."

He stepped into the house, eager for the familiar surroundings of home. He wanted to soak it all in because he knew the day would pass quickly.

Mamm had set him a place at the table for his second breakfast. The others had already eaten, but they all gathered around him on the benches.

"Tell us a story, Andy. What is it like at the Lesters'?" David asked. All the rest of the little voices chimed in at once, the questions rolling in one after the other.

"Every morning, I get up early when Mrs. Lester raps on my door and milk the cows, then Mrs. Lester makes a big plate of sausages and eggs to feed me before I go down the lane to catch the school bus." Andy's ears blazed when he noticed his description of the food caught Mamm's eye. He didn't want her to feel bad that they lacked sausages every morning, so he sighed in pleasure after he licked the tomato gravy clean off the plate.

At the mention of the school bus, his siblings' eyes grew wide. Andy could tell they wanted to ask more questions about his *English* lifestyle, but those subjects were best avoided while Mamm was in earshot. So, he changed the topic and spent the rest of his time talking about his beloved Marie Burton.

"You know Marie Burton has such a shiny coat. I brush her twice a day, and she barely nickers. Her favorite thing is to take a handful of oats from my hand. Her nose nuzzles into my hand, and she always licks me when I feed her."

Eventually, Mamm could no longer delay leaving for church, and she shooed everyone out the door to the wagon. "Please hurry. Church is being hosted at the Yoder farm today, and they live at the edge of the district. We don't want to be late."

Andy helped his siblings pile into the back of the wagon. As they climbed up, Mamm inspected each of them, making sure their clothing adhered to the ordinances. The clothing appeared threadbare and worn, but they wore their best frocks, and not a bonnet string or hat was out of place.

Mamm whispered to Andy before mounting the wagon. "Did Dat tell you that people have been speaking his name as a potential candidate for minister?"

"He told me it was a special service, but didn't mention his name as a candidate." Andy's mind whirled. Being a minister was the most important work a man could have. If Dat became minister, the status of their family would elevate. Dat would surely want him home and not farmed out to an *Englisher.* A sprig of hope sprang up in his heart.

Dat ambled out to the wagon from the barn, took his place beside Mamm, and clucked Cookie forward. Mamm held baby Abraham on her lap. Andy noticed Dat wore his best hat with the widest brim. The wider the brim, the more important the status at church. If Dat became minister, Mamm would make him a new one with an even wider brim.

At ten o'clock on the dot, Dat turned into the Yoders' lane. Buggies lined up in rows by the barn, each appearing as a dark speck against the bright green of the late spring.

"Woah!" Dat exclaimed as he halted Cookie and parked the buggy.

Everyone tumbled out of the back, eager to see their friends, but Mamm stalled them with a stern look. "Don't you go off yet. We need to wait for Dat to put up Cookie."

Dat strode off with Cookie towards the barn. Upon his return, he gave permission for everyone to go off and greet their groups. He took the young boys with him and joined the men standing in a line close to the barn, while Andy and David took off to the neighboring buggy barn with the older boys and teens.

In the buggy barn the young men stood quietly, making shy grins at each other, all wearing the same black vests, white shirts, and hats.

Dat began the formal greetings, starting at the front of the line. He greeted each man by shaking their hand and pecking their cheek with the holy kiss. Andy's younger brothers, Roman, Eli, and Alvin, followed Dat's example.

After everyone had arrived, and the greetings were all given, they entered the house. First to enter were all the single young ladies. After shaking hands with each one, the Bishop led them to the living room, where they sat together. The married ladies came next, taking a seat behind the girls. The boys, the unmarried men, and finally the grown married men followed and sat on the opposite side of the room. The Bishop entered. Silence permeated the room in holy reverence. The only sounds heard were the occasional sniffle or cough and the adjustment of bottoms on the benches.

Deacon Detweiler handed out the *Ausbund* hymnals. Their worn covers showed their age. Only when they fell apart were they ever replaced. Deacon Detweiler led off with the first song, *"O Gott Vater,"* and everyone joined in.

Amish singing was unlike anything Andy heard on the radio in Mrs. Lester's living room. *"O Gott Vater"* started off in a slow, mourning chant that rose to a crescendo and then a wail. He winced at the noise, now realizing how their music lacked melody. He thought a song titled "O Good Father" should be a more joyful tune, like the songs Mr. Lester sang in the barn.

All around him, the congregation sat with their heads bowed, singing the wailing song. Andy could hear the neighboring Mr. Yoder singing a bit too loudly, off tune as always, and he pursed his lips to hide the smirk that threatened to escape. The song sung in High German, the official church language, dragged on for a full fifteen minutes.

A second song, *"Das Loblied,"* followed, and while Andy sang, the Bishop and ministers from other districts rose and wrestled their way into the hallway.

Andy kept his eyes down, occasionally sneaking a sideways glance, curious to see what the ministers were doing. Their hushed murmurs joined as an undercurrent to the singing. Andy figured they were discussing the content of the sermons for the day, coordinating who would give the different parts of the message, and preparing for the special ordination service.

When the song wrapped up, the three ministers came back into the living area.

Andy listened as the minister delivered the first pre-message. He didn't understand it well because the minister spoke only in High German. After the first message, the minister invited the congregation to kneel for a prayer.

Then Mr. Yoder rose and read another scripture. Andy tried to remain attentive, but his thoughts wandered to Marie Burton. *What was she up to? Would Dat buy her?*

The third minister rose and started preaching the primary message. Andy shifted in his seat, trying to get comfortable, knowing that the sermon could last for hours. His mind drifted again to the baseball game and peanut butter sandwiches that awaited him after church, and then back to Marie Burton. If Mr. Lester sold her to a stranger, how would he survive? Her presence had made living away from home bearable. Maybe Dat would become a minister, then he wouldn't have to go back to the Lesters. The thought of leaving his newly found *English* lifestyle also tore at him. *What did he want?* He knew he wanted a different life. Neither an Amish nor an *English* life, he realized, provided the answer.

Halfway through the sermon, Andy's eyes followed Mrs. Yoder as she disappeared into the kitchen. She returned with a big bowl of snickerdoodle cookies and handed the bowl to a child sitting in the front row. The children passed around the sweet treats, digging their little hands into the bowl to pick out a cookie. Andy smiled as they licked the sugary crumbs from their fingers. He wished he wasn't too old to have a snickerdoodle, but it warmed his heart to see his little brothers and sisters enjoy the best part of the church service.

Church dragged on for what seemed like an eternity. Andy forced his eyes to stay open as the minister droned on. Finally, the Bishop arose and took over, piquing his interest. "As you well know, today we have a special ordination service. In a few minutes, we will proceed with the nominations."

Nomination Sundays were rare, and Andy had never experienced one before. The men in church leadership shuffled their way into the hallway and into an adjoining bedroom. Then the Bishop signaled for the women members to file into the hallway. Each woman took a turn, pressing their lips against a crack in the bedroom door and whispering the name of their preferred candidate. Mamm returned to her seat with a solemn look on her face. Andy wondered if she had nominated Dat.

Next, the men took their turn. When everyone had passed through, they all sat silently on the benches while the leadership tallied the votes and prepared the lots. Andy stole a glance at Dat. He sat, head bowed, hands clasped together, a light tremor in his leg.

Dat's leg always shook when he was nervous. *Did Dat want to become a minister?*

The leadership filed out of the bedroom with five hymnals in tow, each bound with twine. Mamm had told him that only one had the special slip of paper tucked into its pages.

A deacon arranged them, standing upright on a table in the front. Then the Bishop came and rearranged the hymnals again to make sure that no one knew—which one hid the paper—before speaking. "We have five nominees for this district. The Lord will show us which one has the special calling on their life." He withdrew a slip of paper from his back pocket and read the five names. Andy clenched his fists tight in anticipation. "David Yoder, Merle Byler, Amos Stoltzfus, David Schwartz, and Eli Troyer."

The faces of the chosen men paled except for Dat. He stared straight ahead; no emotion registering on his face.

Mummie told him once that when a man became a minister, he held the weight of the souls in his charge before God. Who would want to answer for the souls of others? He had a sneaking suspicion Dat didn't care about the responsibility. He wanted the title.

One by one, each nominee rose and collected a hymnal from the front and opened it to *"O Gott Vater,"* looking for the slip of paper. Merle Byler went first. He grabbed the hymnal in the middle, undid the twine, and opened the book. The page sat empty. Relief flooded his face as he sat down. Next came David Schwartz, then Amos Stoltzfus. Neither man had the special slip of paper. It was down to the final two candidates, Dat and David Yoder.

Andy snuck a glance across the aisle. Mamm's lips held in a tight line, and her face grayed. Dat had a steely look of determination in his eyes. *Would Dat or David Yoder have the slip in their book?*

Dat stood and walked forward, choosing the hymnal on his left. When he returned to his seat, his fingers undid the twine and flipped the pages. Tucked in the crease lay the paper. He fingered it and looked up as the Bishop spoke the words written in Acts 1:24: "And they prayed, and said, thou Lord, which knowest the hearts of all men, show whether of these five thou have chosen."

Dat flipped the hymnal shut. The Bishop extended his hand. "Will Eli Troyer rise to receive this charge for his ministry?" Dat stood out of his seat and shook the Bishop's extended hand. "God will strengthen you for this new work," said the Bishop. Then he gave Dat a holy kiss on the cheek, sealing the ordination.

Mamm started the wailing. Loud heaves came from her bosom, and the rest of the congregation followed her lead. Their sorrow over Dat's new charge for their souls wrapped the room in heaviness, but Andy knew Dat wanted this. *He wanted the power.*

Another song started up again to end the service. Andy's stomach churned with hunger and nerves. They had sat well past one o'clock.

With the flip of a page, their whole lives had changed. Before, the thought of Dat having such an important position hadn't fazed him, but now the pressure made him queasy. Barely anyone knew they had existed. Now, their neighbors and relatives would scrutinize their every move. A minister's son didn't have a choice but to be perfect. He couldn't face the shame it would cause Dat to be otherwise.

Later that evening, after Andy helped with the chores, he climbed up into the buggy beside Dat to head back to the Lesters'. The pair rode in silence for the first half of the distance until Dat cleared his throat.

"I'm going to tell Mr. Lester that you won't be returning after the spring work is done. Now that I'm a minister and have added responsibilities, I'll need your help around the house."

Andy couldn't hide the grin that crept onto his face. He turned away, not wanting Dat to see his pleasure. His grin faded, though, when he thought about Marie Burton. The thought of losing her stopped his breath.

As if reading his thoughts, Dat responded, "I'll see if Mr. Lester will exchange your services for the rest of the season in exchange for the horse. If it's not enough, then I'll offer my help when the harvest season comes. We'll just have to make do without the extra wages."

This time, Andy couldn't contain his joy. He gave a little bounce in the seat and smiled widely. "Thank you, Dat." He was coming home, and Marie Burton was coming with him.

Andy

1938, Troyer Farm, Burton, Ohio

"Mamm, my throat hurts awful." Linda Ruth rose from the kitchen bench where she had attempted to eat her breakfast.

Andy shoved a hunk of bread into his mouth. Linda Ruth's cheeks flushed the color of a shiny red apple as she lay back down on the bench beside him.

Mamm came over and placed a hand on her forehead. "Child, you are burning up. It's to bed for you. I'll mix up a poultice for your throat and bring you some hot tea." Mamm took her elbow and guided her down the hallway to the girls' bedroom.

Andy thought little of Linda Ruth's illness as he swallowed a swig of hot coffee and headed out to his chores. With so many in the house, someone was always sick.

The next day, Linda Ruth's fever raged on. On day two, David fell ill as well, and by day three, over half of the household became sick.

"I think we should go fetch the Doc," Mamm commented as she washed up the dishes after breakfast. "There may be something he can do."

"I don't know," Dat hesitated. "There might be nothing he can do and then we will rack up a bill. Let's wait a few more days."

"Something tells me this isn't just a normal flu. At least go into town and see if others have fallen ill in the community."

Dat closed the prayer book he studied for this week's sermon and sighed. "Alright, I'll head into town and make a stop at the general store. Andy, you come with me."

Andy didn't want to go into town. He had avoided Dat's company ever since he became minister. It scared him that Dat's enhanced connection to God would see right through to his soul. He knew there was far more evil than good in there.

Mamm spoke. "Since Andy is going along, pick me up a sack of flour while you are in town."

Dat hitched up the horse and drove at a leisurely pace, seeming unconcerned about the illness at home. He pulled into the general store and tied up the horse.

"What brings you in today, Eli?" Walter Fitch, the proprietor, asked as the door creaked shut behind them.

Dat placed three quarters on the counter. "Here to pick up some flour for the Missus and hear the news. Half the family's nursing fevers. Mary is worried it could be something more serious."

Mr. Fitch fingered the coins. "Sure hope not. I hear the measles are going around." He clucked his tongue and shook his head. "Hope you haven't caught a bout of 'em. Tell the Missus I give her my best." The cash register dinged as he deposited the coins and handed Dat his change.

Andy grabbed the sack of flour and carried it out to the buggy. Mr. Fitch's news swirled around in his head. Maybe something more serious was going on. It seemed every time they got ahead, disaster struck.

Dat looked up at the clouds swollen with pending rain. "Let's go pay Doc Aldon a visit and see if he can tell us about the measles."

Andy stroked Marie Burton's neck. "I'll be right back," he whispered to her. Then he followed Dat down two doors to the doctor's office. A bell jingled as the door squeaked open.

"Be out in a minute!" Doc bellowed from the back.

Dat stood straight with his hands clasped together. A clock ticked away, seeming to increase the pressure of waiting. Dat fidgeted with the brim of his hat. He looked down at Andy, with lips pressed together. "I sure hope Mamm appreciates the effort this is taking."

After a few minutes, Doc Alden emerged from the back in his white coat with his stethoscope around his neck. He dried off his hands on the towel that hung on a nail next to the sink. "Sorry to keep you waiting. What can I do for you, Eli?"

"The wife wanted me to come and see if there is anything you can do for our young 'uns. Several of them have taken ill with fever."

"How many?" Doc Alden's forehead wrinkled in question.

"Five."

"There seems to be a severe case of the measles going around these parts. I was just over at another homestead down towards Middlefield. Real touch and go there for a minute, but the family seems to have pulled through. All ten of them had the measles. Do you know what to look for?"

Dat shook his head.

"First, they'll be a fever followed by a sore throat. On day two or three, a rash starts on the face and hands and then spreads all over the body. Anybody have a rash?"

"Mary has mentioned no rashes. She would've told me if she had noticed one. Is there any medicine you can give?"

"I'd like to examine them before I make recommendations. This afternoon I'm heading over your way to see another family. I'll stop by the house. Tell Mary to look for the rash, and meanwhile, keep applying cool compresses to the children's foreheads to keep the fever down. If that doesn't work, give them a cold bath. Also, monitor their breathing. If the chest has to work hard to go up and down, come and fetch me. I'll let you know this afternoon if I think it's measles. I pray that's not the case, because if so, I'll have to place your household under quarantine."

Dat gave his goodbyes and exited. Andy didn't know anyone who had measles before. Mummie had always told him they'd choke you to death. Andy thought that would be a miserable way to die, letting the rash close your throat tight until no more air could get through.

Once out on the street, Dat took off in a jog back to the buggy. Andy kept pace with him, also wanting to get home to see if anyone had a rash.

When they arrived home, Dat plopped the bag of flour on the kitchen floor. Mamm stood with her back to him at the stove, fixing a poultice.

"Well, what did the Doc say?" she prodded.

"He doesn't know until he stops by this afternoon and examines the children. Says there's been several cases of measles reported down towards Middlefield. He wants to rule that out."

"I doubt it's measles. Why did you tell him to come? How in the world are we going to pay his fee?"

"I don't know. If need be, I'll ask the Bishop if the church can help. Do any of the children have a rash?"

"Why do you ask?"

"Doc said that could be a major symptom."

Mamm's face blanched. "Lindy Ru just came down with a rash this morning. Started on her face and hands and it's spreading. She's the first one."

Dat drummed his fingers on the table. "It may be the measles, then."

"*Unser Vatter*," Mamm whispered.

"Doc said to make sure we pay attention to the little ones' breathing. If they struggle, we are to fetch him."

Mamm pumped water into the kitchen sink, wetting several rags with cold water. "I need to take these to Linda Ruth and Abraham and trade them out." She sighed as she walked down the hallway.

Mamm wore a path between the boys' and girls' rooms, changing out compresses every five minutes and spoon-feeding broth to the little ones. After a quick lunch of cheese and bread, she sat down at the table. Andy ate his bologna sandwich beside her. When he rose with his empty plate, he saw how she rested her head and closed her eyes. A bead of sweat formed on her neck, wetting the neckline of her dress.

The crunch of gravel caused him to look out the door. The doctor exited his car and walked to the door.

"Mamm," he whispered in her ear. "The doctor's here."

"*Ach*, you shouldn't have let me drift off like that," she fussed.

"You were looking a little tired. I figured you needed the rest. I looked in on Abe and Lindy Ru. They seem to be fine. Are you feeling alright?"

"Just a bit tired. Nothing a good sleep won't fix."

Dat came in from the barn. He looked at Mamm through slitted eyes and placed a hand on her forehead. "You feel warm, Mary. I think you have a fever."

Mamm shrugged him off. "Just tired, that's all."

"Best be careful that you don't come down with whatever it is. I'm going to have Doc look at you as well."

Doc Alden stood at the screen door. "Howdy folks"

"Come on in, Doc," Dat motioned for him.

Dr. Alden entered, carrying his black leather bag.

"I'm afraid that Linda Ruth has started with a rash," Dat told him.

The doctor's lips turned down, and he reached into his back pocket and took out a handkerchief. He tied the ends around the nape of his neck, covering his mouth. "I just need to be careful not to catch it myself." His voice sounded muffled from behind the cloth.

Andy wondered how illnesses spread. Maybe he should tie a handkerchief around his mouth, too. Breathing through the fabric sounded awful. He'd almost rather be sick.

Dat led the Doc down the hallway and into the girls' room as Mamm and Andy trailed behind them.

"Here's my first patient," Doc exclaimed as he planted himself on the edge of the bed. He took his stethoscope from around his neck and listened to Linda Ruth's heart. "Mary, come and help me with this dress so I can see the rash."

Mamm helped undo the tiny clasps on Linda Ruth's night-dress, and the doctor placed the cool round metal piece against her speckled back.

"I also need to see her mouth and throat," he said. Reaching into his satchel, he pulled out the tongue depressor. He pressed the metal against Linda Ruth's pink tongue. "Say ahhh." Linda Ruth sat up weakly, leaning against Mamm, her eyes half closed, too tired and sick to fight.

"I think I've seen enough. She has all the telltale signs of the measles—fever, rash, and white spots on her throat. How many in the family have symptoms?"

Dat cleared his throat. "So far, only five, but I'm worried about Mary as well. She feels warm and achy."

Doc placed a hand on Mamm's forehead. "Mary, you have a fever. I must caution you to rest. It is likely that the entire family will come down with the disease. The only way through is to let it run its course. Measles are the most dangerous to the little ones. Linda Ruth is the most advanced in her illness. The others will soon start showing signs of the rash. Keep a close eye on Abraham. He's the youngest and the most susceptible to complications. I'll need to report this outbreak to the health department. Don't leave this house or be in contact with others. They will come by in the next day or two and place a quarantine sign on the front door."

Doc placed his hat on his head. "Can you boil me some water, Mary? I need to sanitize this depressor before I leave."

Mamm nodded, but didn't move from her perch beside Linda Ruth.

"Andy, will you help boil the water?" Dat asked.

Andy headed to the kitchen. Dat and the doctor followed behind.

"She needs to rest," the Doc instructed. "Remember what I told you in the office—keep the fevers down with cold compresses and baths if possible. Make sure they drink water and broth, and if the breathing gets bad, call for me."

"How should we get word to you since we don't have a telephone and can't leave the house?"

Doc rubbed his chin. "I'll pass by here every day. If you need help, tie this apron to the porch rail." He pointed to Mamm's worn apron slung over a chair. "I'll know to stop."

"Thank you," Dat replied. "I'll settle with you when I come into town the next time. I promise."

Andy caught a hint of despair in Dat's voice. They'd come so far—a stable house, work, and even a position in the church. The thought of losing any of their progress pained him. He tried to slap away the fear that buzzed in his head.

Doc put up a hand. "I know you're good for your word, Eli. Please just take care of your family. God be with you all."

Andy turned away and scowled. *God? Where was God in all of this?* He hadn't been with them when their stomachs rumbled with hunger, or when the fire burned down their house. Certainly, He wasn't with them when Dat groveled for work, selling him off to help pay the bills. If God were real, He wouldn't allow another catastrophe to strike their family.

The night passed without incident. Mamm held out for as long as she could, but by morning she could no longer see to anyone's needs because of the illness ravaging her own body. Dat sent her to bed, and she didn't argue. Andy and Dat tended to the sick the best they could. Word spread, and people brought pots of soup to the front porch, too scared to stay or even talk through the screen door.

By noon the next day, Linda Ruth seemed to be on the mend. Her fever broke and the angry rash faded to a darker color. Abraham, however, took a turn for the worse. Mamm lay in bed next to him. She slipped in and out of consciousness as the fever racked her body. While Dat did chores, Andy did his best to see to everyone's needs.

Mamm woke up late in the afternoon. "Something's wrong." She couldn't lift her head.

"What is it?" Andy responded.

"Look at Abraham."

Abraham lay still. His restlessness had ceased, and his cheeks burned hot with the fever. His pale and cracked lips bled at the corners. Most alarming, however, was the shallow, fast breaths that came in quick puffs out his nose as his chest labored to rise and fall.

"Eli," Mamm croaked, her voice sounding like a rough piece of bark.

"Mamm, it's me. Dat's out at the barn."

"Go fetch him. Something's wrong with Abraham. Look at his breathing."

Andy ran to the barn without hestitation and summoned Dat back to the house.

Dat stood beside the bed, the wooden floorboards creaking under his weight.

Mamm smoothed Abraham's blonde hair, with half-closed eyes.

Adrenaline surged through Andy. "What do we do?"

Dat took charge. "The Doc said to call him if the breathing got bad. I can put the apron out, but it may not be until tomorrow that he can get here. The fever is too high, let's try a bath. Go get a washbasin and fill it with cold water."

It took a minute for Andy to process Dat's instructions. He'd only bathed himself before.

Dat lifted Abraham into his arms. "Stop standing there dawdling. Go get the water ready."

Andy bolted to the pump, making four trips back and forth to fill up the washbasin he had set on the kitchen floor. Dat didn't bother to take Abraham's clothing off. He submerged his body into the basin, and Andy poured buckets of cold water over him. The baby's clothing clung to his ribs, and a groan escaped his lips when the water touched his feverish skin. The cold bath seemed to help. Andy noticed Abraham's breathing became less rapid. He even opened his eyes for a brief second.

"Go to the boys' room and fetch some dry clothes and a towel," Dat said while he struggled to keep Abraham's slippery body in an upright position.

Andy returned with a fresh white shirt, long johns, a cloth diaper, and a towel. He helped wiggle Abraham into the clothes, and Dat carried him back to the bed, placing him next to Mamm.

Hope rose in Andy's heart, when Abraham later took a few sips of Aunt Rachel's soup. After checking on his sisters, Andy settled in his own bed, wishing this was all a bad dream.

A hush fell over the house. The sky darkened outside, and the lamps burned low. Sleep overtook Andy like a fog, rolling in and settling over the hills. The day exhausted him. His eyelids drooped low, and his breathing slowed.

Andy woke to Mamm's cries the next morning. He ran across the hall with a racing heart. Abraham's little body lay next to her, still and gray. "Noooooo...." she howled.

Andy didn't understand. *Why was Abraham's skin so gray? Surely, he couldn't be dead.* He fought the urge to flee and vomit at the same time. "What is it, Mamm?" Andy stammered. Maybe the fever had gone to their brains.

"He's gone!" she wailed. "Abraham's gone."

Dat rushed into the room, fresh from the chores. He pushed Andy aside and placed his hand on Abraham's chest. Then Dat spoke the words Andy feared, "He has gone yonder."

Mamm curled up in a ball, her arms drawing Abraham close. Andy's chest tightened, squeezing with such force, a lone teardrop fell down his cheek, escaping the pressure. He pinched his arm and winced; this wasn't a dream. A strange feeling mixed in his stomach. A soup with ingredients he didn't recognize. He left the room feeling like he should stay but not knowing what to do.

All morning long, he poked his head in the door. Mamm lay in the same position, holding Abraham tight until she no longer cried, and Doctor Alden's frame darkened the doorway.

Doc Alden knelt beside her. "I'm so sorry Mary, I wish I could have been here to help the young lad." His voice sounded muffled from behind his mask. He placed a hand on her forehead, checking for fever. "Eli, can I have a word?" Doc motioned toward the hallway.

Dat stepped out into the hallway. The men's hushed words carried into the adjoining bedroom, where Andy helped feed David. Andy sat on the bed, unsure of what to feel. A disaster of this magnitude would crush anyone, but strangely, it didn't crush him. He'd known all along that God didn't like his family. He only wished Abraham hadn't been collateral damage.

"How do you want to handle the burial and funeral?" Doc asked Dat.

"It is customary to have a viewing, but I don't know how we will manage a showing while we are under quarantine."

"I could take the body to the hospital morgue. You could postpone the funeral until you are out of quarantine."

"No, we need to have the funeral the next day. The Bishop wouldn't approve of waiting." Their voices faded as they got further away.

Andy strained to hear their words.

The two men were now in the living room. "What do you think, Doc? You think we could lay him out in the window and folks could file past for the showing?"

The window. Andy shuddered. Its cavernous glass would eat Abraham's soul.

The Doc responded, "I think it's a fine idea, Eli, considering the circumstances. You want me to notify the Bishop of your plans?"

"Yes, please. We'll plan to lay out Abraham in his burial clothes at ten o'clock in the morning. Andy and I will make the burial box today and have it ready for the graveside service. After the showing, Bishop Miller can preside over the burial at the cemetery."

The men returned down the hall. Doc looked at Mamm curled up holding Abraham close, then whispered to Dat. "Mary cannot stay in bed with the boy; he needs to be put in a cool place to slow the decay of the body. Do you think we could take him to the basement?"

Dat swallowed hard.

"I'll explain it to her and take the boy from her arms, so you don't have to," Doc said.

Dat dipped his head, then turned down the hall and waited. It bothered Andy that Dat hadn't done the task himself.

Doc spoke softly to Mamm as he knelt beside her. "Mary, Eli and I are going to put Abraham in a safe place until the viewing and burial."

Mamm's eyes were vacant as she looked up at him. "Please, no."

Andy wanted to close his eyes and put his hands over his ears to shut out the images of Mamm's unraveling, but he couldn't bring himself not to pay witness to the moment.

Doc gently peeled Mamm's hands away and lifted Abraham into his arms, as if he were holding a newborn. Silent tears streaked down her cheeks.

"We are going to give you a proper burial, wee one," Doc spoke tenderly. "Mary, I know you'll want to be at the viewing tomorrow, so it's important you rest today, drink fluids, and gain your strength. Before I leave, I am going to give you some medicine that will help you sleep." Doc turned and carried Abraham over the threshold and down to the basement. Mamm's sobs filled all the empty spaces in Andy's heart.

The next morning dawned sunny and cool. Dozens of Amish buggies rattled down the lane at quarter till ten. Aunt Rachel sent over a burial outfit for Abraham. Mamm dressed Abraham carefully. His small body lay on the white built-in bench, with his wheat-colored hair glowing in the morning light, reminding Andy of an angel.

Andy set up two kitchen chairs behind the body, and Mamm and Dat took their seats, keeping their hands in their laps and their eyes fixed on Abraham.

A line formed at the front door and, one by one, each member of their district walked by to show their respects, nodding at Mamm and Dat through the window.

Mamm looked like she might crumble and dissolve into a pile of ash at any moment. Dat sat unblinking, expressionless. Their dark clothing contrasted with all the white and sunshine, making them look like two crows sitting on a wire. The people came to see Abraham, but all eyes were on Mamm and Dat—two dark specks against the light.

Andy stood behind Dat, trying to be strong, but his insides quivered. He couldn't stop the anger that rose inside and threatened to erupt. *I want answers*, he thought. *What kind of God would allow this?*

Daniel 2:27-28

Daniel replied, "No wise man, enchanter, magician or diviner

can explain to the king the mystery he has asked about,

but there is a God in heaven who reveals mysteries."

ELEVEN

Sylvia

1945, Slabaugh Farm, Burton, Ohio

Sylvia tossed and turned in bed, wrestling to stay asleep. Sweat beaded along her thighs, causing her nightdress to stick to her legs. In her dream, Betty ran towards her in an open field of flowers, her blonde curls bouncing up and down around her chubby cheeks. She grew up as Sylvia imagined she would. Sylvia's heart squeezed with a strange mixture of delight and sadness at the sight of her. She wanted to tell her she was sorry. To beg for her forgiveness.

The sun beat down on the top of Sylvia's dark hair; the heat spreading to the tips of her outstretched fingers matched the warmth in her heart. Betty's smile stretched from ear to ear as she pointed in Sylvia's direction.

"Yes, Betty, come!" Sylvia cried. She couldn't wait to hold her in her arms again and tell her how she missed her.

The anticipation made Sylvia's arms ache, but Betty ran right past her. The brush of her dress against Sylvia's bare leg made the hairs on her arm rise. Sylvia called after her, "Wait, don't you see me? Betty!" She stomped her foot in frustration, her eyes following the mass of curls until they focused on a man in front of her shining bright as the sun.

His white clothing shimmered, reflecting the colors of the black-eyed susan's, fireweed, and bachelor's buttons that spread out across the horizon. He had long hair, a deep laugh, and a twinkle in his eye, yet his presence commanded honor. Sylvia almost had in mind to curtsy before him.

"Dat!" Betty cried. Her arms fully outstretched, reaching for him.

Dat? This man looked nothing like Dat. How could Betty forget us, her own family?

The strange man picked Betty up and swung her around. The edge of his long robe rustled against the surrounding grasses. He threw her up in the air. Her curls extended past the top of her head and spread out like a peacock displaying its feathers.

She giggled. "Again!" she pleaded.

The man chuckled and tossed her up in the air again, his strong arms catching her. This time, he hugged her close to his chest. Betty sighed and buried her face in his white robe.

"Let's go home, Dat. This is a beautiful place, but I miss our house."

"Yes, little one," the man agreed. "It's time. Our work here is complete."

The man looked at Sylvia as he spoke. His eyes filled with a magnetic power so strong it seemed to pull her soul right to him. She knew how Betty felt in his arms because she felt it, too; held, weightless.

Sylvia wanted to bask in his presence, but a hard reality set in—he was taking Betty away from her again. She looked into his eyes and dared to raise her chin a hair.

He addressed her. "I have prepared a place for you, too, Sylvia. In my house are many rooms. One day, you will come and stay with us."

Sylvia stood speechless. He knew her name. Every fiber of her being wanted to follow this man. "I want to come now," she sputtered. "I'm ready."

"It is not your time yet. You have much to accomplish, my child."

What do I have to accomplish? One poor decision I made as a child has marked my entire life. At least let me make it right.

As if reading her thoughts, he responded, "You will come in time, when your work here on earth is finished." He winked at her and gathered Betty in his arms, throwing the corner of his white robe over her body, and they floated off the ground gently up into the heavens. Her sister's blonde hair melted into the sun's rays, and the man's robes blended with the clouds till they were gone.

Sylvia ran after them, her hands reaching as high as they could, grasping for a sliver of the man's robe. Unable to run any further, she bent over, gasping for air, then collapsed on the ground, squinting up at the sky.

Scenes from the day Betty died flooded her mind. Betty's hand with blue fingernails hanging over the side of the kitchen table, would forever haunt her. *What purpose did that serve?* The sun still beat down, but the warmth seemed to have left with the man.

Sylvia's eyes flipped open, and she inhaled deeply and sat up in her bed. She looked down at her shaking hands and placed one on her chest to still her thumping heart. She looked around, trying to gain her bearings. *Where was she?* The familiar pattern of the quilt spread across her bed focused her. *It was just a dream.*

After her pulse fell to a normal level, she climbed out of bed, vowing to keep the vision to herself.

As she dressed for the day, she noticed her sleeves fell an inch above her wrist. She'd need to ask Mamm to get her some fabric at the store to sew a new dress. In the past year, her limbs had lengthened, and her body had thinned out, taking on the shape of a woman rather than a young girl. Her metamorphosis seemed to happen the minute she turned sixteen. She reached for her *kap* and bonnet, wound up her long dark hair and secured the head covering. She put on her stockings, apron, and wet her lips before heading to the kitchen.

"*Gut* morning, daughter." Mamm sat at the table nursing a cup of coffee. "How did you sleep?"

Sylvia's cheeks flushed at the mention of sleep, and she shrugged. The smile of the man from her dream curved around the perimeter of her thoughts. It was hard not telling Mamm about him, but no way would she slice open that wound again.

"Dat should be in from the barn any minute. Help me dish up breakfast." Mamm rose.

Sylvia placed slices of the toast onto a platter while Mamm ladled the steaming sausage gravy into a bowl and carried it to the table.

Dat's heavy footfall on the porch steps announced his presence. He opened the back door, took his hat off his head, and hung it on the peg. "*Gut* morning," he grunted as he ran a hand through his curly hair, grazing his ears.

"Let's sit up. Breakfast is ready." Mamm flitted around the table, filling the glasses with milk.

Three chairs sat around their small table. Mamm had taken out the extra leaves after Clara and John married and left home. With both of them out of the house, Sylvia had her parents all to herself. At first, she'd worried about how she'd relate. She felt as if her solo presence reminded everyone of the empty place at the table that was painfully missing, but they'd settled into a routine. She filled most of her days out of the house with chores and visits to Alma.

Dat sank his heavy frame into a chair and scooted up to the table. He gripped the handle of the coffee mug and took a big gulp. "*Yough*," he proclaimed, expressing pleasure as the coffee hit his tongue.

Mamm smirked, "Same as any morning, Jake."

They settled into silence as they sopped up the gravy with slices of toast and stabbed at eggs with their forks.

After breakfast, Dat bowed his head, and Sylvia followed suit as they said their silent prayers. Then Dat pushed his chair back from the table. "Anything new to tell Sylvie?" His voice rumbled with warmth.

Sylvia didn't know what news he pined for, but Dat's question cracked the door open, and she couldn't shake the feeling she had to tell him about her dream. How could she, though? They would think her foolish and perhaps even troubled. She paused, stuck on what to do next. Then the words came spilling out of her like water pouring out of a breached dam, so powerful she couldn't stop its substantial force.

"I had a dream last night."

"What was it about?"

"Betty was there," she whispered, moving her eyes to her lap.

Mamm straightened up in her chair. She took her napkin and folded it neatly in her lap, then she unfolded it and placed it beside her plate.

Sylvia hesitated, unsure if she should continue, or should stop. "Betty looked older and so real. Her curls fell to her shoulders, and there was a man there in the field she kept calling Dat. It confused me because it clearly wasn't you, Dat, but I knew he was safe, and I felt so alive standing next to him."

The room stilled.

Dat rested his hand on his chin, one finger to his lips. At last, he spoke. "I think you have had an encounter with the divine."

"You mean God?"

Dat smiled, and Sylvia relaxed, grateful he believed her.

"You could say that. I think you met *Yeses*."

"*Yeses*," the word solicited a smile from her lips. Her spirit lurched in confirmation, but the man she met seemed so different from the Jesus she had learned about at church. She'd always imagined him as a dour man, lecturing wherever he'd go. "I'd like to know more about this, Jesus. Can you tell me about Him?"

"I'd better do my own study first, Sylvie. I'll talk to the Bishop about this and see what clarity he can provide. Give me some time and I'll let you know what I find out."

Sylvia nodded, her chin resting in her hands, as she pursed her lips together. "I liked him, and I think Betty is in a *gut* place."

"*Jah*, your dream comforts me, too."

Mamm didn't speak but stood and began washing the dishes.

Dat gave Sylvia a knowing glance and dipped his chin in acknowledgment. He shifted in his seat and changed the subject. "You are sixteen now, Sylvia. It is time to consider more spiritual things in your life. The time is drawing near when you will need to decide whether to join the church through baptism."

Sylvia kept her eyes on Mamm as she responded. "I haven't given it serious thought. I understand when I join the church, I am committing for life, and this would make you and Mamm happy." She bowed her head. "But I want to be sure."

A pulse threaded in her ears. She hoped her response didn't add more disappointment to Mamm.

"You are entering a time when you will consider such things. You are now old enough to attend the singings for the young people. This will help you make your decision to join the church." Sylvia raised her head, a grin replacing her worry.

"Are you serious, Dat, about the singings?"

"One is being held at the Bylers' next Sunday evening. I've already talked to Alma's folks, and they agreed for both of you girls to attend. You can hitch up Charlie and take the buggy together."

Sylvia jumped up and clapped her hands in excitement.

Mamm looked at Dat disapprovingly. "Jake, I don't like the girls out alone after dark. It seems like they should have a chaperone. Maybe you could take them."

"We'll talk about it later, Lizzie," Dat said. "The Yoders will be here any minute with their wheat load. I need to hitch up the team to the threshing machine."

He rose from the chair and placed a hand on Mamm's slender shoulder. Sylvia noticed the tremble in her hand stopped, and Mamm's shoulders relaxed for a spell.

Mamm grabbed the lunch pail she had prepared. "Packed you some ham sandwiches."

Dat reached for the food and his thermos of water and winked in Sylvia's direction before heading out onto the back porch and to the barn.

Sylvia couldn't contain her excitement as she tackled her household chores. Singings meant the start of the courting season. There would be boys. Young people would pair up. Perhaps she would even find a boyfriend and start going steady. She focused her thoughts on the singings, trying to force the dream to fade to the background, but no matter how hard she tried, it remained, a steady hum to her every move. She hurried through her chores, anxious to see Alma. There would be so much to talk about.

Andy

1943, East Claridon, Ohio

"It's time," Dat said as he overturned a bucket and sat down beside Andy, who milked a steady stream into his pail. "You are of marrying age and need to decide about your future with the Amish."

Andy squeezed the cow's udder a bit too firmly, and she lowed. He wasn't ready to have this talk with Dat.

"Folks have been asking me why you haven't gotten baptized into the congregation yet. I tell them you've been busy working and have shown no interest in a young lady, but we've put it off as long as we can. If you don't commit soon, tongues will wag, and the Bishop will want to have a private meeting."

Dat's words froze Andy to the core. There could be nothing worse than seeing the Bishop coming down the lane to have a chat. He'd never enjoyed living Amish. The hardship, the rules, all of it seemed so restrictive and unnecessary, but Dat wouldn't understand his hesitations. *How could he hide them any longer?* "I know I need to decide soon, but I've had so many questions, and I don't know who to ask about them."

"You can ask me. I am a minister, you know," Dat chuckled.

Andy paused, choosing his words carefully. "All my life, I've wondered who God really is. Who do you think He is?"

Dat looked past Andy and out the barn door. His eyes glazed. "God is distant. He is mighty. He chooses who to bless and who to curse."

Dat's words lit a spark deep inside Andy. "Why would I want to serve a God who lets my brother die? Who burned down our house? Why is He cursing us?" Once Andy opened his mouth, the questions came one after another like the endless sea of corn tassels in the summer fields, and he instantly regretted his decision to lay himself bare in front of Dat. Even at eighteen, he still fell under his father's authority, and it wasn't respectful to question Dat's beliefs like this.

Dat steepled his fingers to his chin. "When I was young and ready to make the commitment to the church, I had the same questions."

Andy tried to imagine Dat young. *Did he also dream of a different life?* That part of Dat seemed so far removed from who he had become.

Dat continued on, "The decision came easier, though. Our way of life wasn't so different back then from that of the English neighbor down the street. Now it is. Our neighbors have conveniences like electricity. We are more set apart, but our tradition has always demanded our loyalty be measured. If we aren't strict, then the world will creep in and take over our thinking. Without the burdens of worldly things, we can see more clearly how to best serve God."

Andy understood Dat's explanation. He'd seen the differences clearly when he lived with the Lesters and went to school, but Dat still didn't answer the biggest question in his heart. *Why would God allow all this heartache to happen to them?*

As if reading his mind, Dat continued, "God doesn't cause the bad things in our lives to happen. Things just happen on their own. How we react to them shows our commitment to serving Him."

This explanation confused Andy. "How can we serve a God we don't see?" *Either God is in charge or not. If He isn't in complete control, then He must be weak.*

"We can see our fellow brethren. If we serve them, we serve God. God takes all our actions into account and weighs them. Think of it as a big scale. In the end, your good must outweigh the bad to get into heaven."

Dat's description made it sound as if we, not God, were in control of our own destiny. "What are we weighing, Dat? Our actions or our thoughts?"

"God weighs both."

Andy stood up and wiped his hands on his pants. "I'm pretty sure the bad outweighs the good in my case, if you count my thoughts."

"*Jah*, it does for most people, but you need to at least try. It's the only way. Who knows the mind of God? We hope He will at least give us credit for our efforts. Your first step forward is baptism. All our ways of living separately help. But by removing ourselves from the world, we empty our minds of the things this world offers and increase our dependence on God. You will have the best chance of getting to heaven if you remain in our traditions." Then Dat asked him the question he really wanted answered. "Will you commit to the church through baptism?" His voice held a slight tremor, and his eyes narrowed.

Andy gulped. If he answered no, it would shatter Dat's pride into tiny pieces, like the fire had shattered Mamm's blackberry jars all those years ago. He didn't want to be that fire, and he certainly didn't want to live in the eternal fires of hell, so he deflected and asked another question instead. "Is Abraham in heaven?"

"Yes, he was too young to be judged. You want to see Abraham in heaven, eh?" Dat cracked a rare smile. "All the more reason to join the church."

Dat strained to bring humor to the conversation, but his words came out full of tension. Andy knew if he pushed any harder something would snap, so he nodded and gave the answer Dat wanted to hear. "I still don't understand, but I'm going to trust you, and do it because I know it means a lot to you and Mamm." It was the most honest answer he could come up with.

Dat's lips upturned into a warm smile that washed over him like the afternoon sun. Dat stood from his perch and placed a hand on Andy's upper back for a moment. He couldn't ever remember a time Dat touched him with such affection. The last time he'd laid hands on him, he'd gotten a whooping for listening to the radio. He wasn't sure about his decision to get baptized, but this was the display of fondness he longed for, even dreamed about as a boy.

"I'll talk to Bishop Miller tomorrow and get you signed up for the baptism classes. The classes will help you understand better." Dat took a full pail out of the barn to dump into a milk barrel.

Andy moved to the next cow. His steady stream hissed into a half-empty pail. The pull and squeeze of the udders were sure and steady. *Why couldn't faith be like this? Known and certain.* His stomach sank with the weight of the conversation. He'd thought deciding would remove the stone of guilt that had settled on his conscience, but now he wanted to escape. *Why had he told Dat he'd commit when he wasn't sure?*

He knew why. Deep down inside, all he'd ever wanted was Dat's approval. His affection. He sighed. Why did he keep circling like a hawk scouting its prey? Round and round but never taking the plunge. Today he'd dove, despite his reservations, committing to put his trust in Dat and the Amish church. It disgusted him that Dat's approval still meant so much. He hoped his decision wouldn't clip his wings and lead to his demise.

——⟨◇◇◇◇◇⟩——

Andy began his baptismal classes on Sunday after church. For five months, he'd meet with Bishop Miller and the six other *youngies* as Mamm called them. They'd study together, learning about their impending commitment to the Amish church.

At the first meeting, Bishop Miller provided copies of the *Dordrecht Confession* to each candidate. He instructed them to take it home and read it. Andy glanced at the pamphlet, but he couldn't read the High German. Maybe Dat could help him decipher it.

The week passed, and Andy failed to gather the courage to ask for Dat's help. He didn't want to engage in such deep spiritual conversations again, so he put it off.

In the following class, the Bishop gave a copy of the *Ordnung*, the written rules of the church. Andy found the *Ordnung* easier to read, since it used everyday language. Glancing through the list caused his throat to tighten a bit. No automobiles, no electricity, hook and eye closures only, no collars, specifics for the hat brims, and so on. Nothing surprised him here except the reality he would live this way for the rest of his life.

These classes delayed the inevitable baptism and gave Andy time to think through his decision. His mind still didn't understand the why, but he knew he faced a crossroads. One path was familiar and well-worn. A road a multitude of ancestors walked down. The other trail dark and overgrown, and he knew no one who had returned reported the outcome. Andy rationalized the familiar worn path as the most practical, convincing himself his decision had some logic to it and was the right choice.

Baptism Sunday came around the Sunday after he completed the baptismal classes. Andy dreaded the day.

Mamm scurried around, making sure everyone dressed in their best. She shushed and shooed the entire crew out of the house and into the wagons. They now had to take two wagons because their family had grown so big.

"Let me look at you," she said to Andy before he took the driver's seat in the second wagon. She stood at arm's length, and fussed over his shirt, smoothing out the wrinkles. "This decision makes me happy. We have prayed a long time for this day." The corners of her mouth turned up in a grin.

Andy couldn't replicate her glee. He turned away and lifted Alvin up in the back of the wagon.

She quickly changed the subject, the tender moment passing. "Let's get going. We don't want to be late for the service."

Andy climbed up in the driver's seat, grabbed the reins, and set out to church.

Andy hated being the center of attention. Today, the eyes of everyone were on him.

At the end of the service, the Bishop began the baptism ceremony. One by one, each candidate went up front. They knelt on the smooth worn floorboards, with their hands clasped in front of them. Bishop Miller asked, "Do you believe Jesus Christ is the Son of God?" After an affirmative response, he followed with two additional questions about obeying the ordinances and a commitment to the church. After the candidates gave their *jahs*, Dat raised up the milk-white pitcher and Bishop Miller cupped his hands over each person's head. The water flowed down their hair and cheeks. "I baptize you in the name of the Father, the Son, and the Holy Ghost," he proclaimed.

Andy's knees trembled as the candidate seated before him rose from the floorboards. He was next.

"Andy Troyer," the Bishop called out.

Andy stood from his seat on the front bench. He went and knelt in front of Dat. Despite his many months of preparation and self-persuasion, his brain fired off warning signals, making his heart rumble. He had a strong desire to run out of the church as fast as Marie Burton thundered across a field, but he couldn't move an inch. Something wasn't right about this. It didn't sit well in his spirit. All his questions remained, but his courage stood stronger than his fear. He knew if he ran, it would crush his family, so his knees hugged the floor, clinging to tradition. Duty and obligation are more important than feelings. *What were feelings, anyway?* Likely the *veech mon's* way of controlling the mind.

"Andy, do you believe Jesus Christ is the Son of God?"

Andy croaked out a yes. Who was Jesus besides the Son of God? He believed that. They had studied His teachings as God's earthly example to follow. The next question followed.

"Do you commit to uphold the *Ordnung* and all its ordinances?"

That question was harder to answer. It meant a lifelong commitment to the rules, some of which seemed silly to him. A weak yes escaped his mouth, even though his tongue tried to hold it back.

"Do you understand this commitment to the church and your fellow brethren? If you do not wish to proceed with baptism, you may reconsider."

Andy's heart skipped a beat. This was his last opportunity to walk away. If he did, what would he be walking towards? Embarrassment? Loneliness? He'd only ever known the Amish ways. It was all any of them knew. So, he forced his mouth to utter the right words, "I commit." He closed his eyes tight as he squeezed out the world around him. The cool baptismal water hit his scalp and trickled down the side of his face, past his ears, and rolled over his shoulders and arms. A wayward drop dripped off his elbow and hit the floorboards, leaving a splatter in the shape of a tear.

There was no peace in this moment, only regret. When he opened his eyes, they fell on Mamm. She sat, hands clasped, with a smile. Unshed tears shone in her eyes. Her expression almost made it all worth it. Seeing her happy and proud.

He rose from the floor, and Bishop Miller extended a hand, then gave him his first holy kiss. The Bishop's long beard brushed his shoulder, and the soft peck on his cheek seemed like a whisper.

It was all over. Relief flooded his heart. He was so glad to get beyond this decision, no turning back now. He wanted to retreat into his world of obscurity and solitude, wishing everyone's eyes would also go elsewhere, and he would no longer be the center of attention. He'd carve out his place in this world and work to create a life he was proud of.

THIRTEEN

Andy

May 1943, East Claridon, Ohio

Andy rifled through the stack of mail sitting on the kitchen table. His fingers rested on a card in the center of the pile. He plucked it out, read it, and shoved it in his pocket, unsure what to do with the news. The edge caught his finger and sliced it. Blood oozed from the cut, and he stuck his finger to his mouth.

"Are you okay?" Mamm asked. "Why are you hiding that card?"

She reached around him and pulled the edge of the postcard out of his pocket.

"Do you know what it is?" he asked.

Mamm shook her head as she read.

"It's a draft registration card. My eighteenth birthday is next month."

Mamm shut her eyes and inhaled sharply. "I feared you'd be getting one of these. I think you'd better talk to Dat about it."

Andy had seen the *We Want You for the US Army* signs hanging from every shop window in town but hadn't given it much thought. By most accounts, the war didn't affect his life, but this little square card brought uncertainty straight to his heart.

"Says I'm to fill it out and drop it off at the local draft board in Chardon."

"I've heard Amish boys have been able to get out of the draft. Dat will know how."

He didn't want to get out of the draft. He wanted to be out from under Dat's thumb.

Mamm dipped a measuring cup into her bucket of flour. Andy could see a slight tremor in her hand as she gripped the handle. She hid her fear well.

He nodded. "I'll talk to Dat this evening." He dreaded bringing up the topic.

After dinner, Dat headed out to finish up the chores. Mamm stayed in her spot at the table, with her fingers curled around a mug of steaming coffee. She gave Andy a knowing glance, they'd always been able to communicate like that, with the widening of their eyes or the raising of a brow.

He got up from the table and followed Dat out to the barn.

He found him scooping feed into the horses' troughs. "Hmm, Dat," his voice squeaked. "Something came in the mail today that I need to talk with you about."

"It's a draft card, isn't it?"

Andy's eyes widened. "How did you know? Did Mamm tell you?"

"No, but she should have. Mose Yoder's boy Joshua got one, too, seemed to be the talk at the cheese plant this morning."

Andy wished he could go back and change his words. Dat seemed unhappy Mamm hadn't told him. He hoped he wouldn't be too hard on her.

"What do I do?"

"You'll fill it out and take it down to Chardon and file as a conscientious objector."

"A what?" Andy's face scrunched up at the strange word. He had never heard of such a thing before.

"It means that you won't fight on moral and religious grounds. You'll have to serve a work term in a camp organized by the Mennonite Central Committee, but the Bishop has taken measures so our boys don't fight or face jail time. We're organizing a group of boys to head down and turn their registration cards in together. The Bishop has agreed to go along as an advocate and speak on your behalf since you all are members of the Amish church."

A smile bit at the corner of Andy's lips. This was his ticket, a way to get off the farm and make a way for himself. He swallowed the smile, forcing the light in his eyes to dim. He didn't want Dat thinking he was happy about this. "Who is organizing this group, and when are they going?"

"The church council. The day after tomorrow. You'll go, and I'll come along as a minister for extra reinforcement."

Andy picked up a pitchfork to busy his hands. Go to war? Fight? The thought made his stomach queasy. The other boys in the school, the ones who teased him, didn't have a choice like he did. They'd be shipped off to kill the enemy and face death. He would never kill another, but he longed to be part of something bigger. Something different. Hopefully, the camp would be his chance.

On Wednesday, Dat guided their buggy next to the others hitched up at the East Claridon post office. Andy joined the boys milling together on the front steps, waiting for the Bishop's arrival.

Joshua Yoder droned on about the crops he had planted this year, when the Bishop's buggy turned in. The Bishop unfolded his lanky limbs and climbed down. Andy's body tingled, and he lost his concentration in the conversation. The Bishop's presence always made him nervous, like trouble lurking around the corner waiting to jump out at him. He assessed his clothing and hairstyle to make sure he'd not broken any ordinances.

Bishop Miller strode up the steps and stood in front of him, holding out a hand. Andy's mouth dried, and he rubbed his sweaty hands on his pants before returning the handshake.

"Good morning, boys!" the Bishop shouted.

Andy noted the Bishop's hat had an extra-wide brim today.

"I understand each of you has received draft notices in the mail. Be assured, other young men in our church have experienced this as well. We've had success appealing before the draft board as conscientious objectors and today will ask for the same consideration. Let's ride over together and have a word with them."

Dat invited Joshua and another young man to ride along with them, and the train of buggies headed north to the county seat of Chardon, looking like a little army of black ants reporting for duty. After the ten-mile journey, the caravan pulled up in front of the brick, town hall and everyone unloaded and entered together.

The group wandered down a windowless long hallway. The air smelled stale. A secretary sat outside a door at a small desk, pecking away at her typewriter. An electric light flickered above. When she heard footsteps in the hallway, she looked up, startled. Her short dark hair framed a thin face with a petite nose and full lips. Andy thought she had to be the most exotic creature he'd ever seen with her short, modern hair and red lips. He became self-conscious of his appearance and of those around him as they huddled in the hallway, taking up the space. "What can I do for you?" she asked, finger poised in midair, ready to strike a key.

The Bishop took the lead. "These boys are here to turn in their draft registration cards and file as conscientious objectors."

"Oh, I see," her lips pursed together and pointed down in a snoot. "You will need to see Mr. Phillips about this matter. Do you have an appointment?"

Bishop shook his head. "No, Ma'am."

"Let me see if he is available." She stood up, her hourglass figure accented by a pencil skirt, blouse, and jacket. She rapped twice on the door behind her. The door cracked open. Muffled voices came from the other side, as she slipped in, shutting it behind her.

At her exit, the boys all took off their hats, smoothed their hair back with their hands, relaxing for a bit. Andy realized the sour smell their combined body odor made in the cramped hallway. He wished he had bathed before making this trip.

After a few minutes, she came back and addressed the group. "Mr. Phillips will see you now." She opened the door wide and ushered them into the room.

Andy entered last and turned to close the door. Before the door clicked shut, he saw the secretary take a little vial of perfume out of her desk drawer and give a few squirts. Embarrassment crept up his neck.

Mr. Phillips stood from behind his desk. "Good morning boys, please hand me your draft cards so I can examine them."

Bishop Miller held out his hand, and they all passed the square cards to him, in turn he handed them to Mr. Phillips. Mr. Phillips took time reading each one. The clock hanging behind the desk ticked away.

"You are all strong and strapping. Our country could sure use you in the service. Are you positive that you want to file as conscientious objectors?"

They all nodded. "*Jah.*"

"It's against our religion to fight," Bishop proclaimed as he looked Mr. Phillips square in the eye.

"Well then, I suppose I'll pass you on to the Mennonite Central Committee and ask that each of you serve your two-year term at a CPS camp. While you are unwilling to put your life on the line for your country, you can still be of use filling in the labor shortages we have around here." He reached to the corner of the desk and picked up a rubber stamp. Pressing it on the ink pad, he stamped each card with the initials, C.O. - MCC - CPS. "You have two weeks to report to your assigned CPS camp. MCC will send you the assignments in the mail. If you don't get instructions from them prior to your report date, please head over to Will Hoover's farm in Middlefield. We can shuffle you around from there. You are dismissed."

"Thank you, Mr. Phillips," Bishop Miller held out his hand again. Their handshake sealed the next two years of Andy's life.

On the morning of his departure, Mamm made him a bologna sandwich and some homemade cookies for the ride. She didn't say many words, but Andy read her looks. The corners of her mouth turned down, and her cheeks complemented the slump of her shoulders. Her eyes hung red-rimmed and watery, a sign she'd been crying. Surely she knew he wasn't going off to fight. Just down to Will Hoover's dairy farm.

He slung his bundle of clothes into the back of the open wagon Dat agreed to let him take. Cookie whinnied as he hitched her up. He'd asked Dat for Marie Burton, but Dat said no. She was essential to the farm. Cookie was getting along in years but was still a good horse, and Andy was glad for her company.

The air was warm, and the sun hit his face. It felt good to think about being free from Dat's expectations. He wanted to make his own way in the world. In this new district, he wouldn't be the minister's son anymore, just a CPS worker. The vision of Mamm's sadness subdued him.

Dat gripped the edge of the wagon. "Make sure you give my greetings to the ministers in the Middlefield district. I told the Bishop to transfer your membership over to them. Be sure to attend the singings; that's how you meet girls." Dat grinned.

Andy sat atop the wagon looking down on Dat, trying to concentrate on remembering his words in case Dat quizzed him later. Mamm came out on the porch and sat in a rocker, hands folded in her lap. After the instructions ended, Andy waved goodbye to Mamm, took the reins and clucked Cookie down the lane. He headed south like a bird migrating back to its home with a song on his lips.

He pulled into the town of Middlefield and smiled at the familiar sights. Up ahead, to his right, sat Patchin's Meat Market. A group of men were out front, just like old times. On a whim, he pulled the wagon into a parking spot next to a car with a shiny chrome bumper and tethered Cookie. It had been years since he had seen Mr. Patchin, and he had a hankering for a cold Coca-Cola.

Mr. Patchin smiled at him. His cheeks sagged a bit more, and deeper wrinkles appeared around his mouth, but his eyes showed no signs of recognition. "What can I do for ya today?"

"I just came by to pay my respects and pick up a Coke." Andy slapped a nickel down on the worn wood counter.

Mr. Patchin stared at him. "You look familiar. Do I know you?"

"I'm Eli and Mary Troyer's oldest son, Andy. I lived here in Middlefield as a boy."

Light dawned in his eyes. "Ah Andy! I haven't seen your family in a long time. Heard you all moved up north. What brings you back down these ways?"

"I'm here to work at Will Hoover's CPS camp."

Mr. Patchin's smile erased from his face, and the light extinguished from his eyes; his mouth set in a firm line. He seemed upset, but Andy couldn't understand why. *Had he said something wrong?*

"I see," he said. He turned and pointed to a picture that sat on the shelf behind him. "See that picture there? It's my boy Tommy. He went over to Europe two years ago and won't be returning. Killed in action. My boy sacrificed his life. I think what you are doing is cowardly, disgusting. I can't believe our government lets you get away with it."

Andy struggled to find words to reply. His cheeks flamed at such a harsh rebuke. Tommy had been a good boy. He remembered him hanging around the shop in the shadows with his nose in a book.

After he'd stopped working for the Lesters, he'd rarely interacted with *Englishers* anymore and didn't go to town as often. He hadn't realized the significance of the war. "I'm very sorry about Tommy," he stammered. "He was a fine boy. I best be going."

Mr. Patchin nodded in agreement. "You best."

Andy picked up his Coke and exited. The bell jingled on his way out. The Coke bottle sweated and dripped down his hand, and he drained it before setting the bottle down on the front steps. Before he rode off, he glanced up at the store one last time. Mr. Patchin had followed him out and stood on the top step. A long stream of tobacco juice exited his mouth and hit a patch of dry dirt at the bottom of the steps in a splatter, a clear sign he was no longer welcome.

Would he ever find his place? Living under Dat's rules didn't suit him. He didn't meet the standards to live in this *English* world. *Where did he belong?*

FOURTEEN

1945, Burton, Ohio

"Sure you know how to drive this thing, Alma?" Sylvia giggled as the buggy bounced along on the road.

Alma flicked the reins. "Of course. Dat lets me drive it all the time."

"Go faster if you can," Sylvia urged. She spread her arms out wide, feeling free as the birds that circled above their heads. The sweet taste of independence touched her tongue. With the wind against her skin and her best friend beside her, she didn't think she could squeeze another ounce of happiness out of the moment. The Bylers' homestead loomed ahead, the destination for the first singing of the season.

"Look, there it is," Alma squealed. "How many young people do you think will be there?"

"I don't know, but let's stick together." A hint of anxiousness laced Sylvia's tone, coloring her excitement gray for a moment.

Alma whispered back, "What if they don't like us?"

Sylvia grabbed her hand. "There's bound to be some other new young people there, too, besides we have each other."

The girls pulled the buggy into the Bylers' yard. Alma jumped out and tied the horse to a nearby tree. They shook out their new dark purple dresses they'd sewn the past week and smoothed out the wrinkles from the white capes that fit snugly around their bodices.

"Is there anything out of place on my *kap* and bonnet?" Sylvia twirled slowly for Alma to examine her head covering.

"Everything looks great. How about me?"

"You look pretty as a peach. Maybe you'll catch the eye of a boy." Sylvia fished in her pocket and pulled out a tiny bottle of lip tint. "I brought something to help us out." Written across the label in flowery script was *Bloom of Roses*.

"Sylvia! You didn't. Where did you get that? Your Dat would be fit to be tied." Alma's face turned down in disapproval.

"He doesn't know," Sylvia grinned. "Consider it part of our *rumspringa*. We can't put on too much or everyone will stare, and word will get back to our folks, but a little will help highlight our natural beauty." Sylvia unscrewed the lid. "Give me your finger."

Alma placed her hands on her hips. "I won't."

Sylvia reached out and plucked a hand from Alma's side. Flipping the bottle upside down, she placed a dot on her finger. "Just try it," she sighed. "Have a little fun for once."

Alma brought the finger to her lips, slowly smearing on the lip gloss. She finished by smacking her lips together to distribute the color. "What do you think?"

"Fancy."

Alma giggled, forgetting her indignation. "Your turn." She took the vial out of Sylvia's hands and pressed a drop onto her outstretched digit.

Sylvia didn't need to ask how she looked. Approval mirrored in her friend's brown eyes as the pupils widened and the corners of her mouth crinkled up into a smile. Putting the lip tint away in her pocket, Sylvia grabbed Alma's hand, and they walked together towards the barn.

As they entered the barn built into the side of a hill, the waning sun warmed the large hand-hewn floorboards. The bottom level housed the stalls for the horses and cows, while the upper level was used to store hay. The Bylers had moved all the bales to the side, swept the floor clean for the event, and had arranged five picnic tables end to end with oil lamps placed in their centers.

On one side of the tables, the boys circled up, talking in low tones. The girls formed their own circle on the other side, and when Sylvia and Alma entered, both circles turned and looked at them.

"Come on over!" Fannie Graber called from the center of the girls, waving at them to join.

Sylvia took in the scene as they walked towards the group. It was all she had imagined and more. An energy sparked throughout the room, unlike the somber church services. Tonight, hope for the future buzzed around them in furtive whispers and glances. A hope of meeting a mate, and of making memories to last a lifetime.

But what about Betty? Shouldn't she be here? The thought slammed into Sylvia with such force it took her breath away. *Betty always appeared.* "Not tonight. Go away," she whispered.

"Who are you talking to?" Alma asked.

She squeezed Alma's hand. "No one. It's nothing."

Fannie interrupted, "Do you see all the new boys here? Ruth says they are from Will Hoover's CPS camp."

The girls giggled.

Sylvia snuck a glance over at the boys' circle. She recognized only a few of them. Their faces glowed in the golden-hour light.

Mr. Byler, the chaperone for the evening, stepped forward. "It's time to begin," he called, motioning for the young people to have a seat at the tables.

Sylvia and Alma followed the rest of the girls to their side and slid in next to each other.

"Number 233," Mr. Byler instructed. The covers of the songbooks rustled open, and he led off, his tenor voice lilting and strong.

Sylvia knew most of the songs, and the ones she didn't know well she pretended to sing along to. She gazed at the faces of the boys who sat across from her. Before tonight, she had never sat so close to a boy, so she took extra care to study the features of each young man. There were boys slight in stature and large-boned, thin-lipped and full-mouthed, some with large hook noses and others with small button-shaped noses. She took in these characteristics, swallowing them and digesting them to recall later when she and Alma were driving home.

She blushed as she realized the boy sitting opposite Alma had caught her staring. She dropped her gaze, but not before she had memorized his features. He was neither small in stature nor large, just medium, but there was nothing average about the thump in her chest when she looked at him.

His dark blonde hair swept to the sides, making his forehead visible, and the corners of his mouth turned up in a perpetual smile. His eyes were very blue, like the color of cornflowers, accentuated by thin brows. He seemed older than the rest, and his air of maturity intrigued Sylvia. *Could she dare to take another look?* After a few more songs, she mustered the courage to do so, and when she lifted her eyes, she found him looking at her as well.

They locked eyes, their mouths moving in unison to the words in the song. Her face blazed, and everything in her told her to avert her gaze, but she couldn't. She smiled, and he mirrored her smile. Sylvia's body tingled; the hair on her arms stood on end. She had to talk to him.

The singing wore on for a few hours and finally, at 9:30 p.m., Mr. Byler closed with a final song. "Mrs. Byler has cookies and pies for everyone in the kitchen. Much obliged if the boys can stay behind and help move the tables back to the corner."

It felt good for Sylvia to stretch her limbs after sitting for so long.

On the walk to the kitchen, she nudged Alma. "What do you know about the boy sitting across from you? Have you ever seen him before?"

"Never."

"I like him. I'm going to talk to him."

"Don't be so bold, Sylvia. You don't want him to think you are crazy."

Sylvia grinned at her friend's admonishment; she knew her antics pushed Alma outside of her comfort zone. They were best friends because they complemented each other, pushing when necessary and pulling back as needed.

If she did things Alma's way, it would be several weeks before she'd even consider approaching the boy. There was no way she could wait that long. Another girl would sink her claws into him. She would only heed part of her best friend's advice, and wouldn't make the mysterious boy her first stop after the cookie table. Instead, she would hold back and wait until the end of the evening to approach him.

Andy's eyes followed the girl he'd caught staring at him during the singing. Hands all around him grabbed at the peanut butter cookies, the sugary crumbs dusting the corners of mouths. The young people drained glasses of milk, leaving cups with white film stuck to the innards littering the table. Those around him paired off in conversations, gaining courage from the milk and cookies.

Andy retreated to the corner, content to observe. The girl was pretty with her dark hair, smooth skin, and silly grin, but what caught him the most was the twinkle in her eye. She looked like she had some big secret to share with the rest of the world, and he wanted to know it. Her presence unraveled something in him, like the first petals of a spring bloom. *Why was he intrigued by this girl?* His interest would please Dat, but he wasn't sure he wanted to please Dat these days. His heart thumped as he saw her heading in his direction, and his mouth dried like a cotton ball. *What would he say?*

"Hello." She extended a hand. Andy's tongue thickened and he couldn't speak. His hard, sinewy hand touched her delicate, smooth skin as he returned the gesture. The touch of her skin sent a jolt to his heart. He marveled at how her hand fit perfectly in his and he didn't want to let go, but felt his palms get sweaty, so he released first. She smoothed down the raised goose pimples on her arms. Her face flushed from the corporeal reaction.

"What's your name?" she asked.

"Andy, yours?"

"Sylvia."

Her name felt familiar, like it had always belonged.

"I've never seen you before. Where are you from?" she asked.

"I'm from East Claridon. Working at the CPS dairy farm over at Will Hoover's."

"First time here at this singing?"

Andy nodded.

"Seems like a good group. Are you coming back for the next one?"

"*Jah*, I think so." Andy didn't know what else to say, so he mumbled, "Guess I'll see you then."

"Sounds good," she whispered, the twinkle in her eye becoming more pronounced. "Nice to meet you, Andy."

He had so many more questions, but his mind went blank. Unspoken words and feelings swirled around in his mind as she turned and walked away. The warmth of her skin seared his hand. His stomach lurched in anticipation of the next time he would see her.

Should he pursue the first girl who ever showed him attention? Dat's words rang in his ears. *Be sure to attend the singings; that's how you meet girls.* Of course, Dat had been right. He should have expected nothing less. Perhaps Dat had even arranged for Sylvia to show him attention.

Andy closed his eyes for a moment. What a silly thought. The earnestness on Sylvia's face framed his vision. She had approached him of her own accord. He'd be mistaken not to find out more about her. The church had planned a volleyball tournament in two weeks. Maybe he could get himself together and come up with some better topics of conversation.

As the girls drove home, Sylvia second-guessed her exchange with Andy. *Were the things she felt real or a figment of her imagination?* He wasn't much of a conversationalist.

"Can you believe tonight? This is what we've been dreaming of. Freedom, *rumspringa*, boys!" Alma exclaimed.

"Andy," Sylvia whispered his name, the infatuation gaining momentum. "Hopefully, he'll ask to drive me home next time. Can you imagine me riding in his buggy?"

Alma looked over at her and smiled. "You give me hope that someday there will be someone for me."

"Did anyone stick out?"

"Not like you, but it takes longer for me. Did you see Jonas Yoder staring at you?"

"Ewhhh. He's my second cousin!" Sylvia exclaimed.

"Saloma told me he fancies you."

"Never in a million years would I want to court Jonas Yoder." Sylvia's thoughts went to Andy. She hoped he would try to talk to her again.

"Do you think they noticed the lip tint?"

"Nah, I don't think so, but we best wet our lips and wipe it off before we get back home." Sylvia licked her lips and took a hankie from her pocket. She removed the color, staining the cloth. She was going to have to get the stain out herself or her Mamm would question where it came from. "Here, use my hankie. Better to only soil one of ours," she laughed as she handed over the square cloth.

Sylvia took the reins while Alma rubbed her lips into the kerchief, finishing up just in time as they pulled into Sylvia's driveway. Sylvia looked up at the sky. The stars reflected in her friend's eyes, causing her whole body to glimmer. If tonight was only the beginning, the future was sure to be amazing.

FIFTEEN

Summer 1945, Burton, Ohio

Ever since Andy had met Sylvia at the singing a few weeks ago, she had been on his mind. Her fiery disposition and forwardness intrigued him, but it also made him squirm. *What should he do with her attention?* The logical next step was to settle down and find a wife, and here he had a fine prospect, but settling down made him nervous. All his life he'd belonged to Mamm and Dat. Now he could carve out his own future—what if he messed up? The blame would fall solely on him. *Slow down. You're getting ahead of yourself.* A buggy ride didn't mean he needed to marry the girl. If he liked the conversation, then he would think through the next steps.

A whistle shrieked, signaling the end of the volleyball game. All around them, the young people laughed and hustled over to the lemonade stand in their bare feet.

He finally mustered the courage to ask Sylvia the question that had been on the tip of his tongue all evening. "Will you ride with me tonight?" He had never asked a girl out before, and his heart hammered, anticipating her reply.

A pleasant warmth spread to the tips of Sylvia's extremities at the words she'd been waiting for all evening. The uncertainties she had harbored these last few weeks washed away. Now that he had asked her, it confirmed his feelings were indeed mutual. Her eyes studied him over the rim of her cup before taking a tiny sip of the tart lemonade he'd brought her. "Sure. I'll need to let Alma know, but it should be fine." A flush rode up her cheeks, and she pursed her lips together in a smile. *This is amazing. I'm going to spend time with Andy in his buggy, alone.* She wanted to squeal, but thought better of it. "I'll be right back." She left his side and slid through the crowd of young people lining the court.

"Alma," Sylvia whispered as she sidled up to her best friend. "Guess what?"

"He asked you to ride in his buggy!" Alma clapped her hands together in glee. "I saw him talking to you earlier and wondered if he asked."

"He spent a lot of time talking about the weather, asking what my Dat farms and so forth. Pretty boring talk if you ask me, but I could tell that he wanted to ask me to ride, and finally he did. Alma, I might faint. What should we talk about? I don't know what I am going to say."

"You mean you didn't give him an answer?" Alma exclaimed. "You can't leave him hanging like that. Go right over there and tell him you'll accept the invitation."

Laughter welled from Sylvia's core. "No silly, I told him I would ride, of course, but what should we converse about? I feel so nervous and am afraid he won't like what I have to say."

"Let him lead the conversation. He is the one who asked you. I know that's hard for you to hear, since you like to march ahead when you want something."

"What if we sit in silence?"

"As long as it's comfortable silence, I don't see any reason to worry. You can enjoy each other's company without constantly talking. Sometimes it's better that way."

"I guess I could ask him about his job, or if he's ever broken an ordinance?" A sly grin appeared on Sylvia's face.

"You wouldn't!" Alma punched her arm. "Let him lead."

"How about this question? How many children do you want?" Sylvia pressed her lips together trying to hide a giggle.

Alma couldn't hold back the howl of laughter that erupted, and tears of joy ran down her cheeks. "If you ask that then we will no longer be friends!" Alma exclaimed.

Their laughter died down. "You always know the best things to say to calm my nerves. Are you sure you'll be fine riding home alone?"

Alma waved her off. "Of course I'll be okay. Don't worry about me."

"First thing in the morning, I'll run over to your house and tell you all about it."

"I can't wait!"

Alma squeezed her hand, and Sylvia hurried back to Andy's side.

—⟨◇◇◇◇◇⟩—

Dusk fell as the volleyball game ended, and the couples paired up. Andy walked Sylvia over to his wagon. Embarrassment pricked his ears. He didn't have a buggy like some of the other boys. His wagon had seen its better days with its aged wood and rusted joints, but Sylvia didn't seem to mind and eagerly pushed herself up into the passenger seat.

Andy settled in next to her and picked up the reins. "Which way to home?"

"Turn right out of the lane and head down Tavern Road about two miles, then you'll make a right onto Jug. Our house is on Jug."

Andy pulled on the reins, and they started off down the lane. Sylvia sat quietly beside him. He didn't know what to talk about. He'd asked all his prepared questions earlier at the volleyball game. The horse's hooves clomped against the pavement, echoing into the night sky. The moon shone bright and washed the landscape in its watery glow, and he listened to the wind rustle through the trees, and the night critters sing in chorus along with the distant hoot of an owl.

About halfway through the ride, Sylvia fidgeted in her seat, and he knew the mood had shifted into the uncomfortable zone. He wracked his mind for topics of conversation but couldn't come up with anything not awkward. Maybe he had misread her intentions.

Doubts started overtaking his mind when she blurted out, "How old are you, anyway?"

Andy turned and looked at her, surprised by the question. "Well, how old do you think I am?" *To answer a question with another question is dumb*, he thought, disappointed he couldn't think of a more clever response.

"I know you are at least eighteen because you are serving in the CPS camp. So, I'll guess eighteen, maybe turning nineteen soon."

Andy gulped. "Well, I'm older. In fact, I turned twenty a few weeks ago."

He watched Sylvia bite her lip at his admission. *He was too old for her.* Any bit of confidence he'd built up flowed right out of him. *I'm sure she'll wonder why I'm not married yet.*

She looked at him through narrowed eyes. "Well, why aren't you married?" she blurted out. A flush of embarrassment rose to her cheeks.

The blush made her look even prettier. He tried to smile kindly to put her at ease. "Guess I haven't found the girl for me yet. Since we are talking about our ages, why don't you tell me yours?"

Sylvia snuck a glance at him. "Well, I suppose I am a teeny bit younger than twenty—sixteen and a half, to be exact."

"Hmm…" he thought aloud. "My Dat was four years older than my Mamm so I guess no one can say anything about that."

His shoulders relaxed. They had overcome the first hurdle. His confidence returning, he continued with the first question to pop into his head. "Tell me a story about your family."

"What do you want to know?"

"Something funny that's happened."

She sat for a moment contemplating. "We have a small family. Not much happens around our place. One time we had lightning strike down six of our cattle in our field, but that's more interesting than funny. What about you? What stories can you tell me?"

Andy clucked his tongue at the horse, digging deep in the recesses of his mind for a story. "Well, I have a much larger family, so mischief is always happening. My brother David and I are close in age, and we often went to school together. Once, the teacher asked David how many brothers and sisters he had. He told her we had three one-of's, one two-of's, and one three-of's. The teacher looked at him in confusion and asked what all those numbers had to do with brothers and sisters. She didn't understand David was telling her 'one of's' were individual children and that we also had a set of twins and triplets. When he explained it, she just shook her head and laughed. It's been a running joke in our family now. Sometimes I even lose track of who is who."

Sylvia smiled. "Well, how many are there of you, anyway?"

"There's eleven of us."

He told her about his life on the farm, the moving about, the fire, and how he went away to work at age eleven. He couldn't believe how easily the words flowed. She sat content to listen, soaking up the details—asking brief questions now and then, but letting him talk most of the time. Andy had never talked about his life to anyone like this before. It was unfamiliar territory for him and left him feeling breathless. After he had finished with the main points, he asked her some questions.

"Tell me more about your family."

"Like I said, we're small. There's only three of us, my older brother John and sister Clara. My parents adopted Clara at a young age, so she's not my blood sister, but you'd never know it."

She gulped. Her voice grew somber. "We had another little sister, Betty. She died when she was eleven months old."

"What happened?" He berated himself for the question. *Why did he feel the need to pry?* All of this was so new to him. She had shared something very personal, and he understood the grief of losing a sibling firsthand, so he cleared his throat and began again. "Truth is, Sylvia, I had the same thing happen. I lost my little brother, Abraham, when he was two. He died of the measles. Dat and I tried to save him, but the fever just overtook him. He died in my Mamm's arms during the night. The rest of us got over the measles, but I think my Mamm is still heartsick over losing Abraham. She lost other children, too, at birth, but Abraham was different. We had all grown to love him."

It had been so long since he'd relived the night of Abraham's death. Life still made little sense.

Tears leaked out of her eyes, carving a trail down her cheek. "If you knew the truth about how Betty died, you wouldn't have asked me to ride with you."

"What are you talking about?"

Sylvia turned away. "If only some illness had caused Betty's death. I was supposed to be watching her, but I went out to play instead. If I had been there, then maybe she wouldn't have died."

Andy pulled the wagon off to the side of the road and put his hands on her shoulders. She turned towards him. Her pain weighed on him. "How old were you when this happened?"

"I was five. The memories have faded with time, but my guilt has not. My Mamm is so different. She worries all the time about us."

Andy nodded. "I understand. Grief has changed my family, too. I am so sorry you carry the blame. It cannot be an easy burden to bear." His eyes lingered on her face, and he wished he could read her thoughts. He wanted to reach over and capture a tear in the pad of his thumb, to cup her face and kiss away the pain in her eyes, but he resisted the urge and changed the subject instead. "Is that Jug Road up ahead?"

Sylvia nodded. "My house is the second one on the right." She used the back of her hand to wipe away the tears. "I'm so sorry to cry on our first date," she sniffled.

"So, this is a date, *eh?*" Andy teased, lightening the mood.

"I'm sorry to be so forward," Sylvia responded, covering her face with her hands as she folded her body in half with embarrassment. They pulled into the lane and stopped in front of the white two-story farmhouse. "I wouldn't blame you if you didn't ask me to ride again."

"Truth is, I feel a special connection with you Sylvia, I'm surprised we have so much in common. Thank you for sharing with me about Betty." Andy let the reins go slack and sat back in the seat. He handed her his handkerchief.

Sylvia straightened at his words and whispered, "Me, too." She used his handkerchief to wipe away her tears.

His heart swelled. *This must be what love feels like.* The stars seemed to twinkle down their approval, enveloping them with their warmth and safety. Something greater was happening, like a force had plucked them straight out of the sky and placed them together.

"Can I talk with your Dat about going steady?"

"I'd like that very much."

He grinned. "I'm glad. I wanted to snatch you up before Jonas Yoder asked."

Her brow furrowed and her lips pursed. "How did you know about Jonas Yoder?"

"Oh, he's told all of us he's gonna court you. I'm sure he'll be quite upset when he finds out I've talked to your Dat."

"I would never have agreed to go with him."

"I'm glad." Andy reached over and took her hand in his. Shivers ran up his spine. Their hands fit together like two pieces of a puzzle.

SIXTEEN

1945, Burton, Ohio

Sylvia sat on the edge of her bed, playing with the hem of Andy's handkerchief. She hadn't meant to take it with her, but liked the fact she had slept with something of his. Folding it into tiny squares and placing it in her apron pocket, she bounded down the steps, interrupting Dat's morning ritual of reading the newspaper. "Good morning, Dat." She hummed as she fumbled around in the cupboard, looking for a mug. She poured her cup of coffee and slathered a piece of bread thick with a coat of apple butter and flopped down in the chair beside him, leaving a trail of crumbs on the floor.

"You're in a good mood this morning," Dat commented. "It wouldn't be because of a special guest who brought you home last night, would it?" He raised an eyebrow.

"Were you spying on me?"

"I might have peeked out the window. Who is the boy?"

Sylvia ignored the question. "Before you tell me I shouldn't be alone with a boy, I want you to know that he is going to come and talk with you before we go out again to make it proper."

"That's all good, Sylvia, but who is he?"

She chewed on the end of her fingernail. "So, he's a bit older than me."

"Okay," said Dat. "You still didn't answer the question? Who is this boy...*eh*, possibly man?" His eyes brightened.

Sylvia blushed. "His name is Andy Troyer. He works over at Will Hoover's CPS camp."

"Andy Troyer." Dat rolled the name around on his tongue. "Doesn't sound familiar, but there are lots of Troyers in these parts. Do you know his parents' names?"

"I'm sorry, I didn't ask, but I know his Dat is a minister, and they are from the East Claridon area." Sylvia grimaced at her lack of knowledge. "I told him you owned a buggy shop. I'm guessing he will pay you a visit in the next few days. His wagon has seen better days. Maybe you could help with a couple of repairs," Sylvia giggled.

"Do you want to see him again?" Dat asked.

A flush crept up her cheeks again, and she averted her eyes. "Yes. I would like to go steady."

Dat drummed his fingers on the oak tabletop. "You remember the conversation we had a month ago about baptism? If you are serious about this boy, then you need to consider joining the church. If he is older, as you say, he will want to consider marriage, and you cannot be married until you have completed your baptism classes."

Sylvia had given little thought to baptism since they'd last talked. The singings had consumed her attention. Dat's suggestion had gone in one ear and out the other, but she realized he was right. If she and Andy became serious, she would need to commit to the church. She wondered whether Andy was a member. Surely, at twenty, he was.

"Well, is Andy a member of the church?" Dat asked.

"I don't know. I didn't ask him." Sylvia winced again at her lack of information. At this rate, Dat would never give his permission.

"So, you don't know who his parents are, or if he is a member of the church? What do you know about this boy? What did you even talk about? You know compatible matches have to do with more than looks and feelings, right?"

Sylvia hung her head. "Yes Dat. You're right." Then she fibbed a little to get him off her back. "I have been thinking about baptism. I think it's a good idea."

"Let me talk to this boy and see what I think of him. If I approve and you still want to continue the relationship, I'll talk to the Bishop about your baptism."

"Okay, Dat." She swallowed her last bite of bread. Hopefully, Andy would make a good impression when he came to visit. "Speaking of the Bishop, have you talked with him about my dream?"

Dat sat up a little straighter. "I'm sorry, I've just been so busy and haven't had the time to get out to see him, but I will. If my conversation goes well with this Andy boy of yours, then we'll go together." He slapped a palm down on the table. "Speaking of being busy, I'd better get over to the shop. There are at least two wagon repairs waiting for me." He stood up, gathered the newspaper, tucked it under his arm, and walked his dishes over to the sink before heading out the back door.

Several days passed before Andy stood at the threshold of Sylvia's Dat's buggy shop, his stomach a flurry of caged wings.

An older man with a rounded belly and curling hair, who he suspected was Sylvia's Dat, looked up from the lathe he used to fashion a spoke. "*Gut* morning. What can I do for you?"

Andy stepped forward, took off his hat, and extended a hand. "Andy Troyer. I've come to see you about courting your daughter, Sylvia." His boldness surprised him.

"Ah. Andy. Sylvia told me you'd be stopping by. I'd begun thinking that maybe you were a creature of her imagination."

His handshake held firm.

"Jake Slabaugh. Come on in and have a seat."

He motioned to a stool next to the wood stove and pulled up his own across from Andy.

Andy cleared his throat. "Sir, I admire your daughter. We met at the singings, and I drove her home the other night. I would like your permission to go steady."

"Before I grant my blessing, please tell me a little about yourself, son. I'd like to get to know you. Who are your parents?"

Unflinching, Jake stared at him, waiting for his answers.

How did he ever think he would be worthy enough for a girl like Sylvia? His voice wobbled before gaining its footing. "My parents are Eli and Mary Troyer. They live in East Claridon. My Dat is a minister and dairy farmer. I came down to Middlefield because of my draft deferment to work at the CPS camp. Before I left home, I received baptism in the church. I have never courted before, but I like Sylvia and have good intentions."

"How old are you? Sylvia indicated you are several years older than her."

"I am twenty. I know most boys my age are already married, but the deferment prolonged things, and I haven't met a girl that caught my interest until Sylvia."

Jake ran his fingers down through his beard, taming the ends. "I admire your coming and talking with me. Sylvia spoke highly of you, and your membership in the church also speaks well. I will give you permission to spend time with her, but I would also like to spend time with you as well. Would you consider joining me for my weekly meetings here at the shop with some of the other men in the community?"

Andy paused at his request. He didn't know how to respond; his Dat had never asked him to spend time together with other men.

What were Jake's intentions? He saw nothing but earnestness in him. *What did he have to lose?*

"That would be fine, sir, as long as it doesn't interfere with my work at the dairy."

Jake nodded. "Of course, we meet here after morning chores for coffee and, if we are so fortunate, some of my wife's good cinnamon rolls." He added with a grin.

Andy stood and put his hat back on. "Well then, I guess I'll see you Wednesday morning."

"I'll look forward to it." Jake tipped his hat.

Outside at his wagon, Andy replayed the exchange in his head while he hitched up his horse. Jake seemed so different from Dat. He took time to ask questions. He wanted to know who he was as a person. Most of all, he saw the kindness in his eyes. Dat would have intimidated any potential suitors, making sure they understood the importance of his position in the church. He pitied his poor sisters. Their suitors would leave terrified after such conversations. He muttered a prayer of thanks towards the sky for his good fortune and couldn't help but grin as he climbed into the buggy and bid Cookie forward, back to Will Hoover's camp.

The next morning, Sylvia joined Dat on a visit to Bishop Mast.

"First, we will tell the Bishop about your desire to be baptized, then I'll approach the subject of studying about Jesus."

"Do you think he will approve?"

"I don't know," Dat replied.

He spoke little for the rest of the ride. Sylvia wondered what he would do if the Bishop denied his request. How shameful that would be. Nervous energy coursed through her veins.

"Looks like Malon Miller's here visiting as well," Dat commented as he tethered their horse.

Malon, a preacher in their district, was often at odds with the Bishop over his preaching. Sylvia enjoyed hearing him preach about being born again, even though she didn't understand.

"Having Malon present may help me. He'll be on my side," Dat whispered as they climbed the porch steps. He stood at the door and straightened his hat before giving a sharp rap.

Mrs. Mast came to the door. "Ay, Jake, what brings you to these parts?"

"I'm hoping to see the Bishop. I have some matters I want to discuss with him."

She raised an eyebrow when she saw Sylvia standing behind Dat. "Come on in." She opened the door wider. "*Gut* to see you, Sylvia."

As Sylvia stepped into the farmhouse, she smelled cinnamon and sugar in the air. Mrs. Mast must be baking today. They followed her back into the kitchen. The two men sat at the table with mugs of coffee and a plate stuffed with gooey cinnamon rolls between them.

"Jake." Bishop Mast rose from the table, surprise written on his face. He extended a hand.

Dat took it, then reached for Malon's next.

"Have a seat," the Bishop directed.

A cup of piping hot coffee appeared before Dat, along with a cinnamon roll. "Help yourself. I'm going to head out to the chicken house to collect the eggs and do some chores," said Mrs. Mast as she exited the kitchen, leaving them in privacy.

Sylvia stood awkwardly behind Dat.

Bishop locked eyes with Dat for a moment and ignored Sylvia before speaking. "Glad you stopped by. Malon and I were just discussing church matters. What do you think of salvation, and this being born again talk he has been preaching about?"

Dat paused, and Sylvia knew he was weighing his words. Siding with Malon so early in the conversation wouldn't grant him any favor in the Bishop's eyes. He needed to proceed cautiously.

"Well, it's funny you bring this topic up. I came to talk with you about a few things, one of them related to that, but before we get into it all, I wanted to let you know Sylvia told me this morning she is ready to be baptized into the church and start her classes."

"Oh, that's good news." The Bishop's eyes lit up. He glanced at Sylvia. "It pleases me to see young people choosing our ways. This is a good reflection on you and Lizzie and all you've done to raise a *gut* Amish family. You should be pleased."

The Bishop's words touched Sylvia. Her parents were good people.

Dat rubbed his beard, trying to hide his smile. "I am mighty glad she wants to join the church. Regarding your question about salvation, I don't know. I've not studied it for myself. What does the *Dordrecht* say about it?"

Bishop Mast raised his eyebrows, then narrowed his eyes. He seemed surprised by Dat's question. "The document talks about salvation and all our other theological practices, such as the *bann*."

Malon jumped in. "Why do you consider preaching about salvation a problem then, when our doctrines of faith and the Bible teach it?"

It took little for Sylvia to see the conversation was sliding down a muddy slope straight to a ruin. She wanted to pull tight on the reins and yell, Woah! But could never speak unless spoken to when in the Bishop's presence.

There was no time for intervention because Bishop Mast's face reddened and the little vein in his neck bulged out. Malon had pushed a bit too far.

The Bishop's jaw clenched, and his words seethed through his teeth. "It is a problem because it doesn't consider the whole story. While salvation might be available, we cannot guarantee it. A person needs to earn it. Salvation and good works go hand in hand. You can't preach one without the other." He pounded his fist on the table in exclamation.

Dat sat paralyzed by the outburst. There was no way he could ask to study the Bible now. He'd only aggravate the situation. A larger theological rift between Malon and Bishop existed than she'd known, and they'd stepped into a gunfight. The nervousness she felt on the ride over returned threefold, and all the saliva in her mouth migrated to the palms of her hands.

Malon sat dumbfounded, the conversation at an impasse. Still, he pressed. "Thank you for your insight. I respectfully disagree with you, Bishop, and feel you would see differently if you studied some specific scriptures for yourself." He reached into his back pocket and pulled out a small Bible. "I brought you this and marked a few passages for you."

Bishop Mast swatted away the gift. "I don't need a Bible. I have one of my own I can look at."

"Very well," responded Malon. "I'll be happy to share the specific passages whenever you'd like, but I'm not stopping preaching about and emphasizing the ordinances, as our forefathers wrote them." He got up from the table, signaling his part in the conversation had ended. "Good day, Jake, Sylvia." He extended a hand. The Bishop didn't take it. It hung in the air, suspended like a buggy hanging halfway off a bridge. "Tell the missus thank you for the hospitality."

"Consider yourself warned, Malon." Bishop Mast waved his finger in the air. "This is the very thing that separates churches. We are called to unity. You would do well to think about how you can promote unity and not division." The Bishop spoke as he would to a wayward child.

Dat also rose from the table. "I need to be going as well. Thank you for your time. Let me know when the baptismal classes will start."

Sylvia exhaled a breath, grateful Dat had sense enough to forgo any other requests. Wait until Alma heard about this meeting.

They followed Malon outside to his buggy.

"Good grief. What was that all about?" Dat asked him.

"He beckoned me here today for a meeting concerning my preaching. I am only preaching from the Bible and emphasizing the things I know to be true. We have drifted away from the core foundation of our faith. It's time we returned to the truth. The souls of our congregation rest on it."

Dat stood with his arms crossed over his body, listening as Malon attended to his horse.

"Truth is, I came here today for another reason—to ask the Bishop for permission to study the life of Jesus."

Malon stopped fiddling with the bridle and looked up at him with wide eyes. "What made you have this desire?"

Dat described Sylvia's dream. "After I saw the Bishop's anger, I didn't want to provoke him more. Guess I'll try again in a few months."

Malon reached into his back pocket. "Don't do that. Here is a Bible you can use to study. It's written in English. All the passages I marked are an excellent start. I have been studying the life of Jesus for a few years now. If you have questions, please come and ask."

Sylvia looked up at the house. Bishop Mast watched their conversation through a window. She spoke up. "Don't give it to him here. We have watching eyes."

Dat replied, "Let's drive out and I can take it down the road a bit."

"Very well." Malon tucked the Bible in his back pocket and climbed up into his buggy.

Both buggies headed down the lane towards the road. Sylvia had a lot to think about. If Dat accepted the Bible from Malon and the Bishop later found out, there would be trouble to pay, but Malon was their minister, and Dat respected his authority, and he'd offered it. *Please take the Bible.* Her heart drummed with desire. She couldn't bring herself to verbalize her inclinations, so she prayed, wishing with all her might that Dat would accept the gift.

At the end of the lane, Dat pulled the buggy next to Malon's, and out of sight from the prying eyes of the Bishop, Dat accepted their first English Bible.

He tucked it onto the seat beside him as they headed home. "I'm going to learn for myself what all the trouble is surrounding this Jesus," Dat said as his hand patted the worn leather cover of the Bible.

SEVENTEEN

Andy

Late Fall 1947, Burton, Ohio

A ndy stood in the circle of men around the wood stove in Jake's shop. The men stamped their feet and rubbed their hands together, trying to keep warm in the cold and drab morning air. Laughter surrounded the group as Malon told a joke. The camaraderie they all shared warmed Andy's heart.

Andy glanced around. The weak morning light enhanced the shadows, bouncing off Jake's many belts and pulleys hanging from the steel shaft that ran across the ceiling and connected to a gas motor outside. Jake fixed anything anyone brought to him. While he worked mainly on buggies, he also took on other side jobs. His gas motor and pulleys powered sewing machines, a table saw, a band saw, and wood joiners along with other equipment.

For the entire six months Andy had been courting Sylvia, he had taken special care to join Jake, Malon, John and Abe in the shop on Wednesday mornings for coffee and talk. At first, the conversations had been awkward for him, but over time, the tension eased as they grew to know each other better, and now Andy looked forward to their morning meetings.

"*Gut* morning," Andy's teeth chattered along with his greeting.

The men echoed a chorus of *gut* mornings in reply.

Abe commented, "I see we had a hard freeze last night. Those ruts in your lane are sure deep. Malon struggled to get his rig over them this morning."

Malon's whole body shook with laughter as he poked back. "You live across the street and can walk. I had to endure riding over them. If it had been a car, I'm sure I would have gotten stuck."

They settled into their chairs around the stove. Jake opened the door and threw another log onto the crackling fire. The scent of coffee wafted from the pot warming on the back. He took mugs and poured the steaming liquid and passed them around.

Andy heated his hands on the toasty ceramic; the warmth coaxing out further conversation. "I'm looking for a new job. Anyone have suggestions of who might be looking for a good, hired hand?"

"Are you leaving Will Hoover's place?" asked Jake.

"The war is ending, and so is my service term. I'll be out of work. Truth be told, I'm not too sad; Hazel Hoover's cooking leaves a lot to be desired."

The men snickered.

"The other day she went out to collect the eggs and found one of her chickens dead from a blowout. Who knows how long that poor chicken had been lying there? Guess what we had for lunch? Dead chicken. A large egg had ripped apart the poor bird's innards. She just cut around it and fed it to us, drowned in a cream sauce. I couldn't stomach knowing where it came from," Andy shuddered. "I've had enough."

Malon looked over at him. "You don't want to head back home and work on the family farm?"

A blush crept onto his cheeks, and he stammered, struggling to come up with a response.

John saved him from the embarrassment and punched Malon lightly in the arm. "You know he's deep into courting Sylvia. I suspect his staying near has something to do with her."

Malon responded, "Ahh, I figured as much. Just giving him a hard time. I heard Al Detweiler is looking for a new hired hand. He lives down yonder on the west side of town, close to the train station. You should check with him."

Andy tucked the tidbit of information away for later.

Al and Vera Detweiler lived on a crop farm in Burton that grew sugarbush and corn. Within minutes of inquiring, Al offered Andy a job with a ten-dollar raise, which would please Dat.

Andy gave Will Hoover a week's notice and packed up his belongings and moved into an upstairs room on the Detweiler farm.

Vera's cooking showed much improvement, but the dinner conversation did not. Many nights, Al and Vera sat around the table in uncomfortable silence while glaring at each other, avoiding any conversation, and talking only to their children. Their relationship vacillated—causing them to be in love one minute and raving mad at each other the next.

One night, Al and Vera's friends, Bill and Esther, came over to play cards. The two couples sat around the table playing rummy while sipping on a large bottle of wine Bill had supplied. The open consumption of alcohol always caught Andy off guard. *Didn't they worry about someone tattling to the Bishop?*

Andy finished getting himself a glass of water and got ready to head up to bed when Al called out to him

"Sit down and chat for a minute."

He had tried everything he could to avoid these wine-fueled evenings but couldn't think of a reason to turn down the invitation without being rude, so he pulled up a chair. Bill offered him a sip from the bottle; he declined.

The men were getting beaten by Esther and Vera.

"Rummy!" Vera cried as she laid out her cards.

Al groaned in disgust and took another long swig.

Andy took this as his signal to depart before things got ugly. "Thanks for the evening, folks. Morning's a coming mighty fast. I'm headin' up to bed."

"Won't you cut in?" whined Bill. "We can't let these ladies beat us."

"Nah, I'm beat. We got a full day of work tomorrow." Andy stood and put his water glass on the counter before exiting, grateful for his escape.

As he lay in bed, he listened as the conversation grew louder and louder. He tried to close his eyes and drift off to sleep, but Al's booming voice invaded his peace whenever his body relaxed. *Why did Al behave like this?* He'd be unable to help with chores in the morning.

Al's fist pounded the table with a thud, and his eyes snapped open again. He sighed. Tomorrow would be a long day.

"Goddamnit Vera. Why'd you have to beat me like that? A man should be able to win in his own household."

Andy pulled the covers over his head. *Surely, God had no part in this conversation.* Then he heard Vera's chuckle. *Wrong response.*

Her voice shrieked, "You think all I'm good for is cooking, cleaning, and baby making? I got brains and can think, too. For once, I beat you fair and square." Andy imagined her swishing her skirts and prancing around the table in a victory lap. Al would not stand for this embarrassment in front of his friends.

A crash sounded, and feet stomped before Vera yelled, "Al, don't you dare!"

The house fell silent. For a minute, Andy wondered if some harm had befallen Vera.

Then she let out a long wail. "Look at what you did! My hair," she sobbed.

Soon after, he heard Bill and Esther's buggy crunch down the lane.

Bill told him later in the week that Al had grabbed a pair of her sewing shears, ripped off Vera's *kap*, and cut off a sizeable chunk out of her hair.

Andy's entire body shuddered in disgust at the recounting. He couldn't believe Al had the audacity to commit such an act of disrespect. Even his Dat, whom he feared more than anyone, would never treat Mamm in such a way. Someone should report him to the Bishop. Maybe he should report him. He shrugged the idea aside. Best to stay out of it.

Al and Vera didn't speak to one another for a week. Their icy silence permeated the entire house, making everyone miserable. They glared at each other, asking the children to pass messages back and forth. "Tell your father I won't have lunch ready today because I'll be at the sewing circle."

The child responded, "Mamm, he's sitting right there. Why can't you tell him yourself?"

"Because. I am not talking to your father right now. He did something very, very bad."

This went on and on—the children caught in a bewildered circle of confusion. Andy took many of his meals over at Jake and Lizzie's that week to avoid the tension. Grateful for the extra time to spend with Sylvia.

Then one morning, a switch flipped like an electric light, and everything returned to normal. He caught Al and Vera kissing in the kitchen. Later in the morning, while they did chores in the barn, Al asked Andy if he would like to go coon hunting on Saturday night.

"I've never been coon hunting. I don't know if I'll be much help to you all." Warning bells sounded in his head. He didn't know if he wanted to associate himself with Al and his friends after all he'd seen this past week.

"Come on, it'll be fun. There is a group of us guys that go every year. We'll tell you what to do."

Andy shrugged, unsure of how to respond. "Who's going along?" Part of him felt flattered they wanted him to attend. He never had much time for himself these days, and an evening of hunting sounded fun.

"Well, Bill, of course, and several others." Al listed off some church members.

Andy recognized only Joshua. He knew him from the ride over to the draft board. He seemed respectable enough and not cut from the same cloth as the revelers. One night of fun wouldn't hurt anyone. "Okay, I'll come with you," he responded.

Tread lightly, his mind whispered back.

He pushed the apprehension aside. *It's good for me to have friends.*

Saturday evening turned out to be the perfect night for coon hunting. The clouds knit together, blocking out the light from any moon and stars, causing an inky black darkness to settle over the farm. A thin layer of snow peppered the ground. A group of Al's friends gathered in the yard carrying lanterns. Among them were Bill and a few other men Andy had seen around in the community. Their breath produced hazy puffs when they talked. Andy searched their faces for Joshua but couldn't find him anywhere. He guessed he'd chickened out or thought better of it.

Al had bred coonhounds for several years now. He had trained his two newest pups, Maisey and Daisy, every day for several months. He started their training by tying a string to a raccoon tail and trailing it along the ground and up the trees. Then he got rid of the string and started placing the coon tail in random trees. Maisey and Daisy were smart and learned which trees had the scent of the coon and would stand at the bottom and howl. Tonight was their first time treeing live coons, a test of sorts.

The party set off walking along a trail in the woods. Al and Bill led the way with the two dogs on leashes. A quarter mile down the trail, both dogs caught scent of a coon and tugged the men ahead.

"Okay, girls, it's go time." Al patted the dogs' rumps as he bent down and released the clasp holding the canines to their leashes. They were off, tearing through the woods as fast as the wind whistling through the trees. In minutes, the men heard their telltale howls in the distance. Maisey's quick bark followed by a long *ahooooooo* cried in the darkness. The men all hustled to where she stood, front paws on bark, snout raised to the sky, baying.

"Bill, raise up your lantern so I can see if she treed one," Al requested. Bill lifted his light, and, sure enough, a pair of beady little eyes stared back at them.

"Ya gonna shoot him?" Bill asked.

"Nah, we'll shake 'em down and have the dogs chase it to the next tree. It'll be good practice for 'em."

"I ain't climbing a tree, old man," Bill proclaimed. "It's a good way to get hurt."

"Which one of you is gonna climb and shake it out?" Al swung the lantern around the circle.

The men stood, hands in their pockets, afraid to volunteer.

"I vote Andy. He's a young buck, more limber than us middle-aged men. Get on up there, Andy." Al's eyes gleamed with his request.

Andy didn't want to climb trees in the middle of the night, but he had to obey his employer. He couldn't lose this job. Grunting, he gripped the bottom branch and hoisted himself up.

"Shine that lantern so he can see where the darn thing's at," barked Al.

The higher Andy rose into the branches, the more his legs trembled. The wind swayed in the trees and the limbs became more tender, creaking under his weight. The coon sat ten feet above him. He stopped, not wanting to get too close. Coons were nasty animals that could do some damage to a man in such a precarious situation.

"Now shake 'em down!" Al yelled from below.

Andy took hold of the branch and shook with all his might. The coon's plump body fell through the limbs, its paws grasping for a grip, to no avail. He heard the thud of its body below. The laughter of the men and the frantic yipping of the dogs vibrated off the hills as they took after the poor thing.

Andy climbed down to a round of applause. He smirked and took a bow. As he lifted his head, his chest puffed with pride.

Al howled with laughter, and Bill reached for his flask and took a large swig. "Here you go son, you earned this one." He handed Andy the flask.

Andy sniffed at the lid, the sour scent of hooch reaching his nostrils.

"Don't be a ninny. One swig will calm your nerves," Bill encouraged.

Andy had seen what the drink made Al do to his wife, and he wanted no part of it. He didn't want to explain to Jake or his other friends why he had taken to drinking. This could compromise his relationship with Sylvia. However, one sip would hurt no one, and he hated being called a sissy. He trepidatiously pressed his lips to the rim and took a short swallow. The brew burned his throat all the way down and settled in his stomach like a warm blanket. His eyes widened, and he sputtered, trying to hide his surprise with a fist to his mouth.

Bill clapped him on the back. "Atta boy. Let's go get the next one."

The men could hear the dogs howling in the distance as they continued their trek through the woods. As the night wore on, Andy lost count of how many coons he shook out of trees. After each time, he took a celebratory sip from the flask. Bill and the other men took long draws and after a few hours, they found themselves with empty flasks.

"Time to head on back, boys." Al leashed the dogs again, his eyes glassy. The group stumbled through the woods.

"Shhhh." Bill held up a finger to his lips as a branch snapped behind him. "Don't want anyone mistaking us for game," he slurred.

Their footsteps were loud and messy, and they laughed at everything. Andy joined in the fun, feeling light and free. At half past midnight, they stumbled into the yard.

"Be quiet, Vera and the kids are asleep," Al chuckled.

Ignoring him, the men clamored as they climbed up into their buggies to head for home.

Andy went upstairs to his room. He didn't even bother to take off his clothes. He lay across his bed and fell into a deep sleep.

Morning came quickly. The slats of rare winter sun streamed through the windows, hitting Andy's eyelids. He opened one eye, feeling the pounding in his head and bladder. A groan escaped his throat as he rolled over on his stomach, feeling queasy. It took a few minutes to gather his bearings and crawl out of bed. Everything seemed to spin in slow motion. Upon descending the stairs, Vera handed him a cup of coffee. He sipped the hot liquid, letting it settle his stomach and ease the clenching in his head.

"Fun night, *eh?*" Vera chuckled. "Give it a few hours and you'll feel much better."

Andy nodded, afraid to speak lest he vomit all over the floor. He handed the mug back to her and slipped out to the barn.

As the day wore on, the dizziness and nausea subsided, but another burden settled into his gut. He felt awful for breaking the *Orndung* rules, but heavier than that was the power his actions held. This "night of fun" could destroy everything he held dearest, his relationship with Sylvia. He hadn't felt this heavy since childhood, when he'd snuck out to listen to baseball games. He'd paid for that sin with Dat's wrath. This sin was far more serious. *What would the punishment be?*

EIGHTEEN

1947, Burton, Ohio

Andy sat opposite Jake in the repair shop, fiddling with his hands. Guilt over his sin ate him up all week. The weight of it pulled him under like a drowning man. He needed to confess. He figured it would be better to come out and tell Jake than for him to hear about it from someone else. A conclusion that surprised him. Confessing to Dat was out of the question, but his gut told him to trust Jake; besides, Sylvia deserved an honest man.

His stomach twisted. "I need to move out of the Detweiler house. I messed up."

Jake cocked his head to the side. "What do you mean?"

"Last weekend, I went coon hunting with some of Al's friends. I shouldn't have gone, but it sounded interesting. It wasn't long before they brought out the flasks and began drinking. They kept offering it to me, and I partook." He hung his head at his admission, afraid to see Jake's reaction.

Jake didn't speak.

Andy continued, "I'm going back home. Mamm and Dat have moved back to the homeplace to care for Mummie and Daughty on the other side of Burton, and I'm going to live with them." He wanted to say, "till I'm married," but bit back the words. He loved Sylvia and couldn't imagine life with anyone else, but his mistake had put it all in jeopardy. He didn't deserve her. *How could he talk to Jake about marriage when he couldn't even control his own sin?*

Jake cleared his throat. "I suspect we all make mistakes. It seems like you have learned from yours and are taking some actions not to repeat them."

Andy exhaled. Relief flooded his chest and lifted his shoulders a bit, giving him confidence to meet Jake's eyes. In them, he saw kindness.

"Should I confess to the Bishop?" The words sent shivers through him as he said them.

Jake ran his fingers through his beard for a moment. "No, you confessed to an elder, and most importantly to God. That is enough."

Andy's spirits lifted. The guilt that had pinned him underwater vanished with Jake's words.

"Did Sylvia tell you about the trip the young people are taking to Niagara Falls in October?"

"She did." Andy sighed, grateful to move on to other topics of conversation.

"The cost of the total package is twelve dollars for the train fare, accommodations, and food. Do you think you'll be able to join them?"

"I have some funds saved up. I think I can manage." He counted the extra fifty dollars he had put away from his work after he paid Dat his portion.

"Malon and Annie are going on the trip as chaperones, so it will be good and proper. I'll let Malon know you'll attend. The fees are due by the next singing." Jake rose from his perch and extended a hand to Andy. Andy clung to it for an extra second longer than necessary, grateful for the forgiveness it represented.

"You have my permission."

Andy let go of his hand, confused. "For what?"

"To marry Sylvia."

A deep red crept up Andy's neck. "I never asked you, sir."

"You didn't need to, son. I can think of nobody better for my daughter."

Andy stuttered, struggling to come up with words. Unshed tears poked at the corners of his eyes. He didn't deserve such forgiveness.

What would it be like to be married, and have a brood of children underfoot? To run his own household? Hope unfurled at the thoughts, and an idea took root. He would talk to Sylvia about marriage on this trip. Hopefully, they would get a few moments to themselves at some point. *What if she declined him?* The thought felt worse than the daunting task of confessing his sin to the Bishop. He didn't know how he could go on with life if she said no.

Andy spent most of the time on the ride to Buffalo looking out the windows at the speeding countryside. He had never ridden on a train before; the world sped by. The minute he noticed a tree in the distance, it was upon him, whizzing past at breakneck speed. His brain spun, trying to keep up. The slow pace of a horse and buggy allowed for keen observation. When behind the reins, he could take in the world at a slower pace, observing each knoll in the trees. He didn't know which he preferred. Both had their merits, he guessed.

People hustled all around them at the terminal in Buffalo. The instant Andy stepped off the train; he felt the eyes of everyone on him. His plain clothes stuck out like a costume. Eyebrows raised and hands held back giggles as fellow passengers pointed fingers. He rubbed his neck, wishing he could disappear.

People seemed to move at the pace of the train. Their heels clicked this way and that on the polished floor. The ladies wore traveling suits, and the gentlemen carried leather cases. Malon corralled the group together in front of a loudspeaker, shouting out departures and arrivals. He stepped to the front to ask an attendant for directions. The steward pointed them toward a platform.

The group followed Malon, all carrying suitcases except for Andy. Another embarrassment he hadn't considered. He carried a little bundle tied up in a sheet like he had done all those years ago when his family moved from house to house. He kept it down at his side, wishing for a bigger coat to hide it under. They finally reached the platform and boarded a bus, for the final leg.

"Alma, look," Sylvia pointed out the bus window at a tall woman gliding down the platform. She had platinum blonde hair curled under her chin, her tiny waist accentuated by a tight pencil skirt, and shiny kitten heels on her feet. "Do you think she's a movie star?"

"What do you know about movie stars? You've never even seen a movie." Alma nudged her shoulder. "I doubt it. I heard they are out in California."

"She sure is pretty," Sylvia giggled. "Hope she doesn't catch our boys' attention."

"Andy has eyes only for you, and you know it."

As if on cue, Andy glanced across the aisle at her. Sylvia's cheeks grew rosy as he gave her a wink. She grinned back at him.

Alma leaned over. "You notice the way Jonas Yoder keeps staring at you?"

Sylvia glanced behind her only to find Jonas' eyes fixed on her. When a silly grin spread across his face, she quickly looked away. "What does he want?" she whispered to Alma.

"To steal you away from Andy."

"He's creepy."

"Agreed."

An hour later, the bus pulled into the outskirts of Niagara Falls; shops littered the streets with gigantic signs shouting "Souvenirs." Beside them, lodging camps lined the sides of the road with strange names like *Cataract Tourist Camp*. Sylvia wondered which camp Malon had picked out for them. As they neared the town center, shops knit closer together, sidewalks stretched before them with several multi-story buildings rising. Before long, they pulled into the bus station.

Wide-eyed, Sylvia and Alma dismounted, eager to explore the shops and, most of all, to see the source of the roar that hummed in the background.

"Follow me," Malon motioned down the street. They clutched their bags and followed him until he stopped in front of Brown's Tourist Camp, a click outside of the downtown area.

A white clapboard Cape Cod sat in the center of the semicircle of cabins set back from the road. A hand-painted sign mounted to the top of the roof advertised accommodations with full kitchens, beds, and hot showers.

"Wait here," Malon instructed the crew.

He entered the office, and within a few minutes, emerged with several keys. Malon's wife, Annie, instructed the girls to follow her to the left, and Malon took the young men to the right. "Freshen up and meet back here in half an hour. We'll go together to eat dinner at the smorgasbord down the street and see a few sights before bed."

Annie divided the girls up, four to a cabin. Sylvia and Alma roomed with two other girls, Rachel and Mary. The cabin had electric lights, a small hot plate, a sink, and two sets of bunk beds. Clean white sheets and folded blankets were waiting at the foot of each bed.

Sylvia threw her suitcase onto the top bunk. "Alma and I will take this set," she motioned.

Sylvia changed into the new blue dress she had sewn. The sleeves gathered at the wrists, with a small collar dotted with two buttons. At first, she had been uncertain if the collar went against the *Ordnung* but wanted to stand out a bit on the trip. She sewed it in such a way that allowed for easy removal if necessary. Better to ask for forgiveness than permission. Dat's eyebrows lifted at the extravagance, but he didn't comment when she donned her new shawl her parents had gifted her for her eighteenth birthday.

"Can you imagine overlooking the falls with our boys?" Sylvia giggled. "I wonder if Andy will kiss me?"

Alma blushed. "Caleb held my hand once. On a buggy ride home."

"Do you think he'll ask you to go steady?"

"I hope. We have spent very little time together. I hope this trip will allow us to get to know each other better."

"Do you think Andy will ever talk to me about marriage? I don't know how much longer I can wait. We've already been going steady for over a year."

"Maybe he's already talked with your Dat. We are getting into marriage season."

Hope flooded Sylvia's heart at Alma's words. If he didn't talk about the subject soon, she might just need to take the matter into her own hands.

Sylvia went to the small mirror above the sink—a luxury never allowed at home. She adjusted every wisp of her hair, admiring her reflection. Reaching into her pocket, she pulled out her "Bloom of Roses" lip tint. Hiding the tiny tube in the folds of her skirt, she dabbed a bit on her finger and reached up to smear it on her lips. The faintest bit of color added the perfect touch. Her efforts to hide the makeup were in vain as she caught Rachel and Mary standing behind her, staring. "Just freshening up a bit before dinner," she commented, raising her chin.

"Stop hogging the mirror, Sylvia," Alma grabbed her elbow and pulled her to the side. "Are you crazy?" Her hot breath whispered in Sylvia's ear. "You want to get us sent home early? Mary is the Bishop's daughter."

"Don't be so dramatic," Sylvia rolled her eyes. "Loosen up. I should have the freedom to experiment a bit."

Alma's brown eyes pleaded with her. "It's not just you, you need to worry about. Andy will also bear your sin, and both of you are heading towards marriage. Tongues will wag if you keep acting out like this. Don't put him in a bad spot."

Sylvia bit her lip. *She hadn't thought about Andy.* She nodded. "You're right." She licked her lips to remove the stain, grateful for Alma's sensible guidance.

"It's time to go," Alma said, looking at the clock on the wall. The girls linked elbows and headed out the open door to their meeting spot, the picnic tables behind the office.

At the smorgasbord Sylvia piled her plate high with fried chicken, mashed potatoes, and French fries with gravy before squeezing in at the girls' table. She glanced over at Andy, who forked spoonfuls into his mouth. *Would she get any time with him to herself?* After cleaning her plate, she stood and went to the ice cream machine. She delighted in pulling the lever and decorating a cone with a twisty pile of the creamy delicacy. So much easier than hand-cranking the ice cream bucket.

After dinner, they walked back towards their cabins. The air had a sharp edge to it, and Sylvia pulled her shawl close around her shoulders, fingering the embroidered letters of her name Mamm had stitched into the corner. If she had her way, soon her last name wouldn't be Slabaugh anymore.

"Hear that?" Malon cupped his hand and shouted back at the group. "That's the roar of the falls, just a couple of blocks away. Should we check it out at night? I hear the lights are a special sight." An eager chorus of nods and smiles greeted Malon's suggestion, and he veered to the right. The air became damper the closer they got to the falls. A fine mist fell over everything, and wet droplets rested on the top of Sylvia's bonnet. They came to the end of the street and turned a corner to the greatest wonder Sylvia ever beheld.

Sylvia gasped, her eyes widened, and she brought both hands to her mouth, unable to stifle her reaction. "Wow."

The initial murmurs of the group grew quiet as they took in the scene. The falls were far grander than they appeared on postcards. She bet she could have piled three silos end to end and they still wouldn't have reached the depth of the horseshoe carved into the rock. Massive amounts of water spilled over the edge, tumbling down into a giant thundercloud. Different colored lights illuminated each section of the horseshoe, creating a living rainbow.

A group of girls walked to the edge of the railing, and she trailed away from them until she came to a little enclave at the end of the sidewalk. She looked behind her for Andy, wanting to share the moment with him but was unable to spot him in the dusky darkness. She tucked herself against a rock and was so lost in the roar that she didn't feel Andy's presence as he sidled up to her and slipped his hand into hers underneath the shawl. A tingle went up her spine. Only his touch could pull her eyes away from the beauty that beheld her. She turned her head to him and rested it on his shoulder. He smiled at her and leaned in close, his breath hot against her skin.

He brought his lips to her ear. "Marry me?"

Sylvia's heart stopped. *Had he just proposed?* His physical presence made her melt like a block of ice on a warm summer day. She tried to compose herself, but everything about him made her legs rubbery. She turned to face him, letting go of his hand. The lights illuminated the curves of his face. She pictured herself standing at the edge of the falls, ready to make a great, breathtaking leap into the pool of those shining blue eyes. *Should she jump?* Resolve tightened, and the path lay clear before her. *She loved this man.* From the very first singing when their eyes met across the barn in the low lamplight, she knew he was the one for her.

"Yes," she breathed, her words carried away by the roar.

He put his hands on either side of her face and drew her close. Their lips met, and she couldn't help but smile. His lips tasted like the cinnamon Chiclets he liked to chew. A rainbow of lights danced all around them as they swirled together in their cocoon of love encased with the pounding water.

Andy couldn't believe he'd whispered his proposal in Sylvia's ear. He hadn't planned the words, but he could think of no better place to have marked the occasion than the mesmerizing vista in front of them. The power of the falls had caused him to cast off any doubts. At the tourist camp, he'd read about men going over the edge in barrels. He'd thought they were wild for taking such a risk, but now he understood it. The thrill of a definitive jump into the unknown. If he hadn't asked now, then they would have had to wait another year till marriage season rolled around again. The taste of Sylvia's lips pressed against his sealed the love growing in his heart. After they broke apart, she rested her head on his shoulder. He drew her close, always wanting her by his side.

Malon's call broke them apart. "Time to head back to camp!" he hollered.

The group gathered to walk back to the cabins. Andy didn't want to let go of Sylvia's hand but had to do so as they settled back into their formation of leaders in the front, followed by the women and the men in the back. He had a hard time not skipping for joy the entire walk back to camp.

The next morning dawned clear and crisp. The sun worked at melting the frost on the lawn of the campground. Sylvia would have preferred to sleep in a little longer after her late night of whispering and giggling with Alma about wedding plans, but they had breakfast to cook.

Malon had sent the boys to the corner store to buy some eggs, milk, and bread, and they had deposited the groceries on the girls' front porches to prepare egg sandwiches for all. The girls used electric hotplates to fry up the eggs and a toaster oven to brown the bread. Sylvia marveled at how quickly the hot plate came to life and how the pan sizzled after only a few minutes. The constant heat cooked the eggs much faster than the wood burners they used at home. *Being English must be wonderful*, she thought. She pushed the idea out of her head. No use dwelling on something that would never happen now that she had committed to marriage.

After preparing the food, they gathered outside at the picnic tables and quickly consumed breakfast. Malon gave out instructions. "Today is a sightseeing day. This morning, we will break into small groups to explore the falls and the town. We will meet back here at noon. My *gut* wife Annie will prepare some sandwiches for us to enjoy, and then we will go together to ride the Maid of the Mist and the Whirlpool Aero car. Please be back here on time so we can stay on schedule."

Alma nudged Sylvia. "Let's see if Caleb and Andy want to tag along with us this morning. We can do a little shopping, pick up a few postcards, and go see the falls in the daylight." Sylvia nodded and smiled, a flush radiating off her face. She couldn't wait to see Andy again.

"Just imagine, you'll be Mrs. Troyer before the year's out. The first one of our friends to get married."

Sylvia shushed her. "Don't tell anyone yet, Alma. We want our parents to be the first to know when we get home."

Alma closed her mouth in a straight line and bit her bottom lip. "Your secret is safe with me." They found the boys, and the foursome split off from the sizable group and headed down Murray Street towards the falls.

Sylvia spotted a drugstore with an open door on the corner. She tugged at Alma's sleeve and ducked inside. The boys followed. "I want to get a few postcards to mail home," she explained when they were away from the roar of the street traffic and the falls.

It took a few minutes for their eyes to adjust to the dimly lit store. The boys fingered the postcards and picked out a few souvenirs. The girls selected their postcards, then meandered towards the back of the store, looking at the knickknacks for sale. Sylvia's eyes lighted upon a booth tucked into a back corner. Blue block lettering stamped on the side said: *Your photo framed in one minute.* Sylvia looked around and didn't see any other Amish in the store. "Alma, stand watch. I want to get my photo made in that booth."

"Sylvia, you can't. What will happen if Malon or the Bishop finds out?"

"They won't. This is the happiest moment of my life, and I want something to remember it by." Sylvia went into the booth and drew the dark curtain closed. She reached into her pocket and pulled out two quarters to stick into the machine, looking into the big eye in the center that stared back at her, and pulled on the lever. The eye winked, and a bulb flashed. The machine whirred, spitting out a green metal frame with her image.

Sylvia stared at the photo. Her slightly parted lips and pink that brushed up her cheeks made her look pretty. Pleased, she pocketed the picture and stepped out of the booth. Alma stood with her back to her, ready to intercept anyone who recognized them. What a good friend she was. Sylvia put her hand on Alma's shoulder, and she jumped. She laughed, "You sure are nervous."

"Well, are you done?"

Sylvia pulled the little picture from her pocket and let Alma have a quick glance. "You should do it, too. I'll watch out for you."

Alma squealed. "No way. I wouldn't want to risk it."

The girls caught back up with the boys, and they spent the rest of the morning seeing the falls in the light of day and writing notes on postcards to mail home.

After lunch, they got on the *Maid of the Mist* and motored close to the falls. The mist coated everyone in its mystery. As their boat rolled towards the deafening roar, Andy reached over and held Sylvia's hand again.

"When we get home, let's tell our parents first thing."

Andy nodded.

"My Mamm will be so excited to plan a wedding. What will your parents say?"

"I don't know, but I suspect they'll be happy I found a *gut* Amish girl."

Sylvia laid her head on his shoulder. She hoped Andy's parents would like her. Strange that she'd never met them before and now they would marry. Regardless, together, they were complete. Ready to face whatever came their way.

NINETEEN

Thursday, January 1st, 1948, Burton, Ohio

Swollen raindrops hit the window, rousing Sylvia out of her sleep. "Yuck," she groaned, rolling over, wishing she could snap her fingers and change the weather on her wedding day. She stared at her blue wedding dress hanging on a nail in the wall. She hugged her arms to her body and imagined Andy holding her. Tonight, and every night after, she would share a bed with her new husband. The thought warmed her core, bringing a blush to her cheeks.

She threw back the covers and sat up. Her room was a disaster; clothing lay in a disheveled heap. A broken chair in the corner. Reminders of Jonas Yoder's wrath after they'd published their engagement. Yesterday, he'd snuck into the house and destroyed her room, throwing its contents down the stairs. *How could he do such a thing?* Her throat squeezed shut, and her breaths came shallow and fast. She closed her eyes and pictured Andy next to her, holding her hand. The image eased her breathing. Jonas wouldn't be at the wedding. Dat had promised her.

A big flash of lightning interrupted her imagination, followed by a thunderous rumble sounding like a train going down the line. A thunderstorm on New Year's Day? How odd. She took her time getting out of bed, putting on her every-day clothes and then padded down the stairs.

Mamm stood in the kitchen, already at work, moving back and forth from the pot on the stove to a pile of dishes in the sink.

The herbal scent of stuffing and chicken filled the air, one of Sylvia's favorites. She snatched the dishrag from Mamm and assumed putting away the clean pots and pans.

"Coffee?" Mamm handed her a steaming mug.

Sylvia stopped working and took a swallow. The hot liquid hit the back of her throat with its familiar warmth. She set the mug down on the counter and sighed in contentment.

"You sleep well?" Mamm asked.

"As well as expected, before the biggest day of my life. Can you believe there is rain and thunder on my wedding day?"

"It's unusual."

Sylvia put down the dishtowel and sat at the table. The enormity of the day suddenly overwhelmed her, and a twinge of sadness settled in her gut. How she would miss Mamm and Dat. They'd see them every day as they planned to live with her parents, but she would no longer be under their authority. Gone were the days of the three of them living in solidarity. She would answer to Andy now. The mix of their daily lives would forever change. Her sudden melancholy added to the strangeness of the day. *Could excitement and sadness exist at the same moment?* She guessed that if a thunderstorm could happen in winter, then they could.

"What's wrong?" Mamm asked, looking over at her.

Sylvia stood and went to Mamm. She wrapped her arms around her wiry midsection. "I'm going to miss this. You, Dat, and I together in the mornings."

Mamm held her close. "You've always been so strong, Sylvia, overcoming any obstacle in your way. This is a joyous occasion, not a sad one. I see the way you and Andy look at each other. That kind of love can become stronger than even the love of a parent. We aren't going anywhere. Even though things will change, we'll always support you."

Sylvia wiped the tears from her eyes, touched by Mamm's words. She believed her. Mamm was strong, too—releasing her last remaining daughter to marriage had to be hard. Over the years Mamm had softened though, and her sadness and anxiety had mellowed out. Sylvia pulled out of Mamm's embrace. "What else do you need help with?"

"Fannie's bringing over the cake in a few minutes, along with the cookies. You can help her set up the serving table in the dining room."

"Sure." She had been looking forward to Rudy Fannie's famous cake. Folks had been talking about it for decades, but Sylvia had never eaten a slice herself. Mamm said one bite of Fannie's cake would make all others seem as if you were eating sawdust scraped off the floor of Dat's shop. Folks were always after her for the recipe, but she kept it a guarded secret, only offering to make it for special occasions.

At seven, Rudy Fannie's buggy rolled into the front yard. She stepped out holding a big box and waddled her way to the front door, where Sylvia stood ready to lend a hand. "Let me take that." She reached for the enormous box covering Fannie's face and body. Fannie handed it over, and Sylvia carried it into the dining room, easing it onto the center of a serving table. She lifted the lid off the box. "Oh, Rudy Fannie," she gasped. Out of the box came a square three-layer cake covered in mounds of creamy white frosting and dotted with chopped walnuts. "We'll have to keep folks from wanting to eat dessert first when they hear your cake is here. I can't wait to taste it for myself."

"That's right!" Fannie exclaimed. "Lizzie tells me you've never tasted my cake before." Fannie clasped her hands together. "Best one I've ever made. Fitting, it's for the wedding of the daughter of my dear friend."

"Is there more to carry in?" Mamm inquired.

Fanny nodded. "There are boxes of cookies out in the buggy.

We can arrange them on these platters." She pointed to the empty serving dishes lining the table.

Sylvia threw her shawl around her shoulders and opened the door to a frigid blast poking at her in the ribs. The temperature sure had dropped since the thunderstorm; she thought as she headed out to the buggy. Something stung the back of her neck, and she reached back to slap it away. To her surprise, her fingers touched ice. The rain from earlier had transformed into something more lethal. She hustled to the buggy, eager to get away from the slices that pelted her hands and head. Rudy Fannie tried to follow. "You stay, Rudy Fannie!" Sylvia hollered. "I'll get the cookies."

Fannie didn't argue and stood waiting on the porch with her hands on her hips. Sylvia returned carrying four heavy boxes. Inside, she opened them and saw mounds of sour cream cookies, joe mathe's, date balls, and molasses crinkles. The heavenly scents of cinnamon, sugar, and maple cream frosting filled the air, and after Sylvia arranged the platters, she licked the sugar off her fingers.

"Sylvia!" Mamm scolded her.

Sylvia grinned, secretly hoping Mamm would keep fretting over her after the wedding.

"This is crazy weather. Thunder, lightning, sleet, what's next?" Mamm commented, shaking her head.

"Snow, I reckon. You sure are going to have a wedding everyone will remember," Fannie laughed.

Sylvia loved when Rudy Fannie laughed. Her whole body shook like the slinky's in the toy section at the general store.

Mamm pointed up the stairs. "You'd best go on and get yourself ready, Sylvia. It's already seven thirty, and everyone will arrive in half an hour for the ceremony."

—◇◇◇◇◇—

Andy woke up on his wedding morning with Sylvia on his mind. He glanced over at the littlest of his brothers still sharing the bed with him, snoring. Today, he'd leave home for good. He ruffled his brother's hair as a mixture of eagerness and sadness filled him. As much as he wanted to leave this place, he'd never considered the fate of his siblings. His throat itched as he thought about who would take on his workload or be farmed out to help pay the bills. *What would become of them when he left?* He pushed the thoughts aside. Today had no room for sadness, only joy. He rose from the warmth the bed offered and threw on his trousers to go help with the chores.

A faint green light entered the bedroom through the window, casting an eerie glow on the sparse furnishings. A rumble of thunder caught his attention, and he glanced out the window to see dark thunderheads and pelting rain obscuring the barn. He grinned. God may have planned rain for the day, but nothing would dampen his spirits. Today was the day he claimed Sylvia as a Troyer and gave himself to her in marriage.

Sylvia had brought him a love he'd never known before. She had shown him life could indeed be lighthearted and fun again. Her parents had opened their hearts and invested in him as if he was their own. An invisible hand had nudged him along this path of life, and he had embraced its prompt, glad for once he had chosen baptism into the Amish church.

As he entered the kitchen, Mamm looked up from her mug of coffee and piece of bread. She motioned to the loaf sitting on the counter. "Help yourself."

He grabbed a slice, buttered it, and sat down across the table. They ate in their usual silence, letting the drum of the rain meld into their thoughts. Mamm swooped the crumbs left on the table into her hand as she finished the last swallow of her coffee. "What time do we need to be over at the Slabaughs'?"

"Service starts at eight. A bit before should be fine."

Mamm nodded in understanding. "Why don't you stay in this morning? Dat and your brothers are all out doing chores. I don't think they'll miss your help."

"I want to help Mamm. This is the last morning I'll be here on the farm."

Mamm swallowed, her brow furrowed. A frown swept over her face at his words.

He'd lived with them off and on these past few years, but a piece of him always missed Mamm when he was out of the house. Now he would leave for good. *Would she miss him, too?*

"I'll see ya over at the Troyers' then. Be sure to tell Dat we need to be leaving here no later than seven. I'll hang your wedding clothes up in your bedroom."

"Thank you." Andy grabbed his hat hanging on the peg and stepped outside. The temperature had dropped, and the rain had picked up again. He stamped to the barn, trying to avoid getting wet. Before he reached the doorway, the sky opened and rained down sleet. Little bits of ice pelted his forearms and exposed neck. He ran the rest of the way, and when he reached the barn; he stood for a minute, catching his breath.

Dat came around the corner carrying two heavy buckets of milk. His eyes registered surprise at the sight of Andy. "We don't need your help this morning. Don't want you to be smelling like a barn on your wedding day. Go on inside and get ready." He dismissed him.

Andy looked at Dat stooped over, holding the full pails of milk. "Let me at least empty the milk pails." He reached for the heavy buckets. Dat didn't put up a fight.

Deep lines had formed on the bridge of Dat's nose, and a new curve appeared on his back, causing him to stoop. He hadn't noticed how much Dat had aged until this moment. He grimaced. His focus had only been on Sylvia and her family, that he had paid little attention to his own. His parents had met his engagement with silent ambivalence. Their response wasn't unusual, as they only showed emotion when they didn't agree with a decision. Over the years, he understood silence was their nod of approval, but he wished they would have shown some sort of delight.

"Weather sure is interesting today," Dat commented, toeing the mud that had turned to slush. Without waiting for a reply, he turned and went back into the darkness of the barn.

"Mamm says you need to be ready and leaving by seven," Andy called after him. Dat raised a hand in understanding.

Andy emptied the pails into the barrels lining the back of the wagon, ready to be driven to the cheese plant. He put the lids on to keep the rain out and then made his way back to the house to get dressed.

The rain and sleet stopped before he left for the Slabaughs'. On the drive, Andy couldn't help but feel glad. There had never been a place for him under Dat's roof. Now he understood what he'd always felt. He'd only been an object, an extra mouth to feed, a commodity to trade, but not a son. Perhaps Mamm and Dat would find some peace without him here. He slapped Cookie's reins, eager to see his bride.

The wedding ceremony started shortly after eight. The Slabaughs had set up church benches in their living room, and the scent of pine filled the air from the scrubbed floorboards. Friends and family packed the house full to overflowing. Outside, a soft snow fell from the gray clouds; the delicate flakes stuck to the wet earth, covering up the dark mud, and brightening the landscape.

Andy and Sylvia sat in the front row on opposite sides. Sylvia wore her blue wedding dress she had sewn. Andy dressed in his new wedding clothes—a pair of black slacks, a white shirt, and black suspenders topped with a black felt hat. He snuck a shy glance over at his bride. Her face glowed, and she looked beautiful sitting with her hands in her lap, Alma at her side. The song leader started the singing, and friends and family joined their voices together to begin the service. Malon gave the message, and at the end of the talk, he asked Andy and Sylvia to come stand before him to give their marriage vows.

Andy rose. The last time he stood before the church, fear consumed him. This time his heart soared.

"Do you promise together that you will come with love, forbearance, and patience, live with each other, and not apart from each other until God will separate you in death?"

Andy's gaze fell on Sylvia. He couldn't hide his grin. "Yes."

Sylvia responded with her affirmations as well, her eyes sparkling.

Malon motioned for the couple to kneel, and the entire room did the same. Then he led them in a prayer of blessing.

After the prayer the Bishop took Andy's hand and joined it with Sylvia's then said, "The God of Abraham, and the God of Isaac, and the God of Jacob be with you and help you together and give His blessings richly unto you, and this through Jesus Christ, Amen."

When the attendees arose from their knees, it was nearly noon. The gray clouds had broken open, and slats of sunlight spilled into the living room on its occupants like God smiling His nod of approval.

Andy intertwined his fingers with Sylvia's. They now belonged together. Forever.

Andy

Harvest 1948, Burton, Ohio

ndy wiped the sweat from his brow with the handkerchief he kept in his back pocket. He took a swig from the water jug Sylvia had packed him. "Let's take a break," he called to Caleb and Jake.

August had arrived, and with it, the wheat harvest. Jake, being mechanically minded, kept care of the church's community threshing machine and, with permission from the Bishop, provided threshing services for some of the local farmers. Anyone from the church could come and use the machine, but if they wanted the work to be done for them, they could hire it out. Jake had brought on Caleb and Andy to help for the season.

Andy spent most of his day with a pitchfork in hand, shoveling the bound sheaves into the mouth of the machine.

Jake acted as an overseer, walking around the contraption to make sure all the belts and pulleys were in working order to pull the wheat down and separate the germ from the straw. He wafted back and forth from the pulleys to the finished product as it fell into buckets. Once filled, he emptied the buckets into the back of the wagon for the farmer to pull back to their barn. The entire operation required at least two sets of hands and ran optimally with an extra man.

At Andy's suggestion, the men hopped down from the wagon and sat in the shade of a leafy oak next to the barn. They sipped their water and munched on apples and hunks of bread the ladies had packed them. The summer had been exceptionally hot, and the sun beat down relentlessly, its scorching rays bleaching the trees and grasses of their vibrant green. Autumn was coming, and the sultry breezes knew it, making sure their hot breath hit everything it could before Jack Frost appeared.

"It's been a good harvest this year. Glad to have you boys helping, we've made good time today," Jake threw his apple core into the field and rose to his feet, loosening the kinks out of his aging knees. He walked over to the machine and fingered its long belt. "Heat's wearing this one out a bit. Remind me to order a new one the next time we're in town."

Andy made a mental note to remind himself later about the belt as he stood and stretched out his arms. "Let's get back to it. I'm ready for the roast, Sylvia promised me." He licked his lips, thinking of the tender meat and potatoes awaiting him. If he got lucky, they'd have pie for dessert. Sylvia had spoiled him during their first seven months of marriage. She'd proved to be more than he'd dreamed. Smart, kind, hardworking, and always wanting to please him. His admiration and affection for her grew by the day.

The men took their positions, the grinding and shaking of the machine overpowering any attempts at conversation. Six wagons sat full of sheaves, ready to process. Andy estimated they could knock out the last of the work in the next two hours. After, there would be the normal chores of milking and feeding, but the end drew near, and they'd make it home in plenty of time for supper.

The rest of the afternoon passed quickly, and supper proved to be the reward he'd looked forward to. Mounds of steaming beef swimming in gravy, bowls of honey-glazed carrots, and buttery mashed potatoes filled his stomach and stuck to his bones. These types of meals were always a wonder to him after years of blackberry soup and meager provisions provided at home and the camps he worked at. Jake and Lizzie acted like it was normal to eat this well, but Andy knew full well the other side of the coin.

Sylvia looked across the table at him with her doe eyes. "Sure was hot today. I hope you had enough water out there."

Andy replied, "Of course, we had plenty. Great crew today. Caleb will be such a good, hardworking husband for Alma."

Lizzie piped in, "Have they published their engagement yet?"

Andy swallowed his bite. "No, but it will be later this fall."

Lizzie grinned. "Will they live at the homeplace?"

"*Jah.*" Having Caleb and Alma close would be a blessing. He had worried family relationships would get complicated when he moved in with Jake and Lizzie after their marriage, but his fears had been unfounded. They had become even more gracious and gave the newlyweds their privacy by moving into the *dawdy* house they had added onto the main house. They enjoyed each other's company and still shared most meals together.

Lizzie changed the subject. "Church is to be held over at the Yoder farm this Sunday."

"Do you know who is going to be giving the message, Dat?" Sylvia asked. "I sure hope it's Malon. I feel like I learn something new every time he preaches. He keeps my attention."

"*Jah*, it's supposed to be Malon this week. He said the Bishop will be in attendance." Jake pinched his lips together, and the table settled into an uncomfortable silence.

Andy knew what caused the unease. Malon had been preaching in recent weeks about salvation by grace alone. His boldness had put the congregation in a frenzy. Grace a gift? Salvation guaranteed? No one had ever preached like that before. Word had gotten back to the Bishop. More than likely, his upcoming presence at the service said a whole lot about his dissatisfaction with Malon's preaching.

Andy had tried to stay out of the fray. Bishop Miller and his Dat were close friends, and he wanted to remove himself from any association that could hinder his already fragile relationship with his father. He hoped Jake could stay out of it as well, but all indications pointed to the opposite. More than once, Andy had been rooting around in Jake's shop for a tool and had discovered Jake's English Bible hidden beneath a sheaf of papers or in a drawer at the bottom of a cabinet. He knew Jake studied the Bible as a promise to Sylvia to find out more about Jesus, but he never had the courage to ask what he had discovered. Best just to stay out of it.

"Sylvia, why don't you get the dessert." Lizzie broke the painful silence with her request.

"Come and join me." Sylvia tugged Andy up from his seat and pulled him into the kitchen. Once in private, she reached up and kissed him on the lips.

He caressed her cheek. "It was getting a little awkward in there with all the church talk."

Sylvia grinned. "You have me to thank for that, Mr. Troyer. I never should have asked about Malon preaching, but something is stirring. Alma tells me there has been talk in her house as well about the salvation issue. What do you think of all of this?"

"I don't know. I've tried to avoid it. I don't want to upset Dat too much. Seems as if we should be able to study the scriptures for ourselves, though." His mood darkened. *Who am I kidding? Upset Dat too much.* He should be able to think for himself; instead, he found himself worried about what Dat thought.

"That's what I told Dat, too. It's just a big show of power."

Andy held a finger to Sylvia's lips. "All fine for you to say here in the privacy of your home with your husband, but be careful to mind your tongue when you are with your friends. The Bishop has ears everywhere."

Sylvia turned around and pulled the pie from the safe resting on the counter. Andy peeked his head over her shoulder. He licked his lips. "Cherry, my favorite."

"I'll mind my tongue if you give me some space to cut this pie."

"Space?" Andy chuckled. He leaned forward and wrapped his arms around his wife, resting his chin on her shoulder. "I have the best life with my *gut* wife."

Sylvia clucked her tongue. "Take these to my parents." She turned out of his embrace, handing him two generous slices of the oozing red dessert. She followed him into the dining room, carrying their own.

The rest of the dinner conversation revolved around the threshing work at hand and the schedule for the next day. "Are you coming out to the shop tomorrow morning for our meeting?" Jake asked Andy as he headed into the living room to retire to his evening chair. "Malon and Caleb will be there."

Andy swallowed and gave a nod. "I'll come after the morning chores."

"I'll get the coffee ready for you boys tonight, so all you need to add is the hot water," Lizzie said as she cleared the dishes from the table.

The crow of a rooster invaded Andy's dreams, awakening him sooner than he desired. The early morning light made it easy for him to find his trousers, and he thanked the Lord it was at least early autumn and not winter as he bounded down the stairs and out the back door. He strode across the yard to the barn. The morning dew from the grass dampened the hem of his pants as he went about his chores, eager for a cup of hot coffee.

After milking and feeding the cows, he opened the door to the shop and smelled the coffee he'd been pining for. Lizzie had also brought out the rest of the cherry pie from the night before. Andy walked over to the stove and poured himself a cup. He settled onto his usual stool and accepted the piece of pie Jake held out to him. A few minutes later, Malon arrived, followed by Caleb. The men shoveled the pie down, hungry after a few hours of heavy work.

"I don't think there is a better way to start off the day than a piece of Lizzie's cherry pie." Malon chuckled as he licked his fork clean and set the empty plate to the side. "I've been thinking. We've been meeting together for a few years now, trading news, talking about crops, weather, and even family matters. One thing we haven't talked about is spiritual things. It's no secret I've been preaching about salvation at the church meetings. Jake knows I have been studying the scriptures, and I suspect he's done a bit himself. Learning the scriptures by myself has been lonely, and I would like to have a group of men to study together with. Would you consider adding a Bible study to our meetings on Wednesday mornings?"

Andy sat still; his eyes fixed on his empty coffee cup. He swirled the sparse grounds around in the bottom, wishing they would give him some sort of sign of how he should respond. A memory came to him, the conversation he had with Dat prior to baptism when he'd asked why bad things happen. He'd never gotten the answer to his question. Maybe studying the Bible would give him answers, but it came at such a significant risk. To go against the Bishop would bring instant defeat.

Caleb raised his hand. "I'm in."

Andy touched his throat. *How should he respond?*

A relaxed smile came over Malon's face at Caleb's eagerness. "Great." His eyes moved to Andy.

Andy's hands got clammy, and his tongue swelled. He didn't know what to say. Finally, he decided telling the truth would be best, so he mumbled. "I want to, but I also want to follow the rules of the church. I'm afraid it will make my Dat angry." As soon as the words escaped his mouth, he wished he could take them back. They made him sound like a ninny.

"Where do the rules of the church say we shouldn't study the Bible?" Malon challenged him. "Do you still have a copy of the *Dordrecht Confession* they provided to you during your baptismal classes?"

Andy cowered under his words. Of course he'd read the *Dordrecht Confession*. Malon had no idea how he longed for answers to the questions he'd always had.

Malon reached into his Bible and pulled out the tucked-away pamphlet. "Our church is based on this." He waved it in the air. "Let's look and see what it says." He flipped the pamphlet open and held it up to the light of the window to read.

"He (the Christ), by His coming, would redeem, liberate, and raise the fallen race of man from their sin, guilt, and unrighteousness. We confess with all the saints that He is the Son of the living God, in whom alone consists all our hope, consolation, redemption, and salvation, which we neither may nor must seek in any other." Malon paused letting the words settle. "I'm going to repeat that again. He is the one in whom all our hope, consolation, redemption, and salvation rest. Brothers, why doesn't our own Bishop teach these things? At first, I thought I might be mistaken. The *Dordrecht Confession* is a man-made document, after all. Then I studied the scriptures for myself. After my study, I see no error in the doctrine. However, I see an error in the way the church teaches the scriptures."

Malon continued, "The Bishop instructs us that our own efforts and good works can achieve salvation. I am still learning, but

I can no longer preach this falsehood. Only Jesus can provide a way back to God." He exhaled and took a deep breath. "Felt good to say that out loud," he said with a satisfied grin. "This gift of grace is not supposed to be hidden."

Jake raised his bushy eyebrows as he stroked his beard. "Will you preach about this on Sunday when the Bishop is at the service?"

"I have been studying the book of Acts and the beginning of the early church. In so many ways, our church leadership reminds me of the Pharisees. Religious to the core. The truth threatened them. Did Peter water down his message? No, if anything, he became bolder in his proclamation of the truth. As a result, he faced suffering and imprisonment. I hope our church leadership has more sense than the Pharisees. The truth has set me free, and I am not afraid to proclaim it. I'll preach about it from the pulpit every Sunday, Bishop or not."

Jake responded, "I fear for you, but admire your stance. Your points make sense. Sylvia has been after me to learn more about these matters for years after she dreamed about Jesus. I am not ready to be so bold in my inquiry but wish to study for myself and feel comfortable doing so within the confines of this small group." A smile spread across his full lips as he stood from the stool and snapped his suspenders. "Let's do it. We'll meet on Wednesday mornings to study the scriptures here in this shop. Let's keep our studies quiet for the time being. You can lead us, Malon, since you have already begun this journey." He glanced at the clock on the wall. "We need to get to work. There is a lot to accomplish today."

Andy rose from his stool with wobbly legs, grateful the others had decided for him, but still unsure of how committed he could be.

Andy and Caleb headed out towards the barn while Malon went to his buggy.

The threshing job for the day came from Alma's family farm across the street. They had a bumper crop of wheat, with forty full wagons to process. The noise and manual labor gave plenty of time for Andy to think about this morning's conversation. Malon's words of hope, consolation, redemption, and salvation swam around in his head. *I'm not book-learned. How can I understand any of what he's talking about?* Long ago, he had given up hope of being good enough. He'd whittled his faith down to the act of just being Amish. Amish was all there was and would ever be.

The conversation this morning had stirred up a long-lost curiosity for answers to questions he'd always had. A tiny piece of hope germinated like a tender green shoot sprouting from its seed pod. If he took part in the studies, maybe he would find the answers he sought, but his hope was fragile, so he took special care to tuck it deep down inside his heart where he could protect it.

TWENTY-ONE

1949, Burton, Ohio

As time passed, Andy's tender shoot of hope grew into a young plant. The Wednesday morning Bible studies watered it, and his daily readings became the sunlight that fed it.

This evening, he sat up in the bed reading John fifteen. The kerosene lamp glowed, casting shadows around the room. He had been reading his way through the four Gospels; so far, he liked John's account of Jesus' life the best. It seemed a more personal viewpoint than Matthew, Mark, or Luke's.

"What are you reading?" Sylvia snuggled up beside him, looking over his shoulder. She perused the page and read aloud, "I am the true vine, and my father is the gardener. He cuts off every branch in me that bears no fruit, while every branch that does bear fruit, he prunes so that it will be even more fruitful." Her face scrunched. "What do you think it means?"

"I think the gardener is referring to God. The vine symbolizes life. Maybe it means he removes the things from us that don't bring life." Andy liked when she read to him. Her voice made the scriptures come alive. "We used to take pruning shears to our fruit trees to cut off the dead wood and overgrowth. It helped the apples produce better."

"I wish God would take the pruning shears straight to Bishop Miller's heart and trim back some of his hedges. He's a hateful man."

Andy closed the Bible. "You shouldn't say things like that. I think the point is to look at our own lives and see where we need pruning. Bishop Miller isn't the enemy here. He's only doing what he thinks is right."

Sylvia pouted her lips at the admonition. "Why doesn't he want us to think for ourselves?"

"Maybe he fears our learning will lead us away from the flock. His intentions may be genuine. Remember when we read in Matthew about the shepherd who went and looked for his one lost sheep? Maybe the Bishop thinks of us as his one lost sheep."

Sylvia playfully punched him in the arm. "That would mean he's read that story in the Bible. Remember, he thinks studying the Bible is evil, so I doubt he's ever even read it. I don't understand how we are in the wrong."

"I don't know. It doesn't feel wrong, and besides, Malon asked us to. He's our minister, and we are under his spiritual authority." Andy squirmed; there he went again, trying to squeeze out from under the Bishop's authority. He scooted himself up and set the Bible on the bedside table, turned, and gave Sylvia's growing belly a rub and a kiss, then blew out the oil lamp. "Time to get some sleep, little one," he whispered. Before long, they would have a baby to look after.

He turned on his side, needing to sleep, but his mind wouldn't turn off. *Was he a lost sheep?* Right now, he didn't know. There was no road map to navigate life and, most importantly, becoming a new father. This responsibility was beyond his capabilities. He didn't want to follow his father's example. *I want to be like Jake.* The thought hit him with its full weight. Maybe God sent Jake to find him, like the lost sheep. He prayed, pleading with God to make him a good father. After a while, his eyes grew heavy, and when his wife snuggled up against his back, he fell into a deep sleep.

—⟨◇ ◇ ◇ ◇ ◇⟩—

The next morning began uneventfully. Jake and Andy left after breakfast to meet with their group of men. Sylvia picked up her mending and plopped into Mamm's rocker in the living room. Her back ached these days with the weight of the baby growing inside her.

Mamm and Dat had been delighted with the news of a little one, but as her birthing date drew near, she began to see Mamm unravel. Her eyes glazed over, and she appeared lost in some other world—often taking herself to bed to rest. Sylvia knew her pregnancy had opened old wounds for Mamm. A dormant virus had become alive again, like a tapeworm; taking up residence inside Mamm's body again and eating her from the inside out. The wear showed in her aching bones she complained about, and the new patch of gray hair that peeked out from under her *kap*.

Mamm slid her slender body into Dat's rocker beside her and leaned back, closing her eyes. After a few minutes, Sylvia glanced over at her. "You feeling alright?"

Mamm cracked open an eye. "No, it's been hard for me. With the baby coming, I've been thinking a lot more about Betty."

The clock hanging on the wall ticked away. Its tarnished pendulum swinging back and forth provided a place for Sylvia to rest her eyes. If only she hadn't been selfish and had stayed with Betty that day instead of going out to swing. She wished she could hide the ugly truth, but what good would it do? Her guilt followed her everywhere, no matter how deep she tried to bury it.

Mamm's rocker creaked back and forth, and she closed her eyes again. "I dream about her every night. Her birth, her first steps, the golden curls. Sometimes her death. The thump of her head hitting the floor. Her limp blue body in my arms." Tears slid down Mamm's cheeks. "She was a miracle. We prayed so hard for her, then the Lord took her away." She shook her head. "I still don't understand why. I'm hoping a new baby will help me feel less lonely."

Sylvia's heart constricted at her words. "I didn't know you felt lonely." How selfish she'd been once again. She had forged ahead and left Mamm behind, not thinking of her feelings.

"It seems as if everyone else has moved on since Betty's death and found peace except me. Have you noticed the difference in your Dat these past few months? How the slump in his shoulders has disappeared? He has a fresh spring in his step. This time of year, he always grumbles about the workload. Instead, he's taken to helping me wash up the dishes." She wiped her tears and smiled. "Working alongside him makes me feel like we are newlyweds again. What do you think has come over him?"

"I think it's the Bible studies," Sylvia responded.

Mamm looked over at the small table beside Dat's rocker. She picked up the Bible and thumbed through its pages, reading aloud the notations in the margins. She flipped the page and ran her fingers across the words. "Jesus Calms the Storm." She began reading, "That day when evening came, he said to his disciples, 'Let us go over to the other side.' Leaving the crowd behind, they took him along, just as he was, in the boat. There were also other boats with him. A furious squall came up, and the waves broke over the boat, so that it was nearly swamped." Mamm paused.

Sylvia imagined the fear that gripped the men trapped in the sinking vessel, their instinct to claw themselves out of the water for air. She knew that fear well because that's how she felt when Betty died. Scared of drowning in her own sorrow.

Mamm sighed, then picked up where she left off. "Jesus was in the stern, sleeping on a cushion. The disciples woke him and said to him, 'Teacher, don't you even care if we drown?' He got up, rebuked the wind and said to the waves, 'Quiet! Be still!'"

A loud rap on the door startled them both. Like a child caught in a lie, Mamm slapped the Bible shut and shoved it under the folded newspaper on the side table.

"Didn't mean to scare you so," Fannie stood at the open screen door, her sewing basket hooked under her arm.

"Look at the time!" Mamm exclaimed. "Is it Wednesday? Goodness me, I forgot about our sewing hour this morning."

"What were you looking at?" Fannie asked.

"Just reading a bit of news," Mamm replied with a twinge of hesitancy.

Mamm hated lying.

"You seemed to hide it awful fast. Is there something I should know about? Are you making a baby gown or something?"

Sylvia's face blazed red, and even Mamm blushed.

"Well, it's no big surprise. They've been married now for over a year," Fannie chuckled.

Despite her embarrassment, Sylvia breathed a sigh of relief, grateful her pregnancy hid their secret. Even if it had been at the expense of their precious child. She didn't want Fannie to know they owned an English Bible. News like that could travel fast and get into the wrong hands.

"Let's go to the kitchen. I'll fix you a cup of tea and we can spread out at the table," Mamm deterred her friend from the living room.

Quiet. Be Still. The words echoed in Sylvia's mind. Could Jesus squash a storm with just a few words? Seemed too easy of a solution. If it were true, maybe He could do it for Mamm. Ease the pain of her aching heart. *Maybe He could erase her guilt.* She pushed the thought aside. *No, she didn't deserve forgiveness.* She'd pay for her sins the rest of her life. Butterflies bubbled in her stomach, and she pressed a hand to her abdomen. This child was a gift. A gift to Mamm, a replacement for the one she'd stolen all those years ago.

She followed the pair into the kitchen and put the kettle on to boil before turning her attention back to Fannie, asking, "What did you bring to sew today?"

TWENTY-TWO

1953, Middlefield, Ohio

ndy had now been studying the Bible for over two years. Every day he read a chapter, scratched out a few notes, then met with his group of men on Wednesday mornings in the shop to discuss what they'd learned. His knowledge and understanding grew under Malon's teaching, but he wanted to know more. The deeper he dove into the pages of the scriptures, the more complex it became. *Could he remain Amish and believe in salvation?* Jake thought so. Andy didn't want to decide. Malon was all in, and even dropped clues alluding to the fact that he was thinking of leaving the Amish church.

One Wednesday morning, Andy could hold back no longer and asked Malon, "If you leave the Amish, where will you go? What does Annie think about this?"

"Annie's been studying with me, too. She knows if we make this decision, our relationships with the family won't ever be the same, so her preference is to remain."

Jake rubbed his beard. "She's right. Nothing will ever be the same. If you leave, they will shun forever. Your kin will never eat at the same table with you again."

Malon replied, "I reminded her of the passage in Luke about the cost of being a disciple. That passage made us sad. Do you know what I'm talking about?" Malon turned the pages of his Bible till he came to Luke fourteen and read, "If anyone comes to me and does not hate father and mother, wife and children, brothers and sisters—yes, even their own life—such a person cannot be my disciple. And whoever does not carry their cross and follow me cannot be my disciple."

The men sat contemplating the words. Caleb spoke first. "That doesn't seem right. I don't think Jesus would want us to hate our mother and father."

"*Jah*, those are strong words, but let's see what comes after." Malon's eyes twinkled as they often did when he knew something his students had not yet learned. They read on about the man who set out to build the tower but didn't have enough funds to finish what he started, and then about the king who calculated his manpower prior to going to war. "I think Jesus is trying to tell us that before we commit to being His followers, we need to count the cost. Are we willing to see it through to the end, even if our families hate us for our beliefs? Before we commit, we must know the consequences. Christ must be greater than our desire to maintain a relationship with our families. I am ready to take the leap. Annie is not. I wait for the day when she will and pray it comes soon because my zeal for the Lord is growing stronger daily."

The thin pages of Bibles lay open in their laps, and a hush fell over the meeting like a wet wool blanket, dampening the joy they normally felt when they met together.

A hard reality settled in Andy's heart. If he believed Jesus was the way, then moving forward meant no looking back.

Malon broke the silence, clearing his throat. "I hope you all can come to the tent revival meeting across town next week. A traveling evangelist will teach the scriptures. Sources say he's an exceptional storyteller."

Andy took a swig of his coffee. *An evangelist.* The word leapt with promise. He'd love to listen to an *English* preacher.

The crunch of gravel in the driveway interrupted Malon's invitation.

Caleb rose from his stool and went to the window to see who had come. "Bishop Miller," he called out, his face turning white like the sheets Sylvia hung out in the sun to dry. He flew to his seat, grabbed his Bible, and hid it behind a tower of tools off to the side.

Andy didn't know what to do with his and ended up sitting on it to hide the evidence. Jake sighed and took the more mature approach of closing the scriptures and setting it on his workbench out in the open. Malon sat right where he was with the Bible in his lap. The passage they'd just read glared off the page, its words never more applicable.

Jake got up and ambled to the door, opening it after the first knock. "Ah, *gut* morning, Bishop Miller." He extended a hand and motioned for him to come in. "What brings you by on this fine morning?"

The Bishop's eyes dotted around the room. "Word has it you are studying the English scriptures here every week." His eyes rested on the open Bible in Malon's lap. "I thought I made it clear that all individual studies of the scriptures need to be run by me first. You are disobeying my spiritual authority."

The room spun and slowed. Malon, the target of the impending tornado.

Most Amish men would have caved at the rebuke and diverted, but Malon was different. He matched Bishop Miller's gaze eye for eye with deep resolve. "We are doing nothing wrong. I've talked with you about this several times, but there is no reckoning with you. There can be no reason you would be against us learning for ourselves, other than it challenges your authority. Now I understand the *English* saying, 'knowledge is power.' Some of us are hungry to make the faith our own, to live freely, secure in the knowledge of salvation. We can't believe without studying it for ourselves. Surely you can understand that."

Bishop Miller's face reddened, and his eyes turned a steely color as he planted his feet and curled his fists up in balls, ready to defend his position. Turning up his chin, he responded, "This will need to be taken before the council."

Then, with words that stopped Andy's heart, he directed his gaze towards him. "I thought you would have learned better from your father."

Andy's tongue dried at the rebuke, and he bowed his head. So much for trying to preserve his father's honor. Dat would hear about this visit and be making one of his own soon.

Bishop Miller didn't wait for a response. He turned on his heel, strode to the door, and slammed it behind him. A few seconds later, the men heard the snap of stones as his buggy turned out of the lane.

Malon rubbed his long beard in silence for a long time until he spoke. "*Vell*, that was interesting. I suppose there is more discussion to come. I am not quitting studying Jesus and His teachings. In fact, this makes me want to learn more. Like I said earlier, a preacher by the name of Andrew Jantzi is coming to town and is pitching his tent outside of Middlefield. Annie and I will attend the meetings all week and would enjoy seeing you there as well. The services start at seven on Friday evening."

Andy pressed his thumbs into his palms, the pressure grounding him. They must be close to the truth, otherwise Bishop Miller wouldn't be so angry with them. What did it matter if he went to the meeting? His fate was decided. Dat would pay him a visit, regardless. Andy dislodged the Bible wedged underneath him and headed out to work without saying a word. The stakes were higher than ever before.

—⟨◇◇◇◇◇⟩—

Sylvia wrangled her three-year-old daughter onto the kitchen chair. "Clara, sit still. We've got to get your shoes on."

Clara reached for the doll her little brother Ray held onto. "Let go; that's mine," she whined.

Sylvia plucked the doll out of Ray's little fingers and tucked it in her pocket. "If you can't share nicely, then I'll keep it for now." She lifted Ray up in her arms. "We have an important meeting to go to tonight. Please listen, and don't wiggle too much." She took Clara's hand, ready to load up the buggy.

Andy came through the back screen door. "I bedded the livestock for the evening. Jake said to take his buggy, and Caleb's coming over with the horse in a few minutes." His voice quivered.

"Are you sure Dat's okay with us taking his buggy? It puts him at risk as well."

"*Jah*, Jake would like to come, but Mamm Lizzie's not feeling well this evening, so he said to go on ahead. He knows what might happen if Bishop finds out."

Nervous energy coursed through Sylvia's veins; her heart thumped faster as she thought about their blatant disobedience.

At half-past six, Caleb and Alma walked their horse over and hitched it up to the buggy.

Caleb asked, "Do you think it'll work?"

Andy responded, "Hopefully, they'll think we're from another district."

Sylvia shooed the children into the back and climbed in beside Alma.

She looked over at her friend, who clasped and unclasped her hands, a deep crease in her brow.

"I'm not sure this is a good idea, Sylvia," she whispered.

Sylvia grinned back, squashing her own fears. "Don't worry, it'll be fine. Our own minister is the one who asked us to go."

"Why does it have to be in secret, then?" Alma threaded the black curtains she'd sewn through rods above the buggy's windows, then pulled them shut. The interior of the Buggy became a cocoon of darkness.

"I don't know, but Andy feels we need to do this." Sylvia still struggled to believe Andy had even suggested such a thing. It was unlike him to take such a risk.

The ride to Middlefield seemed longer than normal, eventually Sylvia felt the buggy wheels leave the road and churn on a softer surface. Alma peeped through the curtain and exclaimed, "Look at all the people!" Sylvia leaned over her shoulder.

In the middle of a field, the evangelist had pitched a big circus tent. Its two spires rose high into the sky, and the white sides came swooping down to poles driven into the ground. Parked rows of cars lined three sides of the tent, their chrome bumpers gleaming in the light of the sinking sun. A gentleman directed traffic, waving the cars that poured into the grounds into their designated parking spots. When it was their turn, he pointed to the right, and Andy snapped the reins and directed the horse over to the couple dozen buggies parked close to the back of the tent.

"I want to see what's out there, Mamm," Clara reached for the curtain and pulled it all the way back before Sylvia could stop her. "Wow!" she exclaimed.

Sylvia reached over and moved Clara back from the window and closed the curtains, but not before she glimpsed a group of young people from their district in the buggy parked next to them. A girl caught her eye and turned to whisper to her companions. Sylvia sighed; they'd been discovered. So much for the curtains.

Ten minutes later, a clear tenor voice began singing. "I hear the Savior say, thy strength indeed is small. Child of weakness, watch and pray. Find in Me thine all in all."

The words struck a chord in Sylvia's heart. Her strength indeed was small. Tonight, she would watch and pray. She closed her eyes and let the words soak into her bones. The melody was so different from the chants they sang at church. These words brimmed with hope.

"Jesus paid it all. All to Him I owe," the singer crooned.

As she listened, she imagined Jesus. The Jesus she met in the field, His loving eyes beckoning her. His words returned to her, *It is not your time; you have much to accomplish.* She'd always wondered what He meant by those words.

When the song ended, the preacher took the stage. He wore plain black pants, a white button-up shirt, suspenders, and a jacket on top. The jacket wasn't fancy like the ones she had seen *Englishers* wear around town. It had no collar, but it had buttons, a style that seemed to be a mix between their Amish clothes and the modern *Englishers.* He welcomed the crowd and introduced himself as Andrew Jantzi. His blonde hair stayed in place with a thick pomade, and his clear voice carried over the crowd.

Sylvia leaned forward and peered out the front window, yearning to get a closer look, spellbound by his every word. He took a hankie out of his back pocket and wiped the sweat forming on his brow before launching into a story.

"There once was a man who lived any way he pleased. He was rich and had grown up in a family that had not only money but also power. He did all kinds of things that displeased the Lord, especially his direct persecution of the saints. See, he hunted Christ followers, going from town to town sniffing out those who affiliated with Jesus and putting many of them to death, by sword and stoning. He thought he was doing God a favor by weeding out the infidels that taught Christ as the Messiah. You see, Saul didn't think Jesus was the true Messiah. He saw Jesus as a threat to the Jewish people's power."

Sylvia thought Saul sounded a whole lot like the Bishop.

Jantzi gave a dramatic pause, letting his words hang in the air before beginning again. "The Lord, in His great mercy, had a better plan for Saul's life. One day, he traveled with his posse on the way to a new city to hunt down more Christians. Suddenly, a light flashed down from heaven, surrounding the entire group, and God asked in an audible voice, 'Saul, Saul, why do you persecute me?' 'Who are you, Lord?' Saul cried out. 'I am Jesus, whom you are persecuting,' God replied. 'Now get up and go into the city, and you will be told what you must do.' Saul stumbled to his feet, afflicted with blindness. His men took his hand and led him into the city. He lay distraught for three days, not eating or drinking."

Jantzi paused. "I want to stop the story here for a minute. Can you imagine what Saul was thinking? He was doing things according to his convictions. He had channeled his murderous rage into what he felt was productive and good for the Jewish people. After he had this encounter with the Lord, his world flipped upside down. Everything he believed was no longer true. I ask you this question: What do you believe that is untrue? What do you pour your effort and time into that is not pleasing to the Lord? Our ways are often not right. There is only one right way, and it is through Jesus. All other efforts fall short. The story doesn't just stop there, though. God called Saul to something greater. The change in his heart now needed to produce fruit. God orchestrated all of this through a dream he gave to a man named Ananias."

Sylvia's heart quickened at the mention of a dream. Goose pimples rose on her arms.

"Ananias had a vision from the Lord who told him to go pray for Saul. Of course, Ananias felt afraid, but he was more afraid of not following the Lord, so he went to the instructed place. Once he arrived, he saw Saul's condition, blind and belittled and his heart went out to him. He prayed for him, and the scripture says something like scales fell from Saul's eyes and the Holy Spirit came upon him. He baptized Saul that day. Hallelujah!" Jantzi raised his Bible, then thumped it against the pulpit. His body bent low, forearms resting on the wood. He gazed into the eyes of the attendees.

"There are some of you today who are on the wrong path. You have never put your full faith in the Lord Jesus. We are all sinners, and all fall short of perfection. If there was forgiveness for Saul, a man who committed the most egregious acts against the Lord's people, then there is forgiveness for you. Forgiveness is for everyone. For all with big and small sins. You can try your hardest to live a holy life, but in the end our sin still separates us from God. Do you want restoration in your relationship with God? To be forgiven? Put your faith in Him today. Come to the altar."

Jantzi took off his jacket and draped it over the top of the pulpit. Stillness gripped the crowd. Sylvia couldn't stop the fat tears from pouring out of her eyes. A gentle voice whispered in her ear, *If God can forgive Saul, then He can forgive you.* The impact of the words almost caused her to fall to her knees. She looked over at Alma, sure she had been the one to whisper. Alma slumped over against the window with her eyes shut.

The clear voice of the evangelist began singing.

"Just as I am, without one plea
But that thy blood was shed for me
And that Thou bid'st me, come to Thee
O Lamb of God, I come, I come"

Streams of people left their seats and began coursing down the aisles to the front; an invisible hand pushing them forward to receive the gift of forgiveness. Sylvia wanted to jump out to join, but her feet seemed stuck. Guilt anchored her to the seat. *Can You meet me here, God? If I pray, will you accept me like You accepted Saul? Will You forgive me? Release me from this burden?*

The voice whispered back to her, *Come to me, my child. Receive my forgiveness.*

Sylvia wept.

The God of the heavens and earth heard her prayer and met her that evening in the dark buggy. This time He whispered, *Follow me.*

She held out her hands, imagining her heart in them as an offering. "I trust You, Lord," she whispered back. "I want to be Your follower. Please forgive my sins." In that moment, her world shifted. A fullness of heart and peace flooded her soul and mind, and she soaked herself in God's deep pool of forgiveness.

Heartstring

I look at you across the hall
And feel the familiar tug
It is starting, my heartstring
is pulling.
With every step
And every mesmerizing gaze
The pull is stronger
You have my heart on a string.

TWENTY-THREE

1953, Middlefield, Ohio

Sylvia couldn't wait to talk to Andy in private about her encounter with God. On the ride home, she tried to discern his reaction, but he sat quietly with an unreadable face. *What did he think of the service?* She wanted to ask, but the mood didn't feel right. Ray fell asleep in her lap, and Clara slouched beside her. The mysterious words whispered in her ear replayed in her mind. *If God can forgive Saul, then He can forgive you.* Did Andy hear these words, too? Did he experience forgiveness like she had?

Caleb and Alma dropped them off at their door, then unhitched the buggy and walked their horse across the street. After Sylvia tucked the children into bed, she found herself alone with her husband. He hadn't said one word, which perplexed her. She tried not to let his somber mood affect the joy in her heart.

They readied themselves for bed. As Sylvia removed her *kap* and uncoiled her hair, she bit her bottom lip. *Should she keep quiet till morning, or share the miraculous gift she'd received?*

When she could no longer contain her excitement, she went to him and gave him a kiss. "I responded to the message tonight. Something happened. I prayed and believed with all my heart. I know Jesus is the only way to salvation and I'm forgiven of all my sins, of the sin." Her eyes widened as she said the words. "A peace flooded my heart with a joy like I've never felt before. What about you? Did you pray, too?" She heard the earnestness in her voice and wished with all her heart he shared her joy.

Andy twisted out of her embrace and hung his head. "I'm afraid I didn't have the same experience as you. I enjoyed the preaching, but how do I know Jesus is the only true way? Not just a *gut* man."

Her eyes filled with disappointment at her husband's words. "If you knew the peace I am feeling right now, then you would gladly follow Him." *Why had he hardened his heart?* Many a night they'd read the scriptures together, and he knew so much more than she had.

"Can we go back tomorrow night?"

Andy paused. "*Jah*, I do want to hear more."

At least he's willing to go back. Maybe he will respond tomorrow night.

They fell into bed, and Sylvia pulled the quilt to their chins. Her eyes grew heavy, the adrenaline fading, and she fell asleep, her soul at peace.

Andy struggled to settle. He tossed and turned, mulling over the preacher's words. *Could he be free? Free from what?* Sometimes he couldn't even find the words to express what held him back. A piece of him wanted to run away from these decisions, to continue to live the peaceful life they'd created. *Wasn't this enough? When had he become so discontented?* His thoughts kept him awake until the rooster crowed, then he arose.

The next evening, they went through the motions of hitching Jake's buggy to Caleb's horse and pulling shut the black curtains. He didn't want to go, but something compelled him forward. Maybe the shining light in Sylvia's eyes. She seemed more at peace.

They drove into the packed parking lot and lined up again beside the few other Amish buggies. The crowd began singing hymns together. Andy listened to the words as they poured over him. The hymns spoke of hope and longing, peace and forgiveness. All of which he didn't have, and none of which the baptismal waters gave. Baptism had been a hollowed-out promise; this too had the makings of the same.

Jantzi took the stage and welcomed the crowd. He jumped into his message. "Following Jesus is difficult. When we commit to Him, we are so overwhelmed with the joy that floods our hearts we forget hardships will still come, but God promises He will never leave or forsake us. He gives us His Holy Spirit that dwells in each of our hearts when we accept His gift of His salvation. The Holy Spirit strengthens us and helps us when we face times of trouble. Tonight, I am going to tell a story about three friends. How they stood in the face of adversity and how the Lord met them and saved them from the flames.

"Their names were Shadrach, Meshach, and Abednego. In the ancient world, the Persians conquered their land and moved them into captivity. In this unfamiliar country, they were required to dress differently, eat like the locals, and worship other gods. None of the new customs and practices were pleasing to the one true God, but they were strong in their faith and refused to take part. This angered the king. He thought of himself as bigger than God and created an image of himself for everyone to bow down to. The king gave Shadrach, Meshach, and Abednego a choice: bow to the idol or die."

Jantzi stopped. He pulled up the closest stool, once again took off his jacket and sat down. His crystal-clear eyes seemed to bore into Andy's soul, even at a distance. A shock of blonde hair fell away from his slicked-back coif and flopped over his forehead.

"I'm going to level with you. I've read this story more than a hundred times in my life, but I have never put myself in these men's shoes. Take some time tonight and examine your heart. Would you cave to pressure and bow, or would you choose to die? I want to say with all my heart I would die for my Lord and Savior, but the reality is when put in that situation, my faith may not stand strong." He stood and went back behind the pulpit.

"What happens next will encourage you. These men were obedient to God and refused to bow. Because of this, they were bound and taken to the bowels of the palace to be thrown into a furnace. The furnace burned so hot, the guards who threw them in died.

"But the fire did not singe a single hair on the bodies of Shadrach, Meshach, and Abednego as they went into the flames. In fact, the scriptures tell us the ropes that bound them fell off, and they walked around freely. The onlookers stared in amazement, but soon realized something even more incredible. Not only were there three men in the furnace, but there appeared a fourth. How could it be? They sentenced three men to die, but four men walked around alive.

"The king described the fourth man, like the Son of God. Now, we know He was the Son of God, Jesus himself. Shadrach, Meshach, and Abednego followed God to their grave, but God said you won't do it alone. Isaiah 43:2 says, when you pass through the waters, I will be with you, and when you pass through the rivers, they will not sweep over you. When you walk through the fire, you will not be burned; the flames will not set you ablaze. This message tonight is for those who know that following Jesus will cost them greatly."

Andy's heart seized, and he held his breath. This message was for him. All his life, he tried to be compliant and obedient as possible, not for his own gain, but for his father, for Sylvia, for Jake and Lizzie, for the Amish. If he made them proud, then he pleased God, another step closer to his salvation. What misguided thinking. He'd been looking at life through a foggy lens, and now everything came into sharp focus. He couldn't earn his salvation. His futile efforts would never measure up. Dat didn't bring him salvation; Jesus did. Jesus didn't fix the sadness, the disappointment, the unfair things he had faced in this world. He had walked with him through them. Jesus was there as his brother died, as their house burned to the ground, at the Lesters', even during his baptism. *Jesus was the answer.*

Choosing to follow Jesus would produce significant loss, but it would also bring great gain. He hadn't thought of what he'd gain, just afraid of what he'd lose. The gift of unconditional love and approval lay before him. Even Sylvia, in all her efforts, fell short.

Jantzi picked up his Bible and held it high. "The invitation tonight is the same as last night. Follow Jesus; commit yourself to him. His word says in Isaiah 41:10, do not fear, for I am with you; do not be dismayed, for I am your God. I will strengthen you and help you; I will uphold you with my righteous right hand. Brethren, if you want to know this Jesus, the one who will walk with you through anything, come forward. Receive this gift of salvation today." Jantzi started singing.

Softly and tenderly, Jesus is calling
Calling for you and for me
See on the portals He's waiting and watching
Watching for you and for me.
Come home, come home
Ye who are weary, come home
Earnestly, tenderly Jesus is calling
Calling, O sinner, come home.

When the third verse started, Malon's wife, Annie, climbed down from the adjoining buggy and joined the stream of people responding to the call, but she didn't walk alone. Malon joined her every step of the way, gripping her hand. You could hear the murmur of whispers emanating from the buggies, but she held her head high.

Jantzi cried from the pulpit, "Jesus will meet you wherever you are. Open your heart to Him today. Come to the altar or pray with me in your seats. I ask you to open your hands to the Lord in surrender."

Andy couldn't see through the tears clouding his eyes. He never knew anything to be purer than the love he felt. He opened his hands and lifted them up and prayed out loud the words Jantzi led them in. "Jesus, you are the one true God. I trust solely in You for my salvation. Please forgive my sins."

A peace flooded his heart so great that he couldn't stop crying. Sylvia reached from behind and placed her hands on his shoulders, and together they wept.

Andy turned on his side and faced his wife in bed. "What happened to me, Sylvia? I promise you; a spirit entered my body and became a balm to my soul."

"It's wonderful, isn't it?" Sylvia grinned back at him.

"One time when I burnt my hand as a child. Mamm took me over to Mummie Troyer's for treatment. Mummie reached up high on the shelf and brought down her special salve and smeared it all over the burn and bandaged it up. I don't know what was in that medicine, but it instantly relieved my pain. That's how I felt tonight, like the hand of God reached down and smeared a salve all over the broken places in my life, easing the pain. The uncertainty is gone. The striving to be perfect is gone. Words fail me."

Sylvia stroked his face. "You don't have to explain it to me. I feel it, too, it's the mysterious work of God."

"Where do we go from here? What do we do next?"

"I don't know, but Mamm said we should always pray. In the morning, I'll get down the prayer book. Maybe there are some prayers in there for guidance. We'll keep studying the scriptures. This Spirit will tell us what to do."

"I never want things to go back to the way they were," Andy whispered, his eyelids growing heavy.

"They won't. Whatever comes our way, the Lord will walk with us through it."

Andy wound his fingers through Sylvia's and drifted off to sleep facing her. The lost were found.

TWENTY-FOUR

Fall 1953, Burton, Ohio

Andy closed his eyes as Sylvia read aloud from the prayer book. "O Lord, awaken in us a hunger and thirst for You and Your righteousness. Teach us to act according to Your will. You are our God. May Your good spirit lead us along the straight path. We commend ourselves to You; let all our works be blessed and bring honor to Your name and be useful to our neighbors. Make us into tools of Your mercy and let us joyfully go forth and practice our calling. Amen."

"Amen." Andy glanced up from his plate of chicken and noodles and smiled at his wife. His heart swelled in gratefulness for her.

Sylvia closed the open prayer book and set it aside. "Eat your peas, Clara," she urged.

Andy ran his fingers over the seam of the prayer book. He enjoyed hearing the prayers read out loud instead of their usual silent prayers, one little change they'd made over the past weeks. The prayers calmed his mind and refocused his heart on the Lord. Lately, the politics in the church had become almost too much to bear.

He reflected on the past four weeks; so much had changed. His group had continued to meet on Wednesday mornings to study and discuss the scriptures. In addition, Sylvia, Annie, Alma, and Lizzie met as well. To Malon's delight, all members of both groups had committed to following Jesus, and the Holy Spirit worked in their lives, placing in them a hunger and thirst for more of the Lord.

Malon and Annie's transformation exceeded Andy's imagination. Prior to the revival, Malon was passionate about the ways of the Lord. Since his wife joined him in the faith, he became fervent. He feared no one and continued to preach and teach about salvation every opportunity he could. He even invited those who wanted, to gather for extra meetings in his home for prayer and teaching.

This provoked Bishop Miller, who, true to his word, flexed his muscle of power and called a council meeting. The council voted, and despite the close tally, they stripped Malon of his ability to be a minister and placed him in the *ban*.

Their district became divided, some in favor of Malon and Annie, the other on the Bishop's side. The tension became insufferable. Andy tried to stay neutral to keep the peace with his Dat but struggled to do so with his own transformation.

After the *ban,* Malon and Annie hatched a plan to move to a small settlement of New Order Amish in a town an hour south of Burton. They invited all who wished to join them, but Andy declined, believing once Malon left, things would settle down and they could continue studying in their own home. The storm had not quieted, however, and rumor had it the Bishop wanted all the participants in the forbidden meetings to be gone as well. Andy couldn't help but feel they were next.

Despite the impending doom, the discontented spirit he'd felt all his life was gone, replaced instead by a sure, steady calm of knowing of who he belonged to. However, anticipating Dat's reaction to all of this tugged at his peace. *Who would Dat side with?*

One night after supper, the entire family gathered in the living room when a knock sounded at the door. Andy answered it, not surprised to see Bishop Miller and a deacon on his doorstep. He opened the door wider, letting them enter. Normally, a visit of this kind would make his heart flip and his palms sweaty, but tonight he didn't feel any of the usual anxiety. Instead, strength and resolve cemented his core. "Come on in."

The visitors stooped inside, not extending their usual handshakes. Removing their hats, they glanced around the room and asked, "May we have a word with everyone?"

"Yes, have a seat." Andy motioned towards the extra chairs Sylvia had set up. The men settled uncomfortably, their bodies leaning forward.

"You may already know why we are here." They paused for a few seconds, waiting for an answer.

Everyone sat, hands folded in laps, awaiting their judgement.

Bishop Miller picked up the English Bible beside Andy's rocker and set it back down again, as if the pages burned his hand. He scowled. "We have it on good authority that Andy and Sylvia attended the revival meetings. These actions are in direct disobedience of our church membership rules. Consider this visit an invitation to attend Sunday's service and repent, or further consequences will ensue. And you," the Bishop directed his gaze at Jake. "Shame on you for allowing this to happen under your roof."

Jake rocked forward and rose from his chair. His leg trembled.

He's either afraid or angry, thought Andy.

"I think you've said your piece. Now leave us in peace," Jake responded.

Andy could see the anger and hatred seething in Bishop Miller's eyes. He knew then that even if he fell prostrate in front of these men, he would never gain their acceptance again. The Amish church had become the measuring stick, as if it were God himself. *Why did the Bishop refuse to let them study the scriptures? Why were his eyes so blinded?* He'd lived under these same authoritarian rules with his father, playing the game, always striving to earn Dat's respect, all the while ignoring God himself. Enough. His cheeks burned red.

He didn't want Clara, Ray, or any other future children growing up without the knowledge of God's love and grace. They would plan their exit.

He glanced over at his mother-in-law and saw her downcast face. The brine of blood filled his mouth, causing him to realize he'd chewed a sore into his cheek. *What about Jake and Lizzie? How could they leave them? Where would they go?* The reality of the situation loosened his resolve.

Jake showed the men to the door and returned to his chair. Steepling his fingers to his lips, he proclaimed, "The time has come. We can no longer live under such leadership. These men have destroyed the church's peaceful fellowship. I hate leaving this old house here on Jug Road, but what choice do we have? I want peace in my old years." Doubt clouded his eyes as he spoke. "Lizzie and I will head south to the town of Hartville to join Malon and Annie."

Andy set his mouth in a grim line; a buzz sounded in his ears. He couldn't believe it had come to this. Things were moving fast, almost as fast as the train to Niagara Falls.

Jake continued, "There is a need for a buggy shop in Hartville. Malon wrote last week and invited us to join him. I never considered it a viable option until tonight, but we have come to a crossroads."

A stream of tears spilled from Sylvia's eyes and slid down her cheeks at Jake's proclamation. Lizzie handed her a hankie.

"What will we do?" Sylvia asked as she dabbed at her cheeks and reached for Andy's hand. "We can't be apart from you."

"We will go with them after the threshing season is over." Andy squeezed her hand. A part of him wanted to leave now, but the Spirit spoke to him. *Don't just run from your problems,* it whispered. *Face them, face your father and speak the truth.* The thought terrified him. To leave would cause great disappointment for his parents and sever their relationship. They could never share in their fellowship or eat a meal around the same table again. He had to at least try to come to some sort of understanding with them, not for his sake, but for his children.

"*Jah*, that will be good," Jake responded in agreement. "We will help you by looking for housing and work ahead of time and write once we get settled."

Andy did not have to wait long for his first encounter with Dat. Word traveled fast, and in two days' time, Dat's buggy darkened their driveway. Andy's face paled when he caught sight of Dat standing in the barn, observing him work. He jumped down from the wagon and placed his pitchfork to the side.

"Hello Dat, what brings you by?" Andy knew what prompted this visit but feigned ignorance. He extended a hand, which Dat shook weakly.

"Do you have some time to talk?" Dat asked. They walked out and sat under the big oak tree. "I had a visit from Bishop Miller this morning. Told me about his discussion with you. What are you thinking? You know the position this puts me in, a child of mine defying leadership like this."

"I mean no disrespect, Dat, but my heart has changed. I follow Jesus now. He has shown me the truth. I don't place my faith in being Amish. I place it in Jesus." The light in Andy's eyes connected in opposition to the darkness in Dat's. His stomach flip-flopped like a freshly caught fish, but he determined to keep his resolve.

"You know you will be in the *bann* unless you choose to come back to the church and repent." Dat fiddled with the brim of his hat before he spoke again. "Believe what you want in your heart, son, confess publicly, and continue to live out your faith in secret." Dat's face opened in an earnest plea. "It will keep the peace and the family integrity intact. Please consider this option."

Dat's gentle appeal tugged at Andy's heartstrings. He could count on one hand the times Dat had shown him tenderness—when he had dropped him off at the Lesters' house, Abraham's death, his baptism. All his life he had replayed these moments over and over, clinging to the sliver of fondness shown, hopeful each time their relationship would bloom, but nothing ever grew of it. Within a matter of days, the hope had extinguished, and Andy went back to feeling hollow inside.

A long-lost desire for acceptance gripped him, and he longed to lean into it. It would be easy to confess and put a stop to this strife, but the courage of Shadrack, Meshach, and Abednego strengthened him. "I'm sorry Dat, I've kept my studies of the Bible a secret for years and can't continue to do so. I can't hide the joy and peace I have in my heart. Any public confession would be a denial of Jesus. I just can't do that."

Dat's countenance changed, and his mouth drew into a tight line. When he spoke again, it was through clenched teeth, with seething words, "I won't have my eldest son disrespect me like this. After all I have done, how could you do this to me? To the church? You'll ruin my reputation." He stood up, his frame blocking the sun.

Andy leaned back against the tree and raised his head to look at him, his hand shadowing his eyes. The sun's brilliance outlined Dat's figure towering over him; a familiar sight he'd known all his life.

Without waiting for a response, Dat spat in the dirt at his feet. "Don't bother coming around unless you repent. Consider yourself dead to me." He turned on his heel and stomped back to the buggy. The snap of the reins cracked as he exited, leaving a trail of dust in his wake.

Andy leaned back against the tree and closed his eyes. He sat for a long time listening to the birds singing in the trees. *Had Dat meant those words?* He could never imagine saying such hateful things to Clara or Ray, no matter what they did to disappoint him.

After dinner, Andy sent the children to the living room to play so he could have a moment to talk to Sylvia. "Dat came to see me today. He heard about the Bishop's visit and tried every which way to change my mind. Finally, he got so frustrated, he stomped off. Told me I was dead to him unless I repented. He will get over it, right? Time will heal things?" He spoke the words, trying to convince himself, but knew deep inside, a rift had opened between them that would be hard to bridge. Still, hope stuck around, and he wished his heart didn't treat him so.

"Let's take it to the Lord in prayer," she suggested, rubbing the back of his neck.

He frowned. "You don't understand. How could you? Your parents love you. My relationship with Dat has always been complicated." He regretted the words the minute they left his mouth. Sylvia was the best thing that ever happened to him, and now he was pushing her away.

She stopped rubbing his neck. "I read a portion of the Psalms today. There was one chapter that stood out. I marked it to share with you later."

She trotted into the living room and came back with his Bible. Opening to Psalm 27, she read the marked page. "The Lord is my light and my salvation—whom shall, I fear? The Lord is the stronghold of my life—of whom shall I be afraid? When the wicked advance against me to devour me, it is my enemies and foes who will stumble and fall. Though an army besiege me, my heart will not fear; though war break out against me, even then I will be confident. See!" She beamed. "You have nothing to be afraid of. Our victory is in the Lord. Stand strong and be confident in that."

Her eyes held no contempt at his harsh words. Andy pondered the scripture and reached for the Bible, wanting to read for himself. He perused the passage. "Look at verse ten. Though my father and mother forsake me, the Lord will receive me." He sighed and let those words sink deep into his soul. *Thank you, Lord, for that promise.* He desperately needed it.

"I love you, Andy. Even though my family is different, you know I've had my fair share of demons to deal with. Let's keep praying; we have the Spirit now, who won't leave us. We are new people."

Her words spoke truth. Even with Dat's rejection, the waves of his soul had settled and become still and glassy, and the promises of his heavenly father would guide any currents below the surface. He reached across the table and cupped her face in his hands, her skin silky beneath his rough fingers. "I love you, too. We are in this together."

TWENTY-FIVE

Fall 1953, Burton, Ohio

Bishop Miller came calling again a few days later. This time, he brought other ministers and deacons as reinforcements. Andy stood surrounded by the group, including Dat, when the Bishop broke the news. "We can't continue to let you run the community threshing machine."

Andy hung his head. He should have known this would happen, but somehow it caught him off guard. He was good at his job, and the threshing brought in earnings to support his family. The Detweilers planned to begin threshing their crop later that morning. "Let me finish the season and my commitment to the farmers, then you can take back the machine. I planned on leaving at the end of the season anyhow."

"We can't let that happen. The *bann* means you can't do business with church members. Besides, this machine belongs to the church." Bishop Miller directed the men to take apart the pulley system and other components.

"Who will do the work for the farmers?" questioned Andy. "They depend on this service to make their own profit."

"Do you think you're the only one that knows how to use a threshing machine?" Bishop sneered. "There are men who'll be more than willing to take this endeavor off your hands and support their own families. That is what the church does—we support our own, not ones living in sin."

Within the hour, the men had loaded the machine into the back of their wagons and were on their way down the street with Andy's livelihood. Without the whir of the thresher, the farmyard sounded hollow. He turned and stroked Coco's soft mane. She nickered and nuzzled her wet nose in his hand, reminding him he wasn't alone. Horses had always brought him comfort. His heart panged with remorse remembering the elderly Marie Burton, who he'd never see again. Dejected, his eyes fell to his wheat field, yet to be harvested. *How am I going to take care of my family?*

Put your trust in me. I will take care of you. Certainty settled in his heart. His feet held fast to something solid and sure, a hope his parents never had when they faced trouble. Instead of turning back to the Amish church to make his way, he would turn to God.

As he strode to the house, he saw Sylvia sitting on the back porch shelling peas into a bowl. Clara and Ray flicked marbles at her feet, seeing who could make it go the furthest. A pang pierced his side as he watched them play. Doubt crept into the edges of his heart. *Was he a good father?* Somehow, he'd fallen into Dat's economic footsteps, poor without work. *Lord, help me provide for them.* He noticed the smirk on Sylvia's face and wondered what she found so funny after the entire spectacle she'd witnessed. "What's the secret?" he asked, trudging up the stairs.

"Got this today in the mail," she grinned as she reached into the pocket of her apron and removed an envelope. "Word from my folks." She handed him the letter.

He lifted the flap and took out two single sheets. Lizzie's loopy handwriting stared back at him. "Will you read it to me? You know I'm not too good at reading cursive script."

She took it from him and began.

Dear Andy and Sylvia,

We arrived here in Hartville two weeks ago. It is to our liking, a small town with a grain elevator, post office, restaurant, train station, general store, grocery, and a hardware. Everything we need. Life here is quiet and comfortable. There is a small group of Amish believers that meets weekly. We meet in the King Church building and have called ourselves the King Amish Church. Malon leads the service and continues to preach. There are about four Amish families, including us and Malons. A small group, but we hope to grow. We miss you and the children and look forward to seeing you soon. Jake has started a buggy repair shop. There are limited buggies to fix, so he also does other types of woodworking and repairs, some for the Englishers. We live in peace and enjoy our new home. It is up on a hill off the main road. We have several cows and chickens to care for and a small barn. Here is the best news! A farm has come available for rent. The owner, a distant relative, is asking for a reasonable sum, and Jake has already paid for the first month. I hope you are ready to come and join us. Send word. We will be waiting.

Much love,

Mamm

Andy heard Sylvia choke back tears as she read. Lizzie's soprano voice echoed throughout the letter. It was so good to hear from them. He missed them more than he realized.

"The Lord has provided." She folded the letter in thirds and stuffed it back into the envelope.

Andy sat beside her in the empty rocker. "He sure has. It couldn't be more perfect timing. What about work? What are we to do with this house once we leave? It seems so sudden. Are you ready to go?"

"There is nothing left for us here, with our livelihood taken and our community stripped from us. We need to leave with some semblance of our self-worth, otherwise they will take that, too. As for the house, I feel like we need to talk about in person with Dat and Mamm. I'll write back tomorrow and let them know we are coming if you are agreeable?"

He swallowed the lump in his throat, fear clouding his judgement. *Should they abandon the plan?* A vision of Jake's face flashed in front of him. He imagined the sag of his shoulders and the way his eyes fell in disappointment at the news they had changed their minds. "Let them know we'll come. I'll start making the arrangements tomorrow for a driver and a truck to take our belongings."

"What about the livestock? Who will care for them if we're not here?"

"The new place is a farm, so we will take what we can and sell the rest."

Gratitude filled Sylvia's heart for the daylight that crept into their room after tossing and turning all night. Visions of leaving plagued her shallow sleep, and when she got out of bed exhausted, she realized the worst of it all would be breaking the news to her best friend. The thought made her stomach queasy. She'd lived near Alma since she'd been a little girl. They were closer than sisters.

Sylvia finished pushing the scrambled eggs around in the skillet and then plated them along with the bacon and toast. She called the children to the table; nothing seemed to shake the weariness her soul held.

"I'm heading over to Alma's. Can you stay here with the children for a few minutes?" she asked Andy.

"Let's all go. I'd like to tell them together," Andy replied.

She stood and placed their dirty plates in the dry sink. "*Danke*," comforted she didn't have to break the news alone.

After breakfast, the family walked over to Caleb and Alma's. Despite the gloom in their hearts, the sun shone brightly, and the wind whistled through the rows of corn growing in the fields. The ears were getting heavy with kernels, and their tassels bowed over, a sign the harvest neared. Sylvia knew every square inch of this property and fields. She would never forget the many times she raced across the road and down the lane to visit Alma. So many memories made this goodbye the hardest.

They arrived at Alma and Caleb's front door.

"Andy and Sylvia, what brings you by today?" Alma's eyes held confusion as she motioned for them to enter.

Clara tugged at Sylvia's dress. "Mamm, can I go play?"

"Yes, yes, go on. Take care to mind your brother while we talk." Sylvia set Ray down.

"Let's sit out here on the porch so you can mind the children." Alma patted the porch swing, and Caleb brought out a few more chairs so everyone had a seat.

"What's the news? Seems to have been a lot of activity over at your place these past few days." Alma's words were soft. It was just like her to be polite in her inquiry.

Sylvia tried to memorize every square inch of her best friend's face. Her cheeks jutted out at new angles, and dark circles hung around her eyes. Sylvia wondered if the Bishop had also paid them a visit. Leaving her wrung at Sylvia's heart.

Andy cleared his throat, his words coming out a little shaky. "We came to tell you that Jake and Lizzie have secured a small farm for us down in Hartville. We are going to be leaving here within a week's time."

"Oh, Sylvia!" Alma cried. "I'm so happy you are going to be near your Mamm and Dat, but it won't be the same without you."

Sylvia couldn't bear to look her in the eye. "Leaving you will be the hardest. You've always been near my whole life. We're practically sisters."

Caleb interrupted, "Does this have to do with the church division?"

Andy nodded, "Partly. Yesterday, the Bishop hauled off the threshing machine. The same afternoon, we received a letter from Lizzie letting us know they had found a place. We always planned to join them, eventually. Now there is no choice. If we stay here, we'll be in the *bann* and without community."

Caleb's brow furrowed, and an uncomfortable hush fell over the group. It seemed even the birds stopped singing.

Sylvia gathered her courage. "What do you plan to do, confess before the church or go into the *bann* yourselves?" She wanted to know where they stood. If they'd be able to remain friends.

Alma played with a piece of her dress, twisting it back and forth. "I don't know if I can leave all my family behind. Mamm and Dat are getting up in years and depend on us to care for them."

"You're going to confess, aren't you?" Sylvia asked with a wince. She hadn't meant for her words to come out as an accusation. Her vision blurred at the choice her friend had to make.

Alma nodded. "I know it's not right, but what choice do I have? My folks aren't as supportive as yours. All my brothers and sisters have moved away and are building their own lives. I still believe in Jesus and will keep studying, but we can't leave, and we can't go into the *bann*." Alma started crying, tear after tear rolled down her cheeks. "I wish you could just stay and go to Mapleview Mennonite, like all the others who leave. At least then you could visit."

"If we went to Mapleview Mennonite, it would just cause

more problems for you. We might embrace a new church community, but the Bishop would forbid you from seeing us. The consequences would be huge if you disobeyed. It's better for us to be around family, and for our children to grow up knowing at least one set of their grandparents."

"I know. I just wish it were different."

Sylvia found herself at a loss for words. She wished it had turned out differently, too, that this path was less lonely. "I will pray for you. I'll pray that the Lord draws near and gives you strength." She stood up and reached for her best friend and pulled her slender figure tight against her. Alma's tears soaked through her dress and onto her shoulder, leaving a wet patch. They stood for a few minutes, swaying in the wind like the corn tassels in the field. "I'll write, I promise."

"Me, too."

Dat's home loomed ahead in the distance. Andy dreaded this goodbye the most. He hadn't spoken to Dat since their harsh exchange. Clara and Ray bounced up and down on the buggy seat in anticipation, eager to see their grandparents, oblivious to the weight of the mission. Andy held Sylvia's hand, squeezing now and then, wishing he could gain a measure of her strength.

"Andy, Sylvia, how *gut* to see you!" Mamm came out on the front porch as Andy lifted the kids down from the back seat of the buggy. "Come on in. I just made some fresh bread and lemonade."

Andy looked at Mamm through slitted eyes. Hadn't Dat told her yet, they were in the *bann*?

The children followed them up into the house in quiet obedience. "Why don't you go play in the living room?" Sylvia directed.

They peeled off to the cabinet in the corner where Mamm kept a few wooden trucks, dolls, and some games.

Mamm turned to Andy's youngest brother Samuel, the one he hardly knew because he had been born while he served at the CPS camp. "Go out to the barn and let Dat know Andys are here."

Andy settled onto the kitchen bench, and Sylvia sat next to him. The air in the house felt hot and stuffy. While they waited, they made small talk about the livestock and the weather. Andy noted how carefully Mamm avoided asking about the harvest work. She had to know by now about the Bishop picking up the threshing machine. News like that didn't stay hidden.

After a while, Andy began worrying Dat may refuse to see him, but after a half hour, Dat trudged up to the house, followed by Samuel. He stomped into the mudroom, taking his time removing his coat and hat.

Mamm stuck her head out into the vestibule. "Samuel, go play with Clara and Ray," she directed, clearing a space for only the adults to have a conversation.

Dat refused to extend his hand, speak, or make eye contact with Andy, instead he went over to the kettle and poured himself a cup of hot water adding a heaping spoonful of instant coffee and stirred for a good thirty seconds before turning around and speaking. "I hope you are here to tell me you are confessing and putting all this nonsense behind you."

"Dat, we came to tell you we are moving to Hartville. Jake and Lizzie have found us a farm close to them."

Mamm pressed a hand to her abdomen and sank down into a chair.

Dat wrinkled his nose and curled his lip. "You will no longer be in fellowship with the church if you don't repent. Think about what this means for your children and our family. The *veech mon* has got your soul."

"No, Jesus has my soul." He pointed his words directly into Dat's dark and stormy face. "We know the consequences, but I still want a relationship with you, Dat. Sylvia will write often and keep you updated. Perhaps we can come visit from time to time."

"Don't bother. I want no association with you and your new-fangled ideas. I suppose after you move, you'll start driving a car and become worldly."

He turned and addressed Sylvia. "Jake should have used a heavier hand with you. I don't understand why he is abetting you in this sin. You influenced my son down this path."

Andy clenched his fists, his nails biting into his sinewy flesh. "Leave Sylvia out of this. This is my choice. Jake has done nothing but accept me into his family and care for us. He believes in salvation as well and wants to live his older years in peace surrounded by family who love and accept him. This is not a simple decision. We have thought long and hard about what's best for us." Saying these words slammed the door in Dat's face. It would take a miracle to soften his heart. Their leaving would end what little relationship they had.

Mamm whispered one last plea, her face drawn and pale. "Andy, consider your soul. Being right with the church is an essential part of getting into heaven."

Dat gave her a look that put her in her place. "Hush woman. You shouldn't speak about such matters."

Neither their heartfelt pleas nor strong-armed tactics affected Andy's response. "I guess this is goodbye, then. I hope you change your mind and allow us to come visit."

"Humph." Dat let out a grunt as he set his mug down on the counter, and strode out the door to the barn, never once looking back.

"I'm sorry he's acting like this," Mamm muttered. "You know he's hurt. I hope you write and let us know how you've settled. Give him some time and space and he'll come around to another visit."

Andy placed his hand on Mamm's and gave a light squeeze. "Let's go," he said to Sylvia, who peeked her head into the living room to gather the children playing.

Clara and Ray picked up the toys and put them in the cabinet. When they were done, Clara came over to Sylvia and tugged on her skirt. Sylvia bent down. Clara whispered, "Can we just stay a little while longer? We're having so much fun with Samuel."

"I'm sorry, Clara, Dat said it's time to go. He's about to head out to get the buggy hitched up."

Andy wished Sylvia could tell their daughter they would come another time and could play together again, but he didn't want to make false promises.

Clara obeyed and gave a shy wave as she headed out the door. "Bye, Mummie."

Mamm pulled Clara into a tight hug.

Andy searched Mamm's eyes. Tears formed in their corners. He wished it didn't have to be this way. *Why couldn't they just agree to disagree?* He tipped his hat to her as he ushered his family out the door.

On the ride home, Andy clung to Sylvia's hand. As they sat in silence, he thought about the weight of his broken relationships. It felt like someone had knocked him down and placed a boot on his chest. At least they had the Lord and each other. Now he'd have to tell the children about the move. Best get it over with. He swallowed hard. "Tomorrow we will move to Hartville."

"What's Hartville?" Clara asked.

"That's where Mummie and Daughty Slabaugh live," Sylvia chimed in. "Won't it be nice to see them again?"

Clara paused for a moment before responding. "I can't wait to see Mummie and Daughty again. How long will our visit be?"

Sylvia responded, "Clara, it's not a visit. We will live there."

"Can I take my dolly?" she asked, concerned about her hand-stitched doll Mummie Slabaugh made her.

"Yes, of course."

"But I don't want to leave my room. Why can't we just take the house with us, too?"

Andy chuckled at her comment. "That would take a mighty team of horses to move the house. Daughty and Mummie found a new house for us. We will be close to them and can visit often. You'll get to see your cousins, too. Aunt Clara and Uncle Andy J. live there as well. Won't that be grand?"

Clara perked up at the mention of having cousins to play with, and she wiggled around in the seat the rest of the way home.

After they pulled into the driveway, Andy directed the horse as close as he could to the shed in the back. He came to Sylvia's side, helping her down. "The moving trucks and livestock transport will be here in the morning to get everything loaded. I hope Jake and Lizzie got our letter letting them know of our arrival. Remind me to have our new address handy for the drivers in the morning."

She nodded but didn't speak.

He unhitched the horse and led him into his stall in the barn for the last time. He needed to get out of this place, where sorrow weighed on them at every turn. A piece of him wished they could just load themselves into the trucks tomorrow and leave everything behind. They needed a fresh start.

When he returned, he told Sylvia, "Let's sell this buggy and ask Jake to build us a new one when we arrive."

Sylvia didn't respond as she finished unloading the children, and he wondered what lay ahead for them. *Would they even continue driving a buggy?*

TWENTY-SIX

November 1953, Hartville, Ohio

Sylvia sat with the children in the front seat of the moving van. Their belongings rattled in the back as they whizzed up and down the hills at a dizzying speed. Henry, the van driver, had spent most of the trip telling stories. Sylvia, grateful for the distraction, hunched over as her stomach became queasy. She suspected she was with child again but had mentioned nothing to Andy yet. The timing couldn't be worse. She would tell him after they settled.

The livestock truck followed behind them. Andy rode along with the animals in the cab. They brought Coco, a few milking cows, chickens, a sow, and a boar. "Hopefully, they'll breed and produce new little piglets," Andy had explained to the driver as they had loaded.

The caravan rode into Hartville from the east, their first stop, the train tracks. The children pressed their faces up against the glass, squashing their noses, fascinated by the train station. "We are coming up to the town square," Henry commented as he squealed to a stop at the intersection. "On your right, we have The Pantry, Hartville's only restaurant. Beside it, the general store and a grain elevator, across the way, the barbershop and hardware." He shifted and punched the gas again, and the truck lurched ahead. They passed the storefronts and houses lining the downtown street. Sylvia noted which stores were available, eager to get out and do a bit of shopping.

After a few miles, they took a left. Sylvia read the street sign as they turned down Market Street. Mamm had written that their new home was on Market Street. On the corner of the intersection stood a faded barn with a large sign nailed to the front that read: Hartville Livestock Auction.

Henry rolled down the window a crack and slowed the truck. "Sol Miller runs the auction. Farmers come from all over on Mondays, Thursdays, and Saturdays to sell and buy." A mixture of cars, livestock trucks, and a few buggies lined the gravel parking lot.

"I'll bet my husband Andy will want to get over there and see what is going on. He loves things like this," commented Sylvia.

Henry picked up speed, and they took several turns a bit too fast, stirring Sylvia's nausea. Before long, he put on the blinker, and they turned into the driveway. A small two-story farmhouse with a sagging porch and weathered siding sat back from the road, framed by two oak trees. It hadn't seen a paintbrush in years.

Sylvia recognized Mamm and Dat's buggy sitting off to the side. She breathed a sigh of relief. They were here to greet them. The children clambered down from the truck and ran around the back of the house, eager to explore their new surroundings. "Don't go too far!" she hollered after them. Sylvia stretched, glad to be out of the vehicle after the long, bumpy ride.

Mamm and Dat came around the side of the house with the children in tow. "You made it!" they exclaimed. "So, *gut* to see you." Dat extended his hand in greeting and Mamm pulled Sylvia to her side for a hug.

Sylvia's stress melted away in Mamm's arms. She had missed Mamm so much it brought tears to her eyes.

"You ready to see your new home? It's not much to look at, but I'm sure you'll make it a suitable home for you all." Mamm pointed towards the house as the children ran ahead and climbed on the porch, eager to see the inside.

"We'd best get this livestock unloaded," Jake said to Andy. "I'll show you where you can put the animals." He pointed to a small barn behind the house, along with the chicken coop. The driver started the ignition and rolled the truck alongside the barn.

The horse whinnied and pranced its hooves against the floorboards while the cows lowed. Andy climbed up the ramp and undid the gates. "Come on, girl, let's get you into your new home." He grabbed Coco by the reins and guided her down the narrow ramp, her hooves clanking against the metal. Jake opened the stall door in preparation. Andy took note that there were already sacks of grain and a modest pile of hay bales ready to service the animals.

"Had the elevator deliver some feed to hold you over for a few days," Jake said.

"Thank you, Dat."

He found himself surprised by the words that fell out of his mouth. *Had he just called Jake...Dat?* In so many ways, Jake had been a better Dat to him than his own. His throat closed with emotion, and he turned away, embarrassed. A cow swatted him with its tail, nudging him to unload the remaining animals into their new home.

The chicken coop had seen its better days. Andy inspected the wood and noted the rot on the west side, and the spots of rust burrowing their way into the underside of the roof. He'd have to fix what he could with supplies found lying around.

Jake shooed him away from his inspections. "Don't fret too much. I have some supplies in the shop that will fix this right up. I meant to do it before you got here, but time got away from me."

Andy carried the last of his chickens, one under each arm, and put them into the coop. "That'll do!" he exclaimed as he fished a dwindling roll of cash out of his pocket to pay the driver. He needed to find a job. Hopefully, Jake had some leads for work. He didn't want to depend on him for too long.

Sylvia ran her fingertip along the kitchen counter. Mamm had cleaned the house prior to their arrival, but it was still in sad shape. The floor sloped at odd angles, and a few of the cupboards hung loose from the hinges. It did have electricity, but no running water. An old pump well sat in the backyard and a washbasin on the counter in the kitchen.

Mamm blinked. "We didn't know if you would want to use electricity or not. Figured we'd leave it up to you."

Sylvia's eyes widened. She hadn't considered they'd have an option. She flipped the switch, and an overhead light illuminated the entire kitchen. An icebox rattled in the corner. "Guess I'll have to talk with Andy about it." But she'd already decided the minute her fingers pressed the switch. They'd use electricity.

The men carried the furniture into the house, unloading the beds and dressers upstairs into the two bedrooms. They placed the rockers in the living room and heaved the table into the kitchen along with the chairs. Dat unrolled a thick braided rug on the living room floor and placed the clock on the mantel. Within half an hour, they'd emptied the truck, and the drivers were both on their way back to Geauga County. Sylvia busied herself unpacking the boxes in the kitchen and loading her canned goods into the cupboard shelves. "I'll need to go to the grocery store tomorrow and gather a few items, but I think I can make do tonight and get something around for dinner."

"You don't need to worry about that. I brought you a casserole to bake in the oven." Mamm opened the door to the icebox and took out a glass dish. Cooked ground beef covered the bottom with mounds of creamy mashed potatoes on top.

"Thank you, Mamm, that's so thoughtful of you, but I do need to get into town to buy supplies, and we didn't bring our buggy with us."

"I'm sure Dat has an extra he can loan you. Tomorrow is Sunday, and we'll have church services. We can pick you up in the morning and team two horses to the buggy. You can come for lunch afterwards and take your horse and a loaner home. It'll be nice to show you around our place."

Sylvia had forgotten what it felt like to be offered kindness and community. The hostility they'd faced back home had made for a few long, hard months. This tiny worn-down house with peeling paint was nothing like their large farmhouse back in Burton, but it represented a community filled with love and acceptance, something way more valuable.

"Do you think it's all right to use electricity?" Sylvia whispered to the ceiling as she lay in bed. Quiet had descended upon the house, and she couldn't sleep. The wind whistled through the old floorboards, and creaks and groans kept her wondering if there was an intruder.

Andy rolled over to face her. "We don't belong to a church anymore. There is no *Ordnung* to follow. I know we are called to live differently from the world, but maybe some modern conveniences are okay. The most important thing is that our hearts are different."

She squeezed her eyes shut. "How will we survive? You don't even have any work?"

"Electricity does cost money," he teased. "We'll trust the Lord to provide."

"I'm pregnant." The secret tumbled out of her before she could stop it. She searched his face, hoping he was pleased.

Andy paused; his brow deepened. He took her face in his hands, his eyes drilling into hers. "A blessing from the Lord." He kissed her softly, with lips turned up in a smile. "Get some sleep. Tomorrow, we get to go to church and see our friends and family. On Monday morning, we will go into town and inquire about work. Remember, the Lord will never leave or forsake us."

Sylvia placed her head on his chest and listened to his heartbeat. The steady thump of his heart never missed a beat. *I am as sure and steady as the beating of a heart. I will take care of you,* the Spirit whispered. Her muscles became limp as her eyelids became heavy, and she fell into a deep sleep.

The next morning, they sat in the back seat of Mamm and Dat's buggy as they pulled into the church service held at the old one-room schoolhouse. Attending church in a designated building instead of the rotating farmhouses felt different, but the service differed little from the services at home. The four families that made up the congregation were warm and welcoming, greeting them with excitement. Malon and Annie beamed and promised a homecoming dinner that week.

After the service, they rode back to Mamm and Dat's place for a pot roast lunch. Sylvia's heart swelled as she looked around the table at all the familiar faces including Clara, her husband, and their growing brood of children. Peace flooded her; they had made the right decision in coming.

Mamm and Dat lived the same way they had back home, with no electricity or modern conveniences. An outhouse served as the main bathroom, a wood stove in the kitchen, and a washbasin sat on the back porch.

"Does the King Church have an *Ordnung*?" Andy asked at lunch.

Sylvia glared at him. Her irritation at the question made her fidget. *Why in the world would Andy bring up doctrine?*

"Not yet," Jake replied. "We have agreed to live separately from the world, but we do not believe in shunning like back home. Those are man-made rules. Nothing in the *Dordrecht Confession* mentions those extreme measures, nor does the Bible, for that matter."

"Are there other districts, or is this the only Amish church?"

"Malon would be best to talk with about that. There are several Mennonite churches in the area. He will know more."

Andy changed the subject, and Sylvia sighed with relief.

"Tomorrow, I need to go into town and look for some work. Do you know anyone needing some help?"

Her brother-in-law, Andy J. piped in, "I hear East Ohio Limestone might be hiring. That would be close to your farm."

Andy nudged her. "Looks like we'll be making a trip into town in the morning."

She grinned, unable to hide her delight.

Sylvia rose early after Andy left to do the chores. She tiptoed down the creaking stairs, finding her way in the darkness. When she made it to the kitchen, she flipped the switch, and the entire room bathed in light. She couldn't believe how easy electricity made things, no feeling around for the matches and lantern. She opened the refrigerator door, and the cold hit her face. No longer would she need to go to the icehouse to gather supplies to make breakfast. She looked over the limited options. Oatmeal it would be, maybe some eggs if the chickens had laid. She'd also get some milk from the cows. Wrapping her shawl around her shoulders, she went out to the barn. Two buckets of milk sat by the door, and her husband's familiar figure lumbered out of the chicken house.

"Did they lay for us?"

"Yep, got us eight eggs."

"Good. I'll make us some eggs and oatmeal for breakfast."

Andy picked up the bucket of milk and followed her back into the house.

As Sylvia finished cooking breakfast, the children came down the stairs rubbing their eyes, disoriented by their new surroundings.

"Sit up and eat. We are going to go into town after breakfast. I need to buy some groceries, mail a letter, and your Dat is going to look for work." She scooped eggs onto plates and ladled hot oats into bowls she set in front of everyone at the table. "Let's thank God for this food He has given us."

Andy opened the prayer book and prayed the prayer of thanksgiving. "Dear holy Father, we give You great praise, honor, and glory, and deep gratitude for Your innumerable and unspeakably glorious kindnesses and favors, indeed for all Your spiritual and physical blessings, mercies, and good deeds. We offer deep and humble thanks for your great grace and rich mercy, and we especially thank You again for Your eternal salvation, which You gave us through our Lord Jesus Christ. Amen."

Sylvia dug into her plate, eager to get on with the day and explore the new town.

⟨◇◇◇◇◇⟩

The IGA grocery store sat close to the town's square. Cars and trucks filled the parking lot—their chrome bumpers gleaming in the sunshine. Andy cringed. He hated driving a buggy amongst all these cars, and he didn't see a hitching post to tie the horse to, so he wound the reins around the bike rack out front. People went in and out of the store, some in more plain dress and coverings without bonnets and strings, others dressed English with curled hair and lipstick. Inside, Sylvia commandeered a cart and started stocking up on essentials: meats, flour, sugar, spices, fruits and other necessities to stock her kitchen.

Andy took a deep breath, gathered his courage, left his wife's side and went up to the cashier, who was in-between checking out customers. "Excuse me? Can you tell me if anyone in town is hiring?"

The cashier pointed him to a bulletin board hanging inside the door with help-wanted notices. He went to it and immediately one caught his eye. *Workers wanted - East Ohio Limestone. Jobs in mining, coal truck driving, and manual labor. Inquire at Midway St.* Andy J. mentioned East Ohio Limestone yesterday. He pulled the notice off the bulletin board and took it back to the cashier. "Can you tell me how to get to Midway St.?"

"Are you new here?"

"Just moved a few days ago. We have a small farm down on Market." He took some time to describe where the house was located.

"Midway is close to you, then." She took a sheet of paper sitting beside the register and drew him a map. "You're here on Market," she pointed to an X she had drawn to mark his house. "Pull out and make a right. Midway will be right here on your left. East Ohio Limestone is at the top of the hill about a mile down Midway. There is a small office at the front where you can inquire about work."

"Thank you so much." He pocketed the map and returned the advertisement to the bulletin board, eager to get on his way. He found his wife in the aisle examining the different boxes of cereal.

"Look, Andy, they have so many choices." She held up a box of Wheaties and a box of Sugar Pops. "Which one would you rather?"

"Sugar Pops, of course, but Wheaties is a much more sensible choice." He eyed the half-full cart. "We shouldn't buy all this stuff until I secure some work. I have a lead on a job, though, so let's get going."

"But I have more shopping to do."

"Let me help you finish up. What else do we need?"

"I still need to pick up some butter and flour yet. I think I can get by with only that."

"Can't we make our own butter? Just until I get a job. We need to save money."

Sylvia frowned but consented. "Okay, but once you have a job, I will buy my butter."

"Agreed."

They rang up their purchases, and Andy's wad of cash felt even lighter than it had a few days ago.

"I was hoping to do a bit of other shopping in the general store, and maybe check out the hardware," Sylvia commented as he helped load the paper sacks of groceries into the back of the buggy.

"It'll have to wait till another time. Let's get home and unload these groceries."

The buggy wove its way through the grid of cars in the parking lot and back onto the street for the half-hour ride back to the house. Cars slowed behind them, then sped around when the oncoming traffic lane cleared. Life would be much easier if they had a car. They could zoom from place to place and accomplish so much more, but he could barely afford a cart full of groceries, never less a car, besides they needed to decide what church to attend, and what rules they would live by. *Rules*. Andy groaned at the word; he didn't want to live anymore by man-made rules. No time to think about this today. He needed all his mental energy to focus on getting a job.

As they clip-clopped past the other stores Sylvia commented, "I wonder if the general store carries fabrics. I could make myself a nicer dress than this, something more modern." She looked down at her dark blue dress, covered by the black cape.

"You look fine. We don't have money for new dresses." Ashamed of the sharp tone in his voice, he tried to be sympathetic and patted her hand. He wished he could give her a closet full of new dresses, but they didn't have the means.

Once home, they unloaded the groceries and Sylvia ooohhhed and ahhhed at the modern conveniences in the kitchen as she placed the meat and vegetables into the icebox. He hadn't realized how much easier electricity would make life for her, for them all.

Clara stomped her foot and pouted, "I'm hungry, Mamm."

Sylvia pulled a package of noodles out of the paper sack and a jar of canned chicken from the pantry. Within a matter of minutes, the water boiled on the stove. "Chicken and noodles coming right up. Do you care for any?" she asked Andy.

Chicken and noodles sounded good, but with the day getting along, he needed to get over to the Limestone mine. "No, I want to get going, so I'm back in time for the chores." He grabbed an apple out of the sack and took a big bite as he headed out the door.

November 1953, Hartville, Ohio

East Ohio Limestone stood at the top of a large hill, and Coco strained against the climb. Andy snapped the reins. "Come on, girl." She snorted in the cold November air.

Hartville's topography featured rolling hills, but the limestone mining had amplified the valleys and peaks. When he came to a stop in the parking lot, Coco panted, and sweat coated her body in a shiny gleam. "I'll let you have a rest, girl. Here's an apple for your trouble." He nuzzled his apple core up to her mouth, and she gobbled it up.

The mining office sat against the bare hills—a single wide trailer. Not what Andy expected of a booming enterprise. An open sign hung on the door, and when he pushed against it, a little bell jingled. A secretary sat at a desk chomping gum and clicking away at a typewriter. She held up a finger, signaling him to wait, barely missing a beat in her cadence. When she came to the end of the row, the typewriter dinged as she slid the carriage back to the beginning of a new line.

"There, just wanted to finish my line. What can I do for you?" She looked up at him through glasses that slid down her nose; a graying perm complemented her plump middle-aged figure.

"I came to inquire about a job."

Her eyebrows raised. "Do you have any mining skills? The Amish around these parts normally stick to agriculture and woodworking."

"I'm not sure what skills are required for mining, but I'm a hard worker."

"You're right; the job doesn't require a lot of skill," she conceded. "But it does help to have experience. The only openings we have right now are for truck drivers to haul the rock up from the bottom of the shaft." She glanced over his shoulder, out the window, pursing her lips at the horse and buggy. "I don't suppose you can drive a truck?"

His breath caught in his ribs at the question. "I've driven a tractor before. It can't be all that different," he appealed. The only time he'd driven a tractor had been years ago at the CPS camp.

"Well, it's quite different, and you need a driver's license to drive a truck. I'm sorry, I just don't think this job is the right fit for you."

Andy would have accepted defeat, but the stakes were different now. He pictured Sylvia and the children at home eating their chicken and noodles. *What would happen when they had no more funds to buy food?* He had no choice but to fight for their sake. "Are you sure there isn't anything I can help with? I just moved here and live close by." He tried to keep the desperation from leaking into his words.

She chewed on the end of her pencil. "Come to think of it, I heard the manager mention a worker got hurt in the loading bay yesterday and is going to be out for a while. You wait here; I'll go down to the site and see if it's a possibility." She grabbed a spare hard hat hanging on a nail and shoved it down on top of her gray curls.

The breath he'd been holding released as he sat down in a vinyl-covered chair against the wall. At least he had a shot at a job. He buried his face in his hands. *God, You led us to Hartville. Don't leave us now. I need this job, please make a way.* Truth was, the past few days had felt a little bleak. Their comfortable life in Geauga County had slipped away, replaced by uncertainty. *How had he led his family down this road the same way Dat had?* Poor and moving from house to house.

A scripture came to mind; *I will never leave or forsake you. Your mother and father may, but I will always provide. Look at the birds of the air; they do not sow or reap or store away in barns, and yet your heavenly father feeds them. Are you not much more valuable than they?*

The door jangled, startling Andy from his thoughts. He jumped to his feet. A man with deep-set eyes followed behind the secretary. Black dust covered every inch of him. He pulled a hankie out of his back pocket and wiped his face the best he could before holding out a hand. "Name's Tony. Elvira here tells me you are looking for a job."

"Yes, sir."

"She said you have limited skills in mining but claim to be a hard worker. Good workers are difficult to come by around here. I don't know many Amish folk, but the ones I do know work hard. I need a general laborer to help with the sorting machines. The pay is $1.25 an hour. Can you start tomorrow?"

"Yes, sir." Andy's voice leapt in pleasure at Tony's offer. "What time do you want me?"

"We start at seven with a break for lunch and get done around four."

"I'll be here."

"You'll need some equipment. I'll supply it but will have to take it out of your pay."

Andy agreed. "That's fine, sir." They would have to be very careful with their money over the next few weeks, but they could make do.

Tony turned on his heel and walked back through the door. "See ya in the morning then!" he hollered over the beeps and rattles of the heavy machinery.

Elvira grinned. "You got lucky. Caught him at the right time. He isn't always generous with walk-ins, and with the pay. Looks like you'll make even more than me." She clucked her tongue.

"Thank you so very much." His heart swelled towards this lady, who had taken a chance on him. He'd need to remember her name. What had Tony called her? "I'm sorry. I don't think I caught your name?"

"Elvira."

"I'm Andy." He shoved his hands in his pockets, unsure of what he should do next.

She circled back to her desk and took a seat and began typing again. "Guess I'll see you in the morning then."

He raised a hand in farewell and left.

"Sylvia, Sylvia!" He let the screen door slam behind him as he yelled into the house. "You'll never guess what just happened. I got a job. Starting tomorrow at $1.25 an hour."

Sylvia came down from upstairs, finger to her lips. "Hush, I just got the children down for a nap. Why all the hollering?"

He picked her up and swung her around. "I got the job. They almost dismissed me, but the secretary took a chance and fetched the foreman. While she was gone, I prayed. The Spirit brought a scripture to mind. The one in Matthew where Jesus said not to worry. Next thing you know, they're offering me the job. Can you believe it? Fifty dollars a week—more in one week than I made in a month!" His mouth dried at the words. How fast he'd fallen into the pit of despair, and yet the Lord had provided.

"Oh, that's wonderful! What an answer to prayer."

"I've got to get the chores done in the barn. But before I go out, let's take a few minutes to read the scriptures together while the children are napping, and thank the Lord for His favor."

Andy settled into his rocker and opened his Bible. He handed it to Sylvia, who read aloud from John six where Jesus fed the five thousand with five loaves of bread and two fish.

"What a perfect passage for today. Seems like He did a similar miracle for us," Sylvia commented when she finished reading.

She closed the Bible and reached for his hand. Andy couldn't contain the inner glow of thanks that reached the farthest corners of his heart. He began praying out loud. "Jesus, thank You for giving me a job. Thank You for feeding my family and for being with us. For bringing us joy and peace. I'm sorry I doubted You. Amen." Normally his prayers came from the prayer book, but today they came from his heart, simple and filled with gratitude. He squeezed Sylvia's hand as they both rose from their chairs.

"I'll come help you with the chores," she offered.

"Appreciate that. I could use all the help I can get fixing up the barn and chicken coop. When we have a little extra money, we should buy more chickens and sell the eggs for extra pocket change."

Sylvia nodded. "Good idea. If I take in some ironing, I can also make a little extra."

He reached for her hand again and squeezed. They would be fine because they had the Lord and each other.

On Andy's first day of work, the rooster crowed early. He rolled over and sat on the edge of the bed, rubbing the sleep from his eyes. He ran his hand through his sandy hair, feeling it matted down in places and sticking up in others. Not a ray of light filtered through the window, but he needed to get up and do chores before work. He threw on the clothes he'd placed on a chair last evening and crept down the stairs, careful not to make too much noise. The clock on the mantel read five o'clock. He'd better get a move on if he was to get done before he had to leave at six thirty.

It took half an hour to milk the two cows and another twenty minutes to collect the eggs. He didn't have time to muck out the stalls. That would have to wait for the evening, but he fed the livestock and the horses. The pigs were another matter. There were not enough scraps left over from their meals, so he gave what he scrounged up, along with some milk from the cows. Dawn was just beginning to creep over the horizon when he finished up.

When he entered the kitchen, Sylvia stood at the stove frying up bacon and eggs. "Sit and eat," she motioned to the place set at the table.

"I don't have time and can't be late on my first day." He grabbed two pieces of bacon off a plate and kissed his wife before bounding up the stairs to change into his second set of work clothes for the day.

"Make sure you don't leave without the lunch pail I prepared for you!" she called after him.

He grinned. *What have I done to deserve this woman?*

Cars filled the East Ohio Limestone parking lot. The cool November sun bounced off the shiny chrome bumpers, making them sparkle. Andy's dark buggy looked out of place, reminding him of a pair of work trousers next to a fancy suit. There wasn't a hitching post, so he tied the horse to a lone sapling beside the office. He bounded up the steps and into the trailer. Nothing could squelch his joy, not today when he had work.

Elvira was taking off her coat and hanging it on the rack. Her eyes widened when she saw him. "You came."

He wondered why she sounded surprised. "Is this where I need to report?"

"Yes, every day you need to come to the office and stamp your timecard." She pointed to a rack on the wall holding pieces of card stock and a stamp next to it on a small table. "Be sure to put your timecard back in the right place. I've alphabetized them." She shuffled through a stack of papers on her desk until she found what she was looking for. "Here you are." She held up his timecard. He took it from her, reading his name with pride. It was official.

He dipped the stamp into an open inkpad and carefully placed it on the first line.

"Put your initials next to the stamp. Once you have filled up the card, let me know and I'll make you a new one."

It took longer than it should have to find the T section on the rack of timecards, but eventually he did, and after completing the instructions he asked, "Where do I go next?"

Elvira produced a hard hat, jumpsuit, gloves, and a pair of safety goggles from under her desk. "Put these on and then head down to the loading bays. There's another trailer next door where you can store your lunch and any other supplies. We use it as a locker room."

Andy stepped outside with full arms. He placed the hat on his head and zipped up the jumpsuit. He pocketed the gloves and snapped the goggles into place. After putting his lunch in the trailer, he headed down to the worksite. The loading bays were at the bottom of a steep hill, and the gravel rolled underneath his boots. He swallowed, brushing aside his pride in wearing such a silly uniform, but grateful for the protection it provided against the November chill.

The mining yard was filled with all kinds of noises, led by the solid beat of a hammer, and the beeping and humming of the large equipment. A whistle shrieked and a large blast shook the ground. Andy jumped, putting his hands up to his ears.

"You'll get used to it. Happens every thirty minutes." Tony sidled up next to him and put out his hand in greeting. "I'll take you down to the foreman at the sorting plant. You'll report to him every day."

The two men walked shoulder to shoulder. "Have to be careful on this road. The haulers go up and down from the blast site to the loading bays all day long. The dust can get so thick sometimes it's hard for them to see much in front of them when they're driving. You'll want to stay to the side."

As if on cue, a truck rumbled past, kicking dust in their faces. Andy could taste the minerals on the tip of his tongue. Before long, they reached the loading bays.

"Let me give you a quick rundown of the operation before I take you over to the crushing plant." Tony stepped to the side of a large dump truck, unloading its contents into a bay. "The men down at the bottom of the mine drill holes into the base of the rock and place explosives. Once the explosives are in position, we sound the whistle. Pay attention to that whistle. You don't want to be anywhere near the site when it explodes. Run if you are." He chuckled, then continued, "The blast creates large chunks of loose rock. An excavator then loads the rock onto trucks, who bring it up to the crushing bays. These crushing bays break the rock into smaller pieces and sort it according to size. Then it gets hauled off to our suppliers. We need some manpower on the hauling side, but until you get your driver's license, I'll use you in the sorting plant. I need a man to make sure the right product goes on the right truck for transport to the suppliers."

Get my driver's license? The idea of driving made him breathe a little easier. It would be so nice just to drive to work or town. *I'll have to talk to Sylvia and see what she thinks about it.* They walked downhill alongside the open tubes, carrying the crushed rock to the sorting plant. Gravity and agitators moved the loose stone into piles.

Tony introduced him to the foreman. "Wayne, want you to meet our newest worker, Andy. He's going to help you make sure the right trucks get loaded."

"Humpft. Do you have any experience in mining?" Wayne's hard, weathered face had the countenance of the limestone he mined. His gray eyes were framed by sunken cheeks. A wiry figure only added to his toughness. He reminded Andy of an old sinewy piece of beef, chewed up and discarded.

"No, sir, but I'm quick to learn and am a hard worker."

"We'll see."

Tony glared at his foreman. "At least give him a shot."

Wayne responded. "You'll be with me today. Lunch break is at noon for half an hour." He turned on his heel and peered at the pile of rock shooting out of the crushing tube.

Tony laid a hand on Andy's shoulder. "His bark's worse than his bite," he reassured and then left.

Wayne shouted over the noise. "This here is the medium grade rock! See how it is half an inch in diameter? This quarry produces eight different grades, all the way from a fine powder to an inch in diameter! The crushing plant oversees the production of each kind and changes up the crushers accordingly! We make sure none of the different grades mix! Right now, we are working on loading the big stuff! After lunch, we will switch to the fine powder! You'll want to have a handkerchief handy to make sure you don't end up eating that stuff!"

Andy followed Wayne around the sorting area as he gave instructions to the loaders scooping cargo into the back of trucks and containers. "This shipment goes to the rail yard. You know how to drive one of these loaders?" Wayne asked.

"No, sir."

Wayne paused before responding. "You're going to learn. You won't be much good to me if you can't drive. Go on and sit up there in the cab with Lester and watch how he does it."

Andy climbed up in the loader, "Yes, sir." *I wonder if he knows I'm Amish.* All his gear probably masked his identity. The thought of his ambiguity brought a smile to his face, but a pit of fear knotted in his stomach at the thought of driving. He was such an impostor. *I must do this for Sylvia, the children, and the baby on the way. God gave me this job. Surely, He approves.* He held onto the grab bar and heaved himself into the passenger seat in the loader.

Lester leaned over and looked at him in bewilderment, unsure why a stranger had crawled up next to him. "Who are you?"

"You'll be training me today on how to operate this thing," Andy explained.

Lester just shook his head and released the scoop into the enormous pile of gravel, getting bigger by the minute.

"How was it?" Sylvia ran her fingers along his head, stroking his hair like she did the children.

Andy could barely keep his eyes open. "Got to learn how to drive a loader. Lester says I'm a natural, and he'll let me fly solo tomorrow."

By the time he had gotten home, filth covered his clothes, and he went right to mucking out the stalls. After chores, the children were all over him, wanting to tussle on the floor. By the time he climbed into bed, the clock chimed nine, and he felt beat. His five a.m. wake up would come quickly. He wanted to talk to Sylvia about driving but couldn't keep his eyes open long enough to form the words. *They needed to consider getting a car, but what would their new church think?*

TWENTY-EIGHT

January 1954, Hartville, Ohio

Sylvia glanced over at Andy as he clucked the horse and buggy down the road. "Do you feel at home in our new church?"

They had been attending the King Church for a few months now and had settled into a new rhythm, but she still questioned if they truly belonged there.

He slackened the reins but didn't respond to her question. "What do you think?"

"In some ways, yes, but in others, no. We don't live like the Amish. We use the electricity, still dress in our traditional clothing, and drive a horse and buggy. No one at the church has said anything about the modern conveniences or asked for a confession, so I assume it's okay. They've been nothing but loving and accepting, but I can't shake the feeling something is missing."

"Me either," he admitted. "If we become members, then I believe things will change."

"Like what?"

"We'll have to commit to following their ordinances. They don't believe in shunning, but we'll have to bind ourselves to certain standards, one of them being no vehicles. Once we become members, it'll be all in or we'll be out. The longer I work at East Ohio Limestone, the more I realize how important driving is to the job. I've got an itch to drive. It would make things so much easier. What would you think of us buying a car?"

"Are you serious?" She cast him a sideways glance. The corner of her lips lifted in approval. "You think I could learn, too?"

"*Ya*, maybe."

She crinkled her mouth with pleasure before a nugget of truth settled in her gut. Carefully, she picked through her words. "But if we drive, then we can't become members of the King Church."

Andy's body stiffened. "I've been thinking. Everything changed when we found Jesus, and I see things differently now. Half those rules were never in place to bring honor to Jesus. They were about control. Our good deeds should come from a love for Jesus, not because we want to please a Bishop or pastor. What would we be teaching our children if we continued to follow such strict rules? I want them to follow Jesus, not a set of rules."

The horses' hooves echoed on the pavement for the next few minutes as Sylvia contemplated his words. "But what about Malon? He loves Jesus and leads the King Church."

"Malon has Annie to think about. She's always wanted to stay Amish."

"If we don't go to the King Church, where will we worship?"

"I've been thinking about that, too. My co-worker Lester invited us to his church. I thought we could try it out. He attends Maple Grove Mennonite on Smith Kramer Road. Would you be agreeable?"

Her spirit lurched and she grinned at him. "Yes, let's do it. How about next Sunday?"

Mennonite. Sylvia mulled the word around in her mind. She'd heard plenty about how the Mennonites were a watered-down version of the Amish. They had some of the same values, only they believed in salvation and drove cars and had electricity. She hoped Dat and Mamm would understand if they left the King Church.

—⟨◇◇◇◇◇⟩—

The following Sunday, Andy and Sylvia pulled their buggy into Maple Grove Mennonite's parking lot. Andy parked in the back and tied the horse to a tree. Sylvia lifted Clara and Ray down from the back seat and smoothed her dress over her growing bump. She adjusted Clara's coat and her fingers combed a cowlick that had sprung up from Raymond's hair. Her nerves pulsed with energy. *Would this church accept them?*

Throughout the parking lot, car doors slammed, and children clung to their parents' hands as they made their way to a set of double doors that opened to let the parishioners in. The church had no steeple, only a plain white building flanked by a row of windows. Sylvia looked down at her plain, dark Amish clothing. She decided at the last minute to wear only her *kap* and not the bonnet. She looked around, comparing her husband to the other men in the parking lot. His black pants, white shirt and plain black coat didn't look that different from anyone else. Maybe they wouldn't stand out so much.

Andy grabbed Raymond's chubby fingers and led them towards the doors. "Let's go; I don't want to be late for our first time."

They cobbled up the front steps, and before Andy grabbed the door handle, the door swung open.

A man on the other side bellowed out a greeting. "Welcome to Maple Grove. Glad to have you worship with us." He motioned for them to enter the vestibule.

Inside the door hung a rack of hooks for coats. Sylvia shrugged the children out of their woolen jackets and hung them on the pegs. They stood on a landing in the middle of two sets of stairs. One led up to what seemed to be the sanctuary, and the other into a basement. Children ambled up and down the stairs carrying their Bibles. Adults chatted with each other, and the scent of coffee wafted up from the basement, permeating the air. The atmosphere was casual and comfortable, the opposite of the solemn church services they were used to.

"First time visiting?" the man asked.

"Yes," Andy replied. "We are new to the area. My coworker, Lester Gingerich, invited us."

"Good. Lester's a fine man." He held out a hand, and Andy shook it.

"My name is Jerry Miller, and I'm the minister here at Maple Grove."

Sylvia eyed Jerry's clothing. *He could be Amish,* she thought. The overcoat lacked a collar, and dark-colored buttons marched up the center. Her Dat wore such a coat. The only difference was Dat's had hook and eye enclosures instead of buttons. She noted the similarities ended with Jerry's haircut and clean-shaven face. No Amish man would ever sport cropped hair and a faint outline of stubble.

The ladies of the congregation wore dresses with capes. The sleeveless garment that sat on top of the upper part of the dress matched the colors and patterns of the fabric. They completed their looks with white *kaps* with strings. She made a mental note to buy some patterned fabric and sew a few dresses so she would fit in better. Maybe she could modify her head covering so it didn't have so many pleats.

They made their way to a pew and settled in. The sermon titled "Jesus Is the Light of the World" lifted her spirits. The message reminded her of the tent revival meetings. After the invocation, Pastor Jerry invited the Miller sisters up for a special song. Their sweet three-part harmony soared above the congregation. Sylvia's spirit swelled along with the music, and several times throughout the song she closed her eyes, concentrating on the words.

And once again, the scene changed. New earth there seemed to be. I saw the Holy City beside the tideless sea.

As the three ladies crooned on, Sylvia spoke to God. *This is my new earth, my new scene, a new season of peace. Thank You, Lord.*

She reached over and squeezed Andy's hand, grateful for this new life they were building.

After the service, several parishioners approached, offering greetings. "Why don't you stay for lunch? We're having a carry-in," said a young lady who looked Sylvia squarely in the eye, her invitation sincere.

"I'm sorry, I don't feel we can stay since I didn't bring a dish to share," Sylvia lamented.

"Don't you worry one bit. There will be plenty. You're our guests today. Please stay and eat with us."

More church ladies eager to meet the newcomers flocked around Sylvia, urging her to attend the lunch.

Sylvia caught Andy's eye. He gave a nod of approval, and she responded, "We'd be pleased to accept your invitation."

The aroma of fried chicken, noodles, and other delicacies drifted up from the church basement. Sylvia gathered the children and joined the exodus of people heading to the food line. For the first time in months, they were in fellowship with a body of like-minded believers.

"I believe we've found our church," she leaned over and whispered in Andy's ear.

"I think you may be right, as long as the food's good," he teased back.

"Let up on the clutch slowly and move the gearshift down while pressing the gas pedal," Andy instructed.

He sat in the passenger seat of their new car in the empty parking lot of the Hartville Livestock Auction, holding baby Viola, their newest daughter born a month ago, while Sylvia practiced driving.

Their car was anything but new, but they had purchased it with earnings tucked away and savings from the last sale of the livestock back in Geauga County. The 1943 Oldsmobile was spacious for their growing family and erased any last vestiges of Amish from their appearance. They were now fully Mennonite, and progressive ones at that.

The car lurched forward, causing Andy to grip the baby to his chest. "*Unfastandi* Sylvie," he creased his brow. "You need to make that transition a little smoother. Try again."

Sylvia shifted again. The lurch was only minor this time, and she looked over at Andy with a grin on her face. "I wish Alma could see me driving."

Andy tried to warn her but she looked so pleased with herself she didn't see the divots ahead and hit a small hill, making the car go airborne for a moment before it slammed back into the grassy field.

The children in the back hit their foreheads on the seats in front of them, and Andy let out a screech. "Put on the brakes!" The car came to an abrupt halt. "You always have to pay attention," he chided.

"Mamm!" Clara squeaked in the back. "That hurt my head."

Andy handed the baby over to Sylvia and stepped out. "That's enough for the day. Switch seats and I'll drive us home." Rising from the car, he shook out the nerves that had accumulated in his limbs and came around to the driver's side and opened the door. "You could have hurt the children. You need to pay attention. This isn't a game," he admonished again.

The incident had turned his mood sour. Normally, Sylvia's enthusiasm and playfulness lifted his spirits, but today, it just seemed unnecessary. His shoulders sagged after the long work week, having needed his normal Sunday nap.

Sylvia huffed and turned her body towards the passenger window as he began driving back home. "I know it's not a game. I'll concentrate harder next time. The real road is much better than this bumpy old field anyhow." She spoke to the stoplight on the corner, refusing to turn and face him. "When can I get out on the actual road?"

"You need to practice taking off and coming to a stop. Once you can master that I'll take you for a spin on the road."

"When?"

"I don't know when I'll have time. It'll probably have to be on a Sunday afternoon," he grumbled. *What am I doing? Teaching my wife to drive. How did our lives take this turn?* The trees rolled past empty winter fields, and he drummed his fingers on the steering wheel to squelch the anxiety threatening to cloud his vision. So much had changed in such a short period.

Navigating this new world created tension in every area of their lives. For the first time, it threatened to creep into their relationship. *Love is patient, love is kind.* The words of Paul surfaced. He needed to be careful not to let the devil get a foothold. He'd pluck out the nasty weed that had taken root and ask forgiveness for his short temper once the thump of his heart calmed.

TWENTY-NINE

March 1955, Hartville, Ohio

Every Sunday afternoon, Sylvia got out her stationery and wrote letters to Alma and occasionally to her in-laws. It had been a little over a year since they had left the Amish, and so far, only Alma had returned her letters. "Do you think we should plan a trip to Geauga to see your parents?" she mused out loud as she placed the pen cap between her lips.

Andy lay snoozing on the couch. "Huh?" he snorted in his sleep.

"Do you think we should visit your parents?" she repeated.

He opened a sleepy eye. "You think they will welcome a visit?"

"There's only one way to find out. If I write today, they'll know to expect us in two weeks." She took out the paper and dated it at the top in her loopy signature script.

Mamm and Dat Troyer

Greetings from Hartville. Today is a beautiful sunny day, although it is cold here. I have noticed that the daffodils are springing up. We are ready for some warmer weather. The children are tired of being cooped up in the house most of the day. Andy continues his work at East Ohio Limestone, and I have taken in some ironing for the ladies in the community. I enjoy the work and the extra income it provides for us. The small farm is also running well. The chickens are laying lots of eggs, and our hogs are almost ready for

slaughter. It's hard to believe it's been a full year since we left Geauga. Andy and I are talking about bringing the kids for a visit on Sunday in two weeks. We plan on stopping by the farm and to say hello. The children are growing fast, and little Viola has the sweetest smile. Looking forward to our visit and catching up. We'll see you soon.
    Andy and Sylvia.

She read it aloud. "How do you think that sounds?"

"Mmm hmm," he grunted from the couch as he pulled the bill of his hat down over his eyes.

She looked over at her husband, and her heart swelled with love. "I'm sorry, I shouldn't have bothered you during your nap." He worked so hard every week, waking before dawn and going to bed long after her and the children. His Sunday nap was one of his only small indulgences, and here she was prattling on about a visit, stirring unpleasant memories. She folded the letter in thirds, pressing the creases to make them crisp, licked the envelope closed, and addressed it. She'd send it along to work with Andy tomorrow to put in the mail.

Two weeks passed quickly. After the church service, Andy ushered his family into the Oldsmobile and took off towards Geauga County. Sylvia had packed some sandwiches and cookies to eat along the way. They chewed in silence, looking out the windows at the small villages. Soon they came to Burton and inched their car along the main circle.

"There's the school I used to attend." Andy pointed out the window at the looming brick building.

Ray looked wide-eyed, and Clara asked, "Did you ride a school bus?"

"Yes, I did. Caught it in the morning after I finished the milking for Mr. Lester."

"When will we get to Daughty and Mummie's house? Will my cousin Samuel be there?" Clara questioned.

Sylvia replied, "Samuel is your uncle, and yes, he'll be there to play with you. Won't it be nice to see Mummie and Daughty again? But first, we are going to stop and see our friends Caleb and Alma."

The kids bounced up and down in their seats with excitement.

Andy thought of all the memories he had accumulated through the years. Never had he dreamed he would drive a car on these familiar roads.

Before long, he turned down Jug Road, the place they'd left just sixteen months earlier. Their old farmhouse sat ready for its new occupants; an empty shell punctuated by tufts of spring grass that had grown with the recent rains. He veered into Caleb and Alma's well-kept place across the road. The cows lowed as they stepped out of the car.

The front door opened, and Alma came running down the stairs. Sylvia's face erupted into a thousand stars as she ran to greet her. They swayed together in a bear hug for a few moments before pulling apart.

"It is so good to see you," Sylvia looked Alma up and down and gasped at the round belly popping out from her narrow waist. "You're expecting! How come you didn't tell me?"

Alma blushed. "It's hardly proper to talk about such things."

"Of course it's proper. You've waited so long for this blessing." Sylvia locked hands with Alma like they had done their whole lives, and the women led the crew into the house.

Alma had set a table filled with pickles and peaches in small bowls, circled by plates piled high with brown sugar cookies. "Won't you get in trouble for eating with us?" Sylvia asked.

"Who's going to know? I'd rather repent in front of the whole church than miss time spent with you."

Andy knew those words touched Sylvia. The Alma they'd known would have never broken the rules.

"This is wonderful, but we can't stay too long. We need to pay a visit to Andy's folks and get back to Hartville in time to do the evening milking," Sylvia responded.

Alma nodded in understanding, and everyone gathered around the table. The children nibbled on cookies and drank their glasses of milk as the adults eased into conversation.

While the guys talked about the work at East Ohio Limestone, Sylvia turned towards Alma and whispered, "What do you know of Andy's folks?"

"You know there has been a church split, right?"

"No, we've had no news. I've written several times but haven't gotten a response."

"The church couldn't come to any agreement on the salvation issue, so the council recommended they divide into two. Bishop Miller, along with Eli and the other conservative folks, formed their own church. The rest of us continued meeting and appointed a new minister. It's been much more peaceful this way."

A pang of regret pricked Sylvia's heart. *Had they waited, they could have stayed, too.*

Alma continued, "I hear very little news about his folks, but a neighbor told me his brother David also left the Amish."

Sylvia bit her lip at the revelation. David's departure meant their strict shunning would continue—Eli would want to prove his loyalty to Bishop Miller. "Do you know where David went?"

Alma shook her head. "I don't know any more besides what I've told you."

The visit with Eli and Mary would not be pleasant. Sylvia was sure of it now. *Should she alert her husband or just let him find out?* No, she'd hope for the best. No sense in causing even more anxiety. *Lord, please let them at least converse with us,* she prayed.

Within fifteen minutes after leaving Caleb and Alma's, Andy turned onto the road leading to the Troyer homestead. He slowed the car down, his nerves pressing the brakes. He hoped there could be some sort of reconciliation, but he knew Dat's pride ran deep. A year may not be enough time to soothe his injured ego. He'd find out. Regardless, his children deserved to know their grandparents.

"Will Mummie give us cookies and lemonade again?" Clara piped up from the backseat. "Her cookies are the best."

Sylvia turned and addressed the two sets of eyes staring back at her. "This visit differs from other times. We will not be eating any refreshments with Mummie and Daughty. We just finished eating a snack at Caleb and Alma's. Please do as you're asked and mind your manners. It's important to say nothing about our visit to Caleb's. That needs to be a secret between us." Sylvia pressed a finger to her lips.

"Sylvia, you can't tell them to keep secrets," Andy clucked his tongue in disapproval.

She had a funny look on her face, but the listening little ears prevented him from saying more.

"Why can't we eat anything? Mummie always has treats," Clara kept pressing.

Sylvia responded to the question. "There were some disagreements between us and your grandparents before we went to Hartville. We love them very much, but sometimes adults don't see eye to eye."

Despite his annoyance with the secret keeping, Andy was glad she took the lead.

"Why don't you just say you're sorry?"

Sylvia gave a cautious smile to their daughter. "That is what we hope to do today. Now you know why this visit is so important."

They pulled up to the house, and Andy parked the car. Taking a deep breath, he opened the door and climbed out. Tension built along his shoulder blades and traveled up to his neck, giving him a headache.

The children clamored out of the back, slamming the doors. The sound made him wince. The familiar rockers sat on the front porch, swaying back and forth in the cool breeze, and a set of wind chimes jingled their forlorn song. Andy rapped on the door; his crew huddled behind him.

Mamm answered, her head down.

Andy held out a hand. "Mamm, so good to see you." She looked older than he remembered. Her cheeks sagged on her round face, and a deep furrow had taken up residence on the bridge of her nose. Reminders that she had done her fair share of frowning during her life. She didn't return the handshake.

Dat came looming behind her. "I made it clear you are not welcome back in this house. You disgrace us. Take that car out of my driveway and go."

So much for the hope that had fluttered in his heart over the past week. Dat had snatched that bird out of the air and thrown it to the ground. *How could he subject his grandchildren to this kind of treatment?* They were innocent and didn't deserve this. "Can I have a word, Dat?"

Dat pushed his way out the door, and Andy followed him off

the porch to the corner of the house. Andy kept his distance and shoved his hands in his pockets.

Andy started. "I know you're not happy to see me, but I want my children to know their grandparents. For their sake, can we at least have a little conversation?"

"I told you before and, I don't know how I can make it any clearer. You are dead to me unless you choose to repent and come back to the Amish church. I can have no dealings with you."

"Just a quick visit out here on the porch? Look how much Clara and Ray have grown, and I want you to meet your granddaughter, Viola." Dat glanced over at Sylvia and the children huddled together. Clara smiled and waved at him.

Dat sighed and stiffened but nodded in agreement. "Okay, but you need to move your car and park it down the street. It will never belong in my driveway." He locked eyes with Andy for a moment longer than necessary. It was just like him to make a point to have the last word.

Andy turned and jogged to the car. He flipped the ignition, sparking the engine to life, and backed out of the drive and down the road a quarter mile till he came to the corncrib lane. He parked the car behind the corncrib and gathered his thoughts for a moment.

He wished with all his heart it didn't have to be this way. He longed for a sugary sweet reunion filled with molasses cookies and lemonade, but his logic told him this relationship would never be sweet again. It had never been. He had at least hoped for a friendly conversation with an extended hand, a truce of some kind. Instead, he received a greeting filled with disdain. Worse yet, a bitterness that had grown and hardened in the year he'd been gone.

Let's just get this over with. He gave himself a pep talk as he jogged back to the farmhouse. The cold spring winds whipped around him. Only the pale sun taking the sharp edge off the winter's lingering chill. Panting, he came to the porch. Sylvia and the children sat on folding chairs in silence, awaiting his return. Sylvia locked her eyes with his; a plea echoed in them for him to ease the tension. He clambered up the stairs and sat down beside his wife.

"Corncrib looks to be fuller than normal. Did you have a good harvest this year?" Andy asked, trying to make small talk.

Eli nodded. "Hmm. Hmm. Good harvest."

Sylvia piped in, "How is everyone's health?" She looked at Mamm, directing the question her way.

Mamm mumbled, "We enjoy good health."

Andy knew Sylvia wanted to know what other news she had missed out on during the year, but asking those questions wouldn't be polite. How strange it must feel for Sylvia to be in this world of broken relationships, so different from her family, yet here she was living out her marriage vows for better or for worse.

Ten painful minutes later, Andy rose from the chair. "It was *gut* to see you again. We won't take up any more of your time. Whenever you get away for a bit, come and visit us in Hartville. You're always welcome."

Mamm and Dat didn't respond to the invitation and gave no parting words. Andy ushered his family down the porch steps and walked to the corncrib in the distance.

"Why couldn't we go inside?" Clara asked. "I'm cold."

Sylvia pulled her close. "Someday you'll understand."

Once they got to the end of the lane, Andy turned and looked at the house. He didn't want to look. He'd rather drive off this land and never return, but something compelled him to do so. Dat had already gone inside, but Mamm continued to stand there; hand raised to her forehead, shielding her eyes as she watched them trudge down the road. Andy lifted a hand in farewell. Mamm raised hers as well. Dat wouldn't approve of her wave. He hoped he hadn't seen her do it.

He snuggled Viola close to his chest. The rare, sweet moments of his childhood flashed before his eyes—the comforting pat on the head, his favorite tomato gravy. He realized how present Mamm was in all of them. She had provided all the nurturing he'd had in childhood. He needed her now, but knew she would never cross Dat. "Goodbye, Mamm," he whispered into the wind, his heart broken.

I will never leave nor forsake you, the Spirit whispered in return—words that eased the aching of his bruised heart. He hoped the image of Mamm standing on the porch waving wouldn't be his last memory of her.

March 1962, Hartville, Ohio

The phone jingled, and Sylvia lifted the receiver off the wall. "Hello."

No one responded. She was about to hang up when a woman's voice asked, "Is Andy there?"

"No, I'm sorry, he's at work. This is his wife, Sylvia. Can I take a message?" *How peculiar. She couldn't ever remember a time when a woman called asking for Andy.*

The voice switched from English to Dutch. "This is his sister Linda Ruth."

"Linda Ruth! It's so good to hear from you." It had been seven years since they'd heard anything from anyone in Andy's family.

Linda Ruth hung silent for a moment before responding. "Can you let Andy know Mamm died late last night? The funeral is going to be tomorrow." Her voice softened. "I thought he'd want to know."

The news sucked the air out of Sylvia's lungs, and she pulled out a chair and sat down at the kitchen table. "Thank you for letting us know. Are the services at the homeplace?"

"Yes, at ten o'clock."

"We'll be there." They said their goodbyes, and Sylvia didn't even bother to get up from the table. She put the receiver down and buried her face in her arms, trying to process the news. The phone let out its staccato beeps, urging her to hang it up. She blocked out the noise.

In the years since their last visit with Eli and Mary, she had continued to write, although not nearly as much as she had the first year, but she'd still never received a response.

How did Linda Ruth find their number? Her brow furrowed, trying to remember if she included it in one of her letters. She must of, or Linda Ruth took it upon herself to look it up in the phone book. To her knowledge, only one Andy Troyer lived in Hartville.

One by one, she ticked off the years they'd been here. Five years ago, they'd moved from the decrepit farm into the house on Edison Street, next to her parents. Long enough for the most recent version of the phone book to carry their new number.

The urge to tell Andy the news overwhelmed her. Maybe she should wait until he got home from work, but then it might be too late to let his supervisor know of his absence tomorrow. She could phone him, but wouldn't it be better to tell him in person? How could she get to him when he had their only car? Dat could run her over in the buggy, but that would take up too much of his day.

She clicked through the day's schedule. The sewing circle at Maple Grove started at ten, and her friend Edna was coming to pick her up within the next hour. She planned. *I'll explain to Edna what's happened and ask her to swing by East Ohio Limestone on the way home. The foreman can call Andy up to the office and I'll tell him. Maybe he can leave early and drive me home.* It seemed the most reasonable plan, since Mamm already planned to watch the children while she was gone.

She went through the motions of getting their five children ready for the day, feeding them breakfast and began haphazardly packing her bag of supplies, finding it difficult to concentrate.

"Let's go!" she called out. "It's time to head over to Mummie's. I'm going to the sewing circle." She placed her youngest son, Marcus, on her hip, took hold of little Andrew's hand, and led them across the path connecting their house to Mamm and Dat's.

"Mamm!" Sylvia called as she opened the back door and ushered the little ones inside. They knew where to go and tore off looking for the toys.

Mamm turned from the sink where she peeled potatoes. "What is it, Sylvia?" she asked, searching her face. "I can see you are upset."

"It's Andy. His Mamm Mary, died last night. Linda Ruth called this morning to let us know." Sylvia sank into a chair. "We didn't even realize she was sick."

Mamm put down the peeler and pulled out a chair next to her. "I'm sorry to hear this. Does Andy know?"

"Not yet. I'm going to swing by his workplace after the sewing circle and tell him. I told Linda Ruth we'd attend the funeral tomorrow."

"I'll keep the younger children for you if you'd like."

"It might be best if all of them stay behind. I'm not sure what kind of reception we'll receive. Even the older children don't even remember much about their grandparents." Tears threatened the corners of her eyes.

Lizzie nodded. "Of course. I'll do anything I can to help." She leaned over and patted her hand.

They sat for a minute, Mamm's hand resting on top of hers. Such a comfort to have her mother's touch. Hot tears pressed against her eyelids as she realized Andy would never get to experience such closeness with his Mamm again.

Sylvia hardly engaged in the gossip during the sewing circle. A headache settled in the nape of her neck as she contemplated the different words she'd use to break the news to her husband. She busied her hands trying to quiet her mind by tying knots in the comforters stretched taut on their wooden frames.

All around her, the women chattered, sharing news and advice with each other. This church family meant so much to her and had become as close as a blood family over the past decade. Sylvia thought they had moved on from the pain of the last visit to Geauga, but here she was again, facing the giant.

Edna leaned over and whispered into Sylvia's ear, "Come now, let's wrap up. I'll take you over to Andy."

Sylvia appreciated the extra care Edna took to keep her words discreet. She knew how quickly a rumor could spread and didn't want the news getting out before Andy knew. They packed their sewing bags and picked up their casserole dishes.

"Leaving so soon?" asked Rachel, the chair of the sewing committee.

"Edna's my ride today, and I can't leave the children too long with my mom." Sylvia averted her eyes. She hated lying but wasn't ready to share the news yet.

Dust trailed Edna's car as it pulled into East Ohio Limestone. Sylvia climbed out and leaned through the window. "Thanks for dropping me off. No need to wait. I'll get a ride home with Andy."

"Are you sure?"

"Yes. He gets off at four anyway, so even if I need to wait a bit, it'll be fine."

Edna sandwiched Sylvia's hands between her padded palms. "I'll be praying for you. Give him my condolences. When you're ready to share the news, let me know and I'll put it on the prayer chain."

"Thank you, Edna."

Edna rolled up her window and put the car in reverse, swinging out of the parking lot. Sylvia looked at the trailer. Uneasy with the news she carried. She opened the door and peered in.

"Can I help you?" a woman asked, sitting behind a desk while smoking a cigarette.

"Yes, my husband works here. Andy Troyer. I need to speak with him."

The secretary reached over and tore a message sheet from a yellow pad. "What is it you want to tell him?"

"It would be better if I could talk with him in person. There has been a death in the family."

The woman glanced up for the first time at her words. She stubbed out the cigarette. "I'm sorry to hear that. I'll call for the foreman to send him up." She picked up the two-way radio and clicked the button on the side. "Wayne, can you send Andy up here to the office? His wife needs to see him."

Static came through the radio. "Roger that. It's gonna be a few. He's down in the pit just about to leave with a load for the sorter."

"Why don't you have a seat?" She pointed to the vinyl chairs lining the wall.

Sylvia went over and sat down with her hands folded in her lap. She curled her toes tight, wishing she could hide. She about jumped out of her skin when the door clicked open, and Andy's face peered around the corner, soot covered his coveralls, and his hard hat sat askew on top of a face smudged with dirt. Despite his messy appearance, her heart still flipped-flopped at his handsomeness.

"Sylvia? What is it?" he asked, worry etched across his features.

"Let's go outside and have a word." She eyed the secretary; she wanted privacy to break this news. They exited the trailer and went off to the side of the building.

"Are the kids okay? You're scaring me."

She took his hands in hers. "I don't know how to tell you this, but I got a call this morning from your sister, Linda Ruth. Your Mamm passed away." A confused look crossed Andy's face, and she could tell he didn't comprehend her words, so she tried again. "Your Mamm died last night."

His legs folded underneath him as he crumpled to the ground. He removed the hard hat and wiped his brow with a dirty hankie. "How can it be? I didn't even know she was unwell."

Sylvia slid down beside him and took the hankie from him. She turned to him and placed both of her hands on the sides of his cheeks. "This is a big shock. I know. The service is tomorrow at ten o'clock. I told Linda Ruth we would be there. Do you want me to go send a message to the foreman that you won't be in to work tomorrow?"

He shook his head and rose from the dirt. "I'll tell him myself." He reached out a hand to pull her up. "It's close to quitting time. I'll see if I can leave a little early today and drive you home."

She went to him, not worrying about dirtying her dress, and wrapped her arms around his strong body. She clung to him, hoping her touch provided some comfort. He pulled away and trudged up the steps. After a few minutes, he returned. "All squared away. Let's go." He took her hand, head down, as they walked to the car.

The next day, Andy drove past the row of buggies lining the street leading up to the homeplace. He turned into the corncrib lane and once again parked behind it like they had seven years ago. No use making Dat upset again. They climbed out of the car, and Sylvia pulled her coat tight around her shoulders. He looked down the muddy lane at the house in the distance and sighed.

"Let's pray," she said. "The last time we came, it didn't go smoothly; we need the Lord's guidance and wisdom."

Andy grabbed her hand, and they both bowed their heads before he began. "Lord, help us know how to interact with my family. Give us clarity and love for them. Remind me that no matter how they treat us, they don't know the peace You bring. Reveal Yourself to them. Be with us, please."

His prayer was more of a plea. A darkness had settled in his soul since yesterday. An anger directed at Dat for keeping Mamm from him. He'd never had the chance to reconcile things with her.

Andy heard the wails of mourners as they approached the porch. They entered the dark house, and it took a minute for his eyes to adjust to the dim light. Bishop Miller stood at the front of the living room with Dat alongside him. Mamm's body lay out on a board while people filed past, paying their respects. Andy strained to see her, but in the crowded room, he could only get a glimpse of her bonnet and nothing more. No one greeted him, so they joined the line of mourners waiting to pay their respects to the family.

The rest of his siblings stood to the side, welcoming visitors. His eyes fell on their faces. He could pick out who was who, but age and weight had changed their features. When they got to Bishop Miller, Andy held out his hand. The Bishop responded with a nod but didn't return the handshake. Andy stuffed his sweaty hand in his pocket. Unsure of what to do with himself.

Next, he came face to face with Dat; words left him as he looked into his father's dark eyes.

Dat kept his hands clasped in front of him, the knuckles white from their tight grip.

Dat spoke first. "You could show your mother honor by coming back to the Amish church."

Andy's mind went fuzzy. *Had Dat said that?* He wished Mamm could defend him, but she lay in front of him, ashen and gone. *Why such a public rebuke?* He could tell Bishop Miller was listening to their interaction, watching to see what happened next. *Lord, give me wisdom. I don't know what to say.*

His answer came from elsewhere. He knew they weren't his words but the Lord's. "Dat, I know you are hurting, and so am I. Let's lay aside our differences for the day and show mother honor by coming together."

"I am allowing you to be here because she was your Mamm, but don't mistake the invitation as my approval of your lifestyle. You remain *banned.*"

Sylvia tugged on his hand, signaling him to move on before making a scene.

Andy bowed his head in respect. "May *Gott* be with you Dat. May you feel His comfort and peace."

They filed past the casket. Andy couldn't believe how much weight Mamm had lost. She'd obviously been sick for some time. That reality made him sad. No one had bothered to tell them.

"Sylvia," someone whispered to her right. Sylvia turned her head as an Amish woman approached. "I'm Linda Ruth," she explained. "Thanks for coming." She placed a warm hand on Sylvia's shoulder.

Linda Ruth had changed since she'd last seen her. She'd put on weight, and her jowls sagged with age. Sylvia smiled weakly. "Thank you for inviting us."

Andy's other siblings whispered words of greeting but didn't engage in conversation.

Sylvia squeezed Andy's hand before heading to a bench on the women's side of the room. "I'll see you after the service." She wished she could sit beside her husband like they did at Maple Grove and at least provide some comfort with her presence.

The service started, and Bishop Miller launched into a long sermon about all the *gut* Mamm had done. Andy glanced around the room; at all the fellow Amish he'd known for years. Aunts, uncles, friends, and fellow farmers framed his vision. His eyes rested on the man seated at the other end of his bench. He wore simple black trousers, a white shirt tucked in with dress shoes. His clean-shaven face designated him as *English*, but his features looked so familiar. *Where did he know him from?* When had an *Englisher* slipped into the service? Andy combed through the recesses of his mind, nixing potential matches until he made the connection. *Could it be David?*

The last time he had seen his brother was eleven years ago at their wedding. The man at the end of the row had the same jawline, stocky build, and wheat-colored hair. Andy's mouth grew dry.

Guilt flooded his heart with the realization he'd left his brothers and sisters behind to fend for themselves all these years without a thought. He had no idea David had left the Amish until Sylvia told him after their last visit. An ache formed in his middle. *Could he have helped make the transition easier for him? How could he face him now? Would David even want to talk with him?*

Bishop Miller finished up the service. "We ask the *gut* Lord to keep her and see all the *gut* things she did when she was here on earth. May her soul rest with Him," he said as he dismissed everyone to the graveside.

Andy rose from his seat. "David?" His voice squeaked with hesitation.

The man looked up; his eyes flickered with recognition. "Andy?" David stood, his face exploding into a grin as he reached for him.

Memories came rushing back as they hugged—the time spent doing chores together, the meals, the walks into town pulling the little red wagon. He held onto his flesh and blood, a brother, born of the same parents, raised with the same values, and now wearing the same shoes—as an outcast.

Andy pulled out of the embrace and looked David up and down before quizzing him. "When did you leave the Amish? Where have you been? How did you hear about Mamm's death? Did they put you in the *bann*?" The questions tumbled out of him faster than David answered.

David chuckled. "Woah man. I always talked your ear off when we were little. I guess it's your turn now." He put his hands in his pockets and paused, picking at his words. "I left seven years ago. You were the one who gave me courage to leave. What we had here wasn't good, and you helped me see that. So, thank you; I'm grateful."

Remorse punched Andy's gut again. "I'm sorry, I didn't know. I should have been there for you to help you through that time. I'm sure Dat treated you awfully."

David's eyes clouded at the mention of Dat. "You left because you wanted to worship Jesus. I left because I wanted to experience the world— see what is out there. Dat didn't understand either of our choices."

"Where do you live?"

"Down in Wooster. Found work at a bar and even got myself hitched." He held up a finger encased in a wedding band.

A bar? "Have you found what you are looking for?"

David grimaced, his mouth tight. "I have found freedom. Dat

made it very clear I am not welcome back in their lives, so I've created my family, between my wife, patrons, and coworkers. I've built a good support network. We got dealt a bad hand, but I've made the best of it. That's all you can ask of anyone in this world."

"You can have more, David. There is true peace available to all who believe in Jesus."

"All this religious stuff is just toxic to me, man. I can't do it anymore."

Andy backed away at his words, not wanting to push too much. "Come and visit me sometime. We can talk more."

"Where do you live?"

"Down in Hartville. Got a job at a limestone mine. Living a good life with a whole brood of little ones."

"How many have you got by now?"

"Five." Andy smiled as his chest puffed with pride.

"That's great. I'm so happy for you. Let's keep in touch." David reached into his shirt pocket and ripped a piece of paper from a small notepad and handed it to Andy. "Write your number down. I'll call you."

"Are you staying for lunch?" Andy asked as he jotted down his number.

"Are you crazy? No way, I'm out of here. Who knows what godforsaken corner they'd put us in to eat? I came only to pay my respects to Mamm. She tried her best, and I owed her that." He turned towards the front door. "Good to see you. Take care." He folded the paper with Andy's number into his pocket and exited, shutting the door behind him.

Andy's spirit deflated as he watched David walk to his car. He wished he'd stayed in touch better with his siblings. *Shoot.* Regret pinged him again; he should have gotten David's contact information as well.

The men moved the benches aside and began setting up the long tables for the noon meal, while everyone shuffled outside and headed down the road for the graveside service.

"Should we stay?" Andy asked Sylvia as they stood in the graveyard after the burial. Before Sylvia could give an answer, Linda Ruth shuffled over.

"Will you be joining us for lunch?"

Andy hesitated.

"We've set up a special table for you to eat at."

"Great," Sylvia responded in a bright, clipped tone. "Where should we go?"

Linda Ruth's ears turned red, and a flush swept across her cheeks.

Andy knew she hoped they'd decline.

"The cel-llar," she stammered.

Andy thought he had heard wrong.

"The cellar?" Sylvia asked, with confusion in her eyes.

Linda Ruth nodded, then walked away.

"Sylvia, I think we should just leave and save the embarrassment. They would be relieved. I think Linda Ruth told us out of pity so we'd decide to leave." Andy tugged at her elbow.

"And do what? Give them the satisfaction of seeing our tail-lights? No, we aren't going anywhere. If they insist on this silly *bann* and serving us in the cellar, let it be. They should be ashamed. Did you hear the stammer in Linda Ruth's voice? They know this is wrong. Who is going to stand up to your Dat? No one." The longer Sylvia spoke, the redder her face became, and she lifted her chin with a defiant tilt. "I will eat my meal in the cellar to make a point."

For the first time today, his lips turned up at their corners. There was no winning this argument, and he loved her even more for it.

—⟨◇◇◇◇◇⟩—

They descended the creaky stairs into the cellar. Musty cobwebs hung from the ceiling, and the oil lamp illuminated the bare dirt floor of the cellar. Rows of preserved vegetables lined the walls. Someone had set up a small card table in the center of the room.

"Milady," Andy gestured as he pulled out the chair for his wife. "Let us enjoy our meal at this fine dining establishment."

Sylvia giggled, easing the tension of the absurd situation. "Let us bless the food we are about to receive." She grabbed hold of Andy's hand and intertwined their fingers. Bowing her head, she prayed, "Lord, we thank You for the life You gave Mary and that we could honor her today. Bless this food and the hands that have prepared it." She paused before proceeding, "Lord, I'm sorry for being so angry. Give me love for this family like You gave us the love we didn't deserve. Show them they can receive salvation and true peace. We ask this in Your name. Amen."

Andy squeezed his eyes tight before opening them, surprised to see Linda Ruth standing in front of their table with two steaming plates of fried chicken, mashed potatoes, green beans, and rolls. She had to have heard Sylvia's prayer.

Linda Ruth gave them a weak smile in response. "I'm sorry; it must be this way. Thank you for coming, Andy." She set the plates in front of them and turned on her heel and ascended the stairs.

Andy shoved a spoonful of mashed potatoes into his mouth, savoring them, and swallowed before calling after her. "Your kindness means a lot. Thank you for the food."

They ate, then rose from the dark cellar and left through the front door without saying another word to anyone. Their eyes squinted against the bright sunlight.

On the way home, Andy squeezed Sylvia's hand. "I love you and appreciate the stance you took by eating in the cellar with me, but we are never going back to visit again. We aren't welcome there.

I've told Dat about Jesus so many times, but he never listens. It can only be a work of the Lord that changes his heart. All we can do now is pray for him."

"But they are your family. You must see them."

"They were my family. Now you are my family, along with Jake and Lizzie and our brothers and sisters at Maple Grove. We aren't going back anymore, only forward." He set his jaw in a firm line.

A few weeks later, a note arrived from Linda Ruth. *Thought you might want a copy of this. Dat typed it out for all the children in remembrance.* Sylvia held up the typewritten card to the light.

"Read it aloud," Andy requested.

She read,

Mary Troyer (Farmwald) was born July 22, 1900, died March 19, 1962 age 61 yrs. 7 mos. 25 days. Was married to Eli D. Troyer Jan. 20 1922. Lived in matrimony 40 yrs. 1 mo. 19 days. To this union were born 19 children 6 died young. Caleb was 14 and died of rheumatic heart. 12 living all married. Mother started with her sickness in the winter 1960. She doctored for sinus but kept getting worse. Till in May she had to go in the hospital for 10 days. Dr. Nelson told me the bad news: she has cancer in sinus pockets. And can't live but two mon. Dr. said we could try radium treatments but promised no cure. We talked over with mother and decided it's worth a try and she took 34 treatments and seemed to help her. She got good enough, so she was able to go away and to church. The last time she was in church was on Nov. 26, 1961, her pains started up again, and kept get-

ting worse. In the week between Christmas and New Year, she was in great misery and pain. After New Year she was in hospital 4 days, got relief as far as pain was concerned, but gradually getting worse through Jan. & Feb. She had to have strong pills every 4 hrs. Till in Mar. on a Thurs. she had no more pains. And we were kind of relieved, thought maybe she started for the better. But by Mon. she was in great misery and pains in the chest. She talked but so weak we couldn't understand everything she said. Once she lifted her hands and said, "Look at those angels," she asked to get up. I slipped my arms under her to help her. She died in my arms, I said oh: no. no. but she was gone. That was on Mar. 19, 1962 about 9 o'clock. I hope the good Lord will never let me forget that evening as long as I live and keep me humble the rest of my life. I am writing this as a reminder so as not to forget her too soon. As you know, she was a softhearted mother, and we have good hopes for her, and I think the angels met her at the shore over yonder. In fact, I think they met her right in the room that evening. I am surely glad we talked things over the way we did, so let's keep doing things the way she taught us. We can honor her, and we get blessed to do it. Remember how the sun shone in her grave on that cloudy day. And when they were singing, how we heard that nice melody about us.

Dat

"Only forward," Andy replied after she finished reading, his voice husky with emotion.

Sylvia knew not to push him, so she tucked the card back in the envelope and put it away in her chest of special things. There may come a time when Andy would want to revisit his past. She would hold on to this for him.

THIRTY-ONE

May 2003, Hartville, Ohio

Sylvia sat on the padded rocker in the living room, waiting. She messed with her head covering, tucking tendrils of white hair underneath the mesh. For the first time in over forty years, Andy's siblings were coming for a visit.

Linda Ruth had written a few weeks ago saying they were making a day trip to Hartville and asked if they could stop by.

When Sylvia told Andy about the letter, his response surprised her. "Let them come. Let's see what happens."

The years had passed as they waded through the thickets of child rearing and young adulthood, then came the grandparenting phase. Their busy life had no room for those that didn't want to be in it. As time went on, they talked less and less about their Amish roots, until some days she didn't even think about where they came from.

She picked up the pair of binoculars that lived on Dat's old library table. How she missed Mamm and Dat.

"You think spying is going to cause them to come more quickly? Put those away," Andy scolded, his tone sharp.

Sylvia set down the binoculars. *What would they talk about?* She had prepared a platter of trail bologna and cheese along with crackers she could pull out of the fridge, but she'd only get it out if they could eat together. She assessed the condition of the living room. She had taken special care to clean, dusting the picture frames and grandfather clock in the corner.

Paul Harvey yakked away on the radio. Andy shuffled into the kitchen and turned the dial on the under-counter radio to the off position. Tension oozed from his face. They both looked out the window as the traveler van pulled into the driveway.

"They're here!" Sylvia declared. "Act natural."

How could Andy act like this was anything normal? He hadn't seen his siblings since Mamm's funeral in 1962, forty-one years ago.

The words of Psalm 34 tumbled over in his mind. *I sought the Lord, and he answered me; he delivered me from all my fears. Those who look to him are radiant; their faces are never covered with shame.* He felt the tension in his neck dissipate as he focused on the scripture. There were no regrets. God gave him a good life. His children were reputable and kind, and because of God's grace, he felt no shame. His siblings may examine his life with a magnifying glass, but there would be little travesty found because he had set his heart on the Lord.

Maybe at long last there would be reconciliation, especially without Dat looming over their shoulders. Dat's shadow still lingered, but without his physical presence, they could at least breathe. Andy wished he had gone to his funeral in 1971, but Dat wouldn't have wanted him there.

The passengers unloaded from the van. A plump woman spoke first. "Andy! How good to see you." She reached out a hand for him to shake.

He returned the handshake and pulled back, taking her in. Her round face looked just like Mamm's, and her blue eyes twinkled. Her hair had turned white, little bits peeping out from under her *kap* and bonnet. He'd recognize her anywhere. His baby sister, Lindy

Ru. The rest of them, though, were questionable. Age had changed all of them.

"Come on in." He motioned to the open door as they climbed up the back porch steps. The entire crew shuffled inside.

"Welcome. Let's sit in the living room and visit," Sylvia said. They sat down on the brown microfiber sofas and recliners backing up against the walls. "What sightseeing have you done in the area?"

"We just got done eating an excellent dinner at The Kitchen," commented a man who Andy guessed to be his brother Alvin. "Some of the best fried chicken I've had."

A woman likely his wife elbowed him. "What about mine?" The entire crew chuckled.

Linda Ruth piped in, "I think we met one of your grand-daughters who works there."

Sylvia's face lit up. "Oh that must be Sarah, she works at The Kitchen as a waitress." She rose and went to the TV console and plucked a photograph from the mantel. "Is this the girl you met?"

"Sure is."

"That's Andrew's oldest girl. Just came back from a missionary trip to Ecuador. She's not married yet."

Grunts sounded around the room, and Sylvia placed the frame back on the console. "Would you care for some refreshments? I have lemonade, trail bologna, cheese?"

Silence eschewed.

Alvin spoke up. "I don't know about everyone else, but I'm stuffed after that fried chicken."

A chorus of "*Jahs*" sounded aroumed the circle.

Andy wanted to roll his eyes, but thought better of it. No Amish man or woman ever turned down lemonade and trail bologna.

"Tell us the news?" asked Andy, attempting to keep the conversation going.

Alvin began talking about the weather, the crops, and how many cows he milked. The conversation stayed surface level, not venturing into any of the hurts of the past. Before long, the chimes on the grandfather clock rang out, striking two o'clock.

Samuel slapped his knee. "We'd best get going. Told the driver we needed to be back home by four."

Sylvia held up a finger. "Before you go, I want to give you all something." She rose from her perch on a kitchen chair and padded into her sewing room, returning with the small quilt blocks she'd sewn. She handed one to each woman. "For you to remember your visit." The ladies admired the tiny stitches and the dark purple colors she'd chosen. She held an extra one in her hand.

Who was missing? Andy counted each face and realized Linda Ruth wasn't among them. "Where's Linda Ruth?"

"I don't know, can you go see where she is?" Sylvia asked him.

He ducked through the arched doorway separating the kitchen from the living room and scanned the empty room. Sensing movement off to the left, in the laundry room, he called out, "Lindy Ru?"

She peeped her head around the corner, looking like a sinner caught in the act. "Sorry, I seem to be a bit lost." Her cheeks glowed with the lie, and Andy could see the blotchy red spots that dotted her neck. *She was snooping.*

"Can I ask you something, Andy?"

"Sure, anything."

"Did we do wrong to enforce the shunning all these years? All this time wasted. I have a daughter who left the Amish. I don't want to live my last years without her in my life."

Andy couldn't believe she had asked for his opinion. He gave the most honest answer he could. "Then don't. The choice seems complicated from where you sit, but I can tell you from the other side it isn't. God is a God of love and forgiveness. Read for yourself."

He walked over to the radio, where a stack of papers and books sat underneath piled on top of each other. He pulled his worn side by side English German Bible from the bottom of the stack. "I've been waiting for the right time to pass this along. Someone gave it to me long ago. This book started my journey. Read for yourself and tell me what you think."

Linda Ruth reached out her hand and touched the leather with affection. She tucked it under her arm and smiled. "I'm glad we came to visit." Tears filled her eyes. "Are all those pictures in the hallway of your family?"

"Yes, our six children and many grandchildren. All of them have followed the Lord." His voice choked with the sudden realization God had changed the entire course of their family history with His faithfulness.

"You have a *gut* family." Her chin quivered.

He wondered if the regret made her sad, or she longed for something more.

"Yes, we do. I'm glad you came to visit. It means a lot. Have you heard from David? I haven't talked to him since Mamm's funeral."

Linda Ruth stared down at her hands. "He's sick, in Mercy Medical Center. His wife died some years ago, and he brought his daughters back to us to raise when he couldn't handle it."

Andy sucked in a breath. Despite David's insistence on living an *English* life, the tentacles of the Amish had somehow wrapped his children back into the fold.

"He's lived a hard life, you know. You should visit him."

"Here you both are," Sylvia interrupted. "I wondered where you two disappeared off to. I wanted to give you this." She held up her quilt square. "To keep in remembrance of your visit."

Linda Ruth took the gift, admired it, and then held it to her chest. "Thank you, Sylvia. This has been the best visit." Her voice cracked with emotion. She straightened her shoulders and looked at the clock hanging on the wall. "Oh my. Where has the time gone? Alvin's probably having a fit."

As if on cue, the rest of the group ambled behind Sylvia into the kitchen. They said their goodbyes, tucked themselves into the van, and were on their way.

Andy couldn't get the thought of David being sick in the hospital out of his mind, so later in the week, he headed for a visit. Fear tried to hold him back, but the words of Psalm twenty-seven brought him comfort. *The Lord is my light and my salvation, whom shall I fear?*

Bright overhead lights gleamed against the shined floors, and the faint smell of antiseptic hung in the air. Andy glanced down at the slip of paper in his hand. Room four-eighty-four. He took one step forward, willing the other leg to follow. Would David want to see him after all these years? He'd never called as he said he would or asked for any other contact. He paused outside the door, comparing the slip of paper with the room number posted on the wall, and lifted a knuckle to the frame, rapping lightly. "David?" He peeked his head around the corner.

A weak voice came back from the farthest bed. "Come in."

Andy moved inside and tentatively stepped towards the bed. David lay pressed against the white sheets, his skin the sickly color of a stormy sky. A man riddled with decay replaced the exuberant boy Andy had grown up with.

David sized him up, trying to place him. When he figured it out, he pressed a fist to his mouth, holding back the emotion that threatened to escape his lips.

"You never called," Andy quipped with kindness, trying to make the mood lighter. "I should have grabbed your number and not the other way around."

David squeezed his eyes shut at his words.

Andy placed a hand on his forearm. "You'll always be my little brother. I needed to see you. I'm sorry to surprise you like this, but I wasn't sure you'd want to see me."

"How could I not want to see my older brother? The one I've always looked up to. You don't know what your courage meant to me. We could never talk about such things then."

"You told me at Mamm's funeral, and I've always treasured your words." Andy sat down on the white sheet and took David's wrinkled hand in his own.

David hung his head. "I made a mess of myself. Better to avoid what I'd done than face it."

"There are some things I want to tell you. Things the Lord laid on my heart." Andy's eyes connected with his. "Last time we talked, you told me you were searching for peace. Did you ever find it?"

"No." David hung his head. "Only regret."

"It's not too late, David. Jesus loves you very much. He is where you will find peace. I am so grateful the Lord saw fit to snatch me into His fold when I was young. All these years, I have walked with Him and have no regrets. It's not too late for you."

"So, you came here to preach at me?" David gave a sly smile.

"Well, I guess you could say that." Andy returned the smile, then became serious again. "When Linda Ruth told me about your condition, I felt compelled to come. I love you and always have."

"I've made some terrible choices."

"Perhaps you have, but who am I to judge? We all have sinned. When I look at you, all I remember is the little boy who chattered all the way to school. Now I see a broken man. We can't fix these earthly bodies of ours, but I can tell you about the one who can fix your soul. Seek the Lord, and He will meet you here and you will find forgiveness for your sins."

"I'll think about it."

"I'll be praying you do." Andy patted his hand, content he'd said what needed to be shared.

"You saw Lindy Ru?"

"Yes. You won't believe it. All our brothers and sisters came to Hartville to visit Sylvia and I."

"That had to be interesting."

"Tell me about it!" Andy exclaimed. He told David about the visit, and then they spent the rest of the afternoon laughing and reminiscing about their childhood.

"Wish I could get me a bowl of that blackberry soup. I spent my entire childhood groaning in disgust when Mamm served it for dinner, but what I wouldn't do for a taste of it on my lips again," David croaked.

"Me, too, brother. Me, too."

Andy drove home from the hospital in silence. He clicked off the radio as he pulled out of the parking garage, wanting space to think and process the visit. A longing budded inside of him. A fresh yearning for reconciliation he buried deep inside of himself after Mamm's death. Maybe the visits with his siblings had unearthed something new. When he'd walked away from his family after the funeral and never looked back, he'd been justified in his actions. He knew that, however, the wound remained, a pain buried so deep he hardly felt its throb until this week.

A new truth unfurled its petals. Reconciliation may never come in the way he wanted, but to heal he needed to forgive, to release the hate that had been bound up in his heart against Dat and the Bishop. Against those who had turned their backs on them.

Forgiveness is for you, the Holy Spirit whispered.

Tears began running in rivulets down his cheeks and onto his shirt and suspenders at the revelation. He pulled the car into an empty parking lot, knowing what he had to do.

He wept. "Lord, I forgive them as you forgave me," he cried out.

Once his sobs subsided, his hurt dissipated. He fingered the raised edge of the scar on his heart. The wound no longer remained. A sense of completion settled over him. He'd accomplished his earthly purpose—to forgive and be forgiven.

THIRTY-TWO

October 11th, 2011

Andy took a bite of buttered toast and a sip of coffee before running his finger down the seam of his open Bible until it came to his favorite chapter.

"What scripture are you reading this morning?" asked Sylvia as she sipped her coffee. The steam rose from her Corelle mug and fogged her glasses.

"Psalm twenty-seven. Listen to this." He read aloud, "I will see the goodness of the Lord in the land of the living. Wait for the Lord; be strong and take heart and wait for the Lord."

Sylvia bit her bottom lip. "What else do we have to wait for?"

He smiled as he closed the Bible. "Heaven, I suppose. I have seen the goodness of the Lord so much in my life. The older I get, the more I realize God is leading us into His promised land just like He did the Israelites. Only our promised land is heaven."

"Do you have your Bible study this morning at the church?"

"Yes, Pastor Myron is going to be teaching."

"Myrtle Beachy called earlier to see if you could pick Andy J. up on your way. She said it would mean so much for him to get out of the house a bit with the guys. I told her you would come by."

Andy glanced at the clock. "Well, I better get going then." He gathered the papers he'd been studying and stuffed them in the front of his Bible. Rising from the table, he came around to the other side and leaned down to give Sylvia a kiss on the lips. "See you around lunchtime."

"You're feeling better these days, aren't you?" she teased as she got up from the chair and gathered the dishes.

He gave a wry smile. "You bet I am." He patted her rump. "Not too bad for an eighty-four-year-old. The oxygen I've been wearing at night is giving me energy during the day."

"Andy!" She shrugged him off, pink still blotting her cheeks after all these years.

"Be careful not to overdo it. If you feel bad, come back home."

He shrugged off her concern, grabbed his cane, and went down the back steps to the mammoth Crown Victoria they'd driven for years. The car hummed to life, and Moody Radio played low in the background.

He turned corners and zipped along the road without a care in the world. Hartville had become a part of him. The place he felt most at home. He turned into Andy J.'s driveway and saw him sitting on the porch. Andy J. shuffled to the car, hanging onto his caregiver's arm. Andy got out and opened the passenger's door for him and helped buckle the seat belt.

"I'll bring him home right after Bible study in time for lunch," Andy said.

Myrtle's brow creased in worry. "You'll have to stay beside him and help him."

"Of course." Andy nodded in understanding. He witnessed firsthand how confusion had taken over Andy J.'s mind. His bright brother-in-law now resembled a sliver of his former self.

He backed out of the driveway and took the first right onto Smith Kramer. Before long, they pulled into the church parking lot. The roofline he'd grown to love over the decades filled his vision. They had built a new sanctuary twenty years ago, but the old church remained, now serving as a fellowship hall.

So many of his memories lived in this church. When he'd arrived in 1953, his faith was childlike. All the years of preaching, fellowship, and Bible study had grown him into something strong, like an oak. His roots were now planted deep in the ground.

He looped his arm through Andy J.'s, and they slowly made their way to the front door. Others greeted them as they walked into the vestibule. It was a perfect Tuesday morning.

"Did you read the passage for today?" Pastor Myron asked, looking around the room at the weathered saints. They were studying the book of Romans, and Andy flipped his Bible open to the passage.

"Paul can get winded, can't he?" Ernest piped up from across the table. "I had difficulty understanding parts of it."

"Let's pick it apart and see if we can dissect the hard bits." Myron asked each man to read a verse and give his interpretation, and, as always, the Holy Spirit brought clarity to the scriptures. At eleven thirty, Myron wrapped up their study. "Andy, will you close us out with prayer?"

"Sure." The men bowed their heads and shut their eyes. Andy began, "Lord, we thank You for this beautiful day. Thank You for these men you brought together to study Your word. Help us be obedient to the call You have placed on each of our lives as we walk out our last days on this earth. You've been so faithful to us; and we want to honor You with all we do. We love You, Lord. Amen."

"Amen," a chorus of voices echoed back.

After the study concluded, Andy headed into the kitchen to clean up. He finished wiping dry the coffeepot and put away all the washed cups while Andy J. sat watching him.

"Come, let's get you back home to Myrtle. I'm sure she'll have a nice sandwich waiting for you." Andy licked his lips, thinking of the lunch Sylvia would have prepared for him as well.

The two men walked out to the car. Andy opened the door and helped his brother-in-law get buckled in. He walked to the driver's side, slid behind the wheel, and fit the key in the ignition. The car smelled of familiar things—coffee, cinnamon air freshener, and winter air. Ordinary things. He took a deep breath. Tightness gripped his chest.

"An—"

The word wouldn't come. His vision blurred and tunneled. He collapsed, the weight of his body pressing against the steering wheel.

His last breath slipped away, and Andy crossed over into the promised land.

The End

Author's Note

My blood runs through this story as one of Andy and Sylvia's grandchildren. What a rich legacy and heritage I have received. Without the Lord's intervention and their obedience, my life wouldn't be the same. All six of their children grew up to follow Jesus and continue to walk with the Lord, leaving a big impact on many.

Grandma Troyer (Sylvia) breathed her last breath on December 1st, 2018. She lived a full seven years and fifty days on this earth without her best friend, soulmate, and lover. She grieved Andy's death and, over time, became more confused, descending into dementia. The family moved her to a nursing community in Amish country, where she passed away surrounded by those who loved her.

I felt the call to memorialize their amazing story in the fall of 2022 while attending a book festival. I always enjoyed reading as a child but during the pandemic picked it back up as a hobby. At the festival, I listened to authors speak passionately about their books, and it ignited the writing spark in me.

I toyed around with writing a novel or collection of short stories about my work as a social worker in senior living, but the clear whisper of the Holy Spirit told me, *Tell Grandpa Troyer's story.* I wrestled with the idea for several months. *Could I do it justice? What would others think of it?* Finally, I obeyed and began writing in February 2023. I had so much fun digging deeper into my family history, interviewing my aunts and uncles, and even paying a visit to their homeplaces in Geauga County, Ohio.

In 2023, I also committed to reading through the entire Bible, and for much of the year, found myself in the Old Testament. I witnessed the provision and care God Almighty provided to the Israelites.

When they lacked a compass, He guided them with a pillar of fire. When they had no food, He provided manna, and as the Israelites grumbled and complained, He continued to show faithfulness. God displayed the same love and faithfulness to Grandma and Grandpa when he brought them out of a life of striving into the promise of salvation, which inspired the title of *Into the Promised Land*.

When I set out to write, I only planned on writing from Grandpa's point of view, but upon further inspection quickly learned this story was as much Grandma's as his. God's sovereignty sewed their lives together, inexplicably bringing together two people that desperately needed each other.

As I wrote, I grew to admire my Grandma's confidence, spunk, and prayer life. Likewise, Grandpa stands tall for his inquisitive nature, and his courage to rise above his circumstances and create the life he always wanted.

Some of my most cherished memories growing up in Hartville were at my grandparents' home on Sunday evenings, when the extended family gathered to enjoy a bowl of popcorn and fellowship. The coffee pot was always full, slices of Swiss cheese (much to Grandpa's disdain) and trail bologna dotted the table, and all enjoyed conversation about Hartville's latest news.

As I grew older, sometimes I would stop in and chat on my way home from work or school. Grandpa and Grandma always asked insightful questions about my life and invested time in me. On one occasion after a visit, Grandpa told me he loved me. I'd never heard him say those words before, and I cried on the way home because I knew he meant them. In retrospect, I am even more touched by his admission of love. He didn't have a loving example to model his parenting after. His parents never expressed love to him through words or physical touch. He learned through the work of the Holy Spirit, and his life reflected the transformative power of Christ.

After Grandpa died, most of his siblings attended the funeral. They arrived early to pay their respects and wept openly when they saw him lying in the casket. I became deeply angry at this display of emotion. They had their chance to make their peace. *Why wait until they no longer could?* In my anger, I hoped they wept with regret, and perhaps they did; however, in my research I learned they likely believed Grandpa (Andy) went to hell for his disobedience to the Amish church.

They refused to eat with the rest of the family after the service, still enforcing the shunning that took place back in the 1940s. The church ladies served them lunch while we were away at the graveside service.

David's family reports that on his deathbed he made a commitment to follow Jesus, and it makes me smile to imagine the two brothers embracing in heaven experiencing true freedom. Linda Ruth's daughter also embraced Jesus as her Lord and Savior and grew to be close to Grandpa in his later years. She became integral to Grandpa's emotional healing as he aged.

I used handwritten stories and oral interviews to corroborate the plot, but changed many names to protect the identities of individuals. I imagined much of the dialogue and settings, creating this hybrid work of fiction.

My prayer is that Grandpa and Grandma's story will somehow open your heart to a deeper understanding of God's love and pursuit of us as He desires to lead each of us into the promised land.

To learn more about my writing, research process, and to see photos of my grandparents, visit sarahheatwole.com.

ACKNOWLEDGEMENTS

All my love to my husband, Jerrel Heatwole Jr. for his support, and allowing me to take so much time away from our family to write. You deserve much of the credit for this project. I love you.

Special thanks to my writer's group, CHARIS, for their cheerleading, critiques, and feedback. Thank you to Linda, my critique partner. You have sharpened my writing skills. "Be gone, passive tense!" To my Monday and Tuesday night writing groups, thank you for your encouragement and excitement; you pushed me to continue through the hard times.

A special thank you to my mom, dad, sister, brother-in-law, and aunts for being some of the first readers of this manuscript and giving valuable cultural insight and feedback. I will always treasure the handwritten critique notes my aunts Clara and Viola provided. I am so grateful they allowed me to share this story.

Paul, I appreciate your detailed description of Jake and your memories of his shop.

To my small group at Lifepoint Church and dear friends— your support means the world.

Most of all, thank you Jesus, for your love and faithfulness. May my words bring You honor and glory.

Love what you see?
Share the story!

Find more great books or
grab another copy for a friend.

———————————

**Enjoy FREE shipping
on your first order!**

———————————

Use promo code: SHIP4FREE

www.masthof.com

9 798896 740384